THE
CHOSEN
ONES

THE CONSPIRACY

A NEW WORLD ORDER

MICHELLE REID

NEWMAN SPRINGS PUBLISHING
320 Broad Street
Red Bank, NJ 07701

First originally published by Newman Springs Publishing 2019

ISBN 978-1-64531-172-0 (Paperback)
ISBN 978-1-64531-173-7 (Digital)

Printed in the United States of America

CONTENTS

PREFACE

I wrote this book for all the people who don't fit in a perfect box and refuse to be controlled and ruled by a certain religion or way of thinking. My aim is to make all aware that at any time, those with power, wealth, and clout can decide that they will pay people, even your family, to make you comply, or take from you something they want. All will follow along in the plot—the conspiracy really—in the name of financial game, and praise from the power holders, the money holders. Beware of your finances, your surroundings, and who you allow into your life, including online with your personal information. I'm not trying to alarm anyone unnecessarily, but you know what I am talking about if you are currently going through it. They study you and find out everything about you over many years; and before you know it, it is too late. They are ready to destroy you. Most vulnerable are women, especially the single or divorced ones, immigrants, children, and anyone they think they can successfully isolate from friends and family. If you are the victim of human trafficking, organized stalking, gang stalking, community stalking (is another term for it), corporate stalking (is also another popular facet of it), harassment, blacklisting, and discrimination, these things are all criminal and illegal activities. Please contact some of the organizations I have listed on the back cover as their vast knowledge and information on the subject can help you. And whatever you do, do not let your family, friends, company, or place of work subject you to mental health testing or drug and alcohol testing if you know that there is no problem, as these are some of the specific tactics they use to get you misdiagnosed and institutionalized, and therefore further control you and your environment. And lastly, there are some great videos online and articles dealing with this subject, but please be aware that with some of their other playbook tactics of spyware and diverting websites, they also like placing misinformation throughout the web, just to further confuse and trick their victims. Be safe, be aware.

CHAPTER 1

THE CHARMED ONE, THE CHOSEN ONES

On a cool spring day on March 23, 1996, a baby girl was born, under the Aries fire sign, in a small town near Salem, Massachusetts, to an outwardly ordinary middle-class family. She was a middle child with one older brother and one younger brother who would soon come a few years later. Her mother was of Brazilian black and Caucasian American decent, a mixture of stuff, but seemed to identify more with being African American, and her father was of Irish American decent, making her and her brothers very fair but biracial kids all the same.

Chantelle was what they called her; and right from the beginning, she displayed the traits of a gifted or magical child, a natural knowing, about the physical world and the unseen world—as they would soon find out in accordance with her astral birth date, time, and year, which all lined up uniquely in multiples of threes, sixes, and nines.

Before the age of five, she would tell her parents of dreams that predicted the future; she would see things like God's or Jesus's hand come from the ceiling, blessing and comforting, her. She would think of a shooting star or specific people, and these things would appear out of the blue. Chantelle knew there was more to this world, and that she was different than others but was unable to express her thoughts and feelings on what she knew with any clarity at such a tender age.

She would tell her parents she was psychic and knew things about their future and past lives, past events, or the way much of the physical world around them worked, such as a person's body changes every seven years—all things she *just knew* to be true, all before the age of five. Her family, being fairly religious and just not believing of such abilities, did not pay her too much attention, or would out right laugh it off as a child's imagination.

Soon Chantelle found herself a best friend, whom she met in grade 3, at the age of eight. Her name was Karen, and they were inseparable. Karen and Chantelle would do all the typical things girls would do—playing with dolls, combing each other's hair, playing dress up and make-believe; but running into the forest and frolicking in nature was by far their favorite thing to do.

On their many jaunts into the forest, they would frolic among the trees and the moss, pick flowers and various herbs, which they would place in jars for later use, all on Chantelle's seemingly expert directions. They would make-believe interacting with fairies, genies, trolls, and other otherworldly dimensional beings. Beings who one day Chantelle confessed to her good friend, of now five years strong, that she was really seeing, and even interacted with, on a daily basis.

Not believing her friend, Karen asked Chantelle to prove it. "What do these beings look like? Do they have a name? And where do you find them?" She puzzled herself with these questions for Chantelle. All great, inquisitive questions from a thirteen-year-old's developing mind; but Karen had to admit—she always sensed something "different" in her friend, and that in all the years of them playing make-believe in the forest, the things Chantelle saw and sensed seemed quite specific, and colorful, for her to just make them up. But Karen never really questioned it until now.

Chantelle looked at Karen in amazement; she could not believe that her friend did not already sense, or know, all these years. She proceeded to explain to her wide-eyed friend how, since a very young age, she had the ability to talk with otherworldly beings, as she liked to call them. That through her bedroom closet, which had become somewhat of a portal for her, she was able to call forth genies, called djinn in some cultures; fairies; other elementals and otherworldly beings; and, of course, deceased humans who wanted to come back to impart information or talk to loved ones.

That evening, Chantelle and Karen spent time together at one of Chantelle's favorite spots—the graveyard. There they mused about days gone by and talked about Chantelle's fascinating, enchanting, yet very unusual and unbelievable childhood and the many magical potions and spells she had taught Karen to make and perform over the years. Spells and potions that Karen had assumed were make-believe and child's play but always wondered why they always came to fruition. Now she knew.

Back at school, Chantelle and Karen were as close and as inseparable as ever, but Karen soon had bad news for Chantelle. Her family was moving to New Orleans this summer as her father had taken a job out there. Chantelle was devastated to learn she would be losing her best friend, the only person she felt she could truly confide in. She felt as though her life was in a tailspin. No one understood her like Karen did—not her mom or dad, and definitely not her brothers. She felt very alone.

Now with her friend's going-away bash an unsettling memory of the near past, and with just over one month left before her scary and uninspiring entrance to high school, Chantelle found her time, when not working at her family's antique shop, being consumed with teachings, visions, and learning lessons from above. Many of her protective otherworldly beings were sent to help her on her tough, but necessary, journey in this world, on earth; and she had much to learn.

Other than a few vivid visions she had as a very young child, such as when "the Creator's," hand came through the ceiling and touched her with a magical, holy type of comfort of knowing and guidance, Chantelle felt emotionally alone. Chantelle spent her days, in her closet, a.k.a. the portal room, practicing healing, love, and other spells, known, deep-seated knowledge of old, and talking, interacting with her friends from other dimensions. She never thought too much about the things she was able to do; even though she knew her brothers didn't have these abilities, she still felt it was a "normal" thing that some people had them. It wasn't until one fateful day, while she and her family were visiting a friend of her father's, Dana, and Dana's mother, that this friend announced to Chantelle's dad and brother's, "You know your daughter is a witch? She is what we call, a Natural Born Witch, and has been for many lifetimes?"

This unsolicited announcement took everyone by surprise; there was a deafening silence in the room, but this information somehow, and in many ways, resonated with Chantelle, and along with Dana's explanation, it explained a lot. The women could not wait to take Chantelle inside and talk to her about what this meant, being from a long line of witches themselves. What followed was a discussion on *how* and *when* her talents would fully come forth in her life—an exact date and time they really couldn't know, but what they did know was that it would come, in "divine time."

Chantelle wrestled with the feeling of being born a witch," which had negative connotations in history and still did in the present. As she would learn and read about the Salem Witch Trials in school, which again cast witches and those accused of witchcraft in a very bad light and warranted death, Chantelle would rather not label herself, always thinking to herself, *I am what I am—nothing more, nothing less.* She always wondered how one could deny what they were, how they were born, who they were. Surely, the Creator, as she liked to call him, staying away from the religious undertones that she so despised due to the fakeness of the many people she encountered under this label, would not want anyone to do so, she pondered.

Chantelle had decided at a young age that she wasn't sure how to feel about the whole "witch" thing or title, but she knew she was different, special, gifted; and she wasn't going to let anyone make her feel bad for having natural gifts and abilities. She would spend hours in her room quietly playing and interacting with beings from the other dimensions. Her family would not think much of it; they thought, how creative Chantelle was, spending hours engaging her imagination. Little did they know.

CHAPTER 2

THE FORMATIVE YEARS

It had been five weeks since Chantelle threw the huge going-away bash for her best friend, Karen. It was September 7, the beginning of her new school year; she was now in high school and in a new school altogether.

Chantelle felt very alone, and detached from her new high school experience. She did not connect to anyone in her family, and now her best friend in this world was gone. With her best friend gone to New Orleans, Chantelle's "big girl" days at her new school began with a terrifying *bang*. No one at the school, especially the girls, seemed to understand her or want to be her friend. They right away saw her as being "different."

While looking out the window during her second-period class, English, Chantelle reflected on her not-so-happy last month of summer break, after her best friend left for her new life in New Orleans. She wondered, was Karen as miserable as she was, or was she adjusting well in New Orleans with new friends, a new school, a school that did not see her as weird and different and shun her like Chantelle's school peers did? As she mused at nature out the window, Chantelle remembered spending the last weeks of her "lazy" days of summer working at the family antiques shop, which wasn't so bad.

Chantelle would think about her mother, who never seemed to be happy for the good events happening in Chantelle's life, a feeling that resonated and resided deep inside her knowing, and being, and one she never understood. She could never understand how a mother could have such deep-seated and unhealthy feelings for her child—an only daughter who's innocent to the world. A mother who would rather give her daughter money than give her, her time. A mother who was smart and attractive, in her time, yet who seemed jealous of her daughter's same attributes and natural gifts, which she always would rather deny were even there.

Chantelle learned at a very young age to not even trust her father who professed to love her so and told her that she was the apple of his eyes but who was very undependable and flawed on many levels. A family like thousands of others that looked good on the outside but had many hidden secrets inside, like her older brother's engrained low self-esteem and lack of a true feeling of belonging that stemmed from many tragic family occurrences. And her younger brother, who was babied and coddled, which led him to feel he was the real king of the family, the only one that truly mattered.

Needless to say, Chantelle's end days of summer were lackluster, but she did enjoy being at the antiques shop as it housed some very old artifacts that her family had collected over the years from around the world, procured but not for sale, like in a museum, for those who wanted to view such examples of history. Being around these extremely old, old world historical pieces always triggered Chantelle's metaphysical side. She had been born with the ability to read and sense energy in things, especially things belonging to the dead. Very old artifacts were Chantelle's favorite items in her family's antiques and collectibles shop, as they had the ability to catapult her back in time. She would take the item into a quiet room, hold or touch it lightly and watch as the room and she were transported to that time period, like in a trance, a movie, with her being the central figure of the scenes.

Many times, while there, Chantelle would see many of her otherworldly friends who would assist her on her journey, such as those djinn, fairies, angels, and some nameless beings. Chantelle would never mention these occurrences to her highly religious family; only her best friend, Karen, knew, and now she was gone. Her religious family, who went to church a couple Sundays a month, would never understand, or want to understand, her abilities and her gifts. Chantelle understood and knew from a young age that she was the black sheep in the family; and such admissions would just cause them to label her as crazy, delusional, or worse.

As the high school years marched on, painfully slowly, in Chantelle's opinion, she longed to see her best friend, whose contact had been reduced to a monthly phone call and the occasional letter over the years. As even though the high school years were prolonged and torturous to Chantelle, it still was a very busy time with homework and working at the shop, which was her only real source of joy during these years, in addition to being with her otherworldly friends, who showed and taught her much over the years. Fine-tuning her abilities and gifts helped Chantelle to pass the time away, giving her life meaning, direction, and purpose. She would have many visions of the future, and predictions that always came true, that her family never understood how she would know these things but refused to believe the answer when Chantelle would tell them. The truth, to Chantelle's family, was too frightening and nonreligious, so denial, and labeling her as problematic was the only option.

Chantelle was excited for graduation because she had planned to finally go to New Orleans to visit her long-pined-for and missed friend of now over four years since she last saw her. With an uneventful high school graduation behind her, she was elated to finally catch her flight to Louisiana and, more importantly, to spend time and catch up with her friend. Chantelle never worried that they had grown apart as she knew they had, and always would share, a special bond, a special connection, and that their meeting, so many years before, was not a coincidence. Chantelle, even at a young age, knew that there are no coincidences in life. Even your family, for good or bad, better or worse, is meant to be in your life; some people are in your life for a long time and some not for long, but never a coincidence—all are there to teach you something.

Chantelle studied New Orleans, Louisiana, and its magical history, steeped in mystery, for months before her trip and was intrigued with its allure and haunting ambiance. People like Madame Marie Laveau intrigued her; so did stories of the French Quarter and the type of French Creole people that Louisiana was made up of due to the type of people who colonized and settled there so many years earlier.

CHAPTER 3

FREEDOM

Karen greeted Chantelle at the Louis Armstrong International Airport, wide-eyed and excited, which was palpable inside both women, their hearts racing to finally see and feel each other after more than four years apart. Chantelle felt at home, as though she had finally been reunited with her real family, her true family, a kindred spirit—even Louisiana seemed oddly familiar to her, beyond all the reading she had done on the place and its people.

Chantelle spent the first weeks in what she felt was heaven on earth, reliving childhood days of splendor, fun, conjuring, potion making, and playing in the woods with Karen. Chantelle and Karen had seemed to have endless things to catch up on; they would talk for hours and hours into the wee hours of the night. Like Chantelle, Karen never had a boyfriend in high school. She managed to connect with friends, something Chantelle couldn't do after Karen left, but no love interest connection. So Chantelle and Karen spent their nights out on the Louisiana town, at nightclubs and endless parties, until the early dawn many a night. They were having the time of their lives, carefree and happy. Chantelle never once missed her family back in Massachusetts. In fact, Chantelle was seriously thinking about staying in New Orleans, indefinitely, as she felt a welcoming kinship, a sisterhood, with New Orleans.

Karen managed to get Chantelle a job at the French Quarter gift shop where she worked, the Mardi Gras as it was appropriately named. The girls not only enjoyed spending this added time together, but Chantelle really did enjoy working at this shop. It reminded her a bit of her family's antiques shop in Salem, pretty much the only fond memory Chantelle had of her childhood back home. The Mardi Gras had some really cool souvenir-type items and also some metaphysical items like incense, candles, dream catchers, tarot cards, and more, following in line with the New Orleans, Madame Laveau, voodoo, and haunted theme of the town. Chantelle loved the whole day and night vibes of the town, and even though she and Karen managed to go out on the town nearly every night they weren't working, they still never seemed to be able to connect with anyone on a love relationship level—not that Chantelle thought much of it; she was having too good of a time and finally feeling herself and alive again to care about a boyfriend at the moment.

Until one fateful Friday at the Mardi Gras shop: while both Chantelle and Karen were working, a very handsome, sophisticated- and prestigious-looking older guy, walked into the shop. Chantelle was immediately drawn to him, not only for his tall, six-foot-two-inch frame and dark-haired, green-eyed good looks, or the permeating confidence he exuded, but for a weird connection she felt to him, as though she knew him from a past life, or maybe even in this life. He right away locked eyes with Chantelle, as her hazel-brown eyes spoke with his and they seemed to engage in a silent, knowing conversation with each other. As he approached Chantelle at the cashier's desk with his naked ladies shot glasses and other party favors, he gave her a wide and warm smile and then mouthed "Bachelor's party" as though he knew she was wondering why he was buying all those erotica novelties.

As he continued to gaze deep into Chantelle's eyes, he opened a conversation with her. "My best friend is getting married next week, and tonight's his bachelor's party."

Chantelle gave a playful nod of approval while gazing back into his brilliant green eyes, smiling and giggling lightly. He reached out his hand and introduced himself as Gary, and she could barely remember her name, but eventually managed to utter a response. "I'm Chantelle," she whispered in a quiet yet deep, throaty voice.

Chantelle never believed in love at first sight, but she was immediately smitten with Gary. His boyish good looks and athletic build aside, she felt a real connection to this person she only met moments earlier; and he must have felt the same way, because he immediately asked her for her phone number and if he could take her out on a date during the week, to which she immediately responded, "That would be nice."

Chantelle tried not to think of her amazing encounter with Gary or jinx it by talking too much about him with Karen, but her heart jumped out of her body when her cell phone rang Monday evening around seven and it was Gary. It seemed like only a few moments that they were on the phone during that initial conversation, yet it turned out to be one and a half hours they talked about themselves, their childhoods, jobs, and future plans. Chantelle was further smitten with Gary after this first phone contact as he continued to shape up to be everything she never knew she was really looking for in a man—a wish list that was maybe in the back of her mind. A list that she always knew would come into play when a possible Mr. Right came forth, a feeling she would know, recognize, and feel deep down in her soul to be right, him being the one.

Karen was excited for Chantelle, like a real best friend should be. Even though she was still without a boyfriend herself, the prospects of all his single friends that she might connect with loomed in her mind, along with the happiness for her friend.

As Chantelle started to get ready for her Wednesday-night first date with Gary, negativity started to creep into her mind: how could she possibly be so happy being here in New Orleans, and now seemingly meeting the man of her dreams? *Something has got to go wrong. Something bad must be going to happen*, she convinced herself. *No one person can have it all, especially not me*, she said to herself, as she was used to all the negativity and unhappiness of the life she had been leading for the last eighteen years before coming to Louisiana. How could it be possible to have it all! She was perplexed.

Karen helped Chantelle get ready for her date with Gary. She was beautifully dressed in a light-colored floral-print dress, a perfect material for the hot New Orleans summer night ahead. The girls were sipping on wine, laughing and giggling as they accessorized Chantelle, readying her for her date, and celebrating the occasion when the doorbell rang. It was Gary, ten minutes early. She could have used the extra ten minutes to calm her nerves, prepare some more, and drink a little more wine with Karen; but she was encouraged that his early timing could be signifying his excitement for the date. It definitely looked as though he took time to get ready because he looked even hotter than he did at the shop, if that was possible, she thought.

Karen watched as Gary walked into the entrance of her family's home and handed Chantelle a beautiful, exotic-looking bouquet of pink, bluish, purple, and white orchids, and then gently kissed her on the cheek. Unexpectedly, his kiss on her cheek sent shock waves through her body, an electricity—you would think it was their first real kiss because the intensity of their first skin-to-skin contact was so intense, even magical. Chantelle was thinking if this kiss on the cheek caused such an intense feeling, she was almost scared to kiss him on the lips but, oddly enough, looking forward to it as well. As they were walking to his beautiful new black sports car, he gently smiled and informed her, "We will be eating at the Rock Wood Country Club."

The Rock Wood Country Club, Chantelle thought as Gary drove. *Between the fancy new sports car, the reservations at the fancy country club, being always dressed in high-quality suits and gentlemen's wear, he must be doing very well at the genetics and engineering corporation he said he worked at as a financial corporate director.*

As they drove deep into the semi-woodsy area, just in the outskirts of New Orleans proper, where the exclusive country club was located, he asked Chantelle, "What made you say yes to going out with me that day in the shop?"

Chantelle let out a cute but slightly uncomfortable giggle, as she was not sure "Because you're hot" was the appropriate answer, yet telling him she felt a deep connection to him, a guy she just met, did not seem like the right answer either. So she decided to turn the question around and ask him, "Well, what made you want to ask me out that day at the shop?"

He again gazed deep into her twinkling brown eyes, like he was reading her soul, and said, "I felt comfortable with you, like I knew you. Also, you were so pretty, yet down to earth. I knew I could not leave there without your phone number, or at least trying to get it."

Chantelle liked his answer, as that was pretty much how she felt upon seeing him, so she replied, "Same." As they pulled up to the country club for dinner, laughing about their seemingly corny answers, they continued to sense an unexplained deep connection between them, like in a movie they had seen before and knew the happy ending.

As the humid July day turned to a slightly cooler evening and then night, Chantelle and Gary spent their first date laughing a lot, with the occasional hand holding, outside in the fresh, intoxicating Louisiana air. And then, right before they both knew they should wrap up the night for another time, Gary leaned over and planted a deep, lingering kiss on Chantelle's ruby-painted lips.

It was as though time actually stood still. Chantelle was floating on air; she was completely and absolutely smitten by Gary, and there was no turning back. And as Gary drove Chantelle back to her living quarters, the kiss and the Louisiana ambience had left them both speechless, yet they knew what each other was thinking and feeling. No words could express their shared happiness with each other at this moment; how blessed they felt to have found each other.

As Gary pulled into Karen's driveway, he asked Chantelle, "Would you do me the honor of being my date and guest at my friend's wedding this Saturday. I have many single friends, and seeing you might not feel comfortable at the wedding, as you don't know anyone, please bring Karen along with you, if she is available."

His offer rang through Chantelle's ears like bells of jubilee, and she knew Karen wasn't working this Saturday and would probably love the opportunity to socialize and meet his single friends, so she accepted the invitation on behalf of both of them. Chantelle thanked Gary for a wonderful night and then sprang out of his car into the house, where Karen sat waiting anxiously to hear all the details of their date, which she knew would be monumental—she just knew. Chantelle quickly showered, got into her most comfortable nightgown, and settled on Karen's bed to give her all the details, many that made her blush, and she didn't even know why.

Karen and Chantelle talked into the wee hours of the night as Chantelle gushed about Gary and all the attributes and personal qualities she loved about him, even though in the back of her mind, she was thinking such outward happiness and excitement was against her code of not talking about such things out loud as it would bring in people's evil thoughts and negativity, causing bad outcome, but this was her best friend, Karen, who never showed or thought of anything but happiness for Chantelle's successes and good fortune. Even when it wasn't Karen's success or good fortune, Chantelle felt safe divulging these innermost, intimate information and feelings to Karen because she knew Karen loved her so and would never want anything bad for her best friend.

Karen was elated to escort Chantelle to Gary's friend's wedding and later reception that beautiful summer day in July. They had a wonderful time like they expected, laughing and dancing the night away and making new friends as Karen met many of Gary's most eligible bachelor friends and Chantelle got to know not only more about Gary but all his childhood friends as well.

Gary being born and raised in New Orleans, to family who had a long history in Louisiana, understood the metaphysical part of life, as many people there did, with the Marie Laveau and voodoo history that preceded it. Chantelle felt very comfortable on dates with Gary when they would talk about the meaning of life, spirituality versus religion; and even though he was brought up a good Southern boy in the Baptist Church, whose family went to church most Sundays and followed the Bible, Gary understood where Chantelle was coming from with her fascination with haunted stuff, the dead, even grave-yards, as he mainly thought it to be imaginative play of her child-hood, and he internalized that Chantelle wasn't far out of being a child, seeing she was only nineteen years old and he would soon be thirty-two. They discussed their fairly significant age difference, him being thirteen years her senior, yet it didn't seem to be an issue when they were together as their mind and feelings seemed to work as one. They had much in common, felt the same about many subjects, and all his friends seemed to really like her, so what was age but a number, they would say.

Through the hot Louisiana summer nights, Chantelle and Gary were falling more and more in love with every date. And even though Gary had, at times, a very stressful job at the biochemical corporation Dyna Corp that seemed to drain him mentally and physically, he still found time to devote to Chantelle, as much as possible; and he always treated her like the queen he felt she deserved to be treated as. After barely one month of close-to-daily dating, Chantelle was invited by Gary's boss, David Candice, to his home for dinner, as David wanted to meet the woman who had stolen the heart of one of their most valued and top executives. The night began with Chantelle taking a cab ride to a small town outside of New Orleans, called Pendle, where Dyna Corp was located. Chantelle met up with Gary there and got the unofficial official tour of the company and a quick overview of its workings. Chantelle was intrigued by this large company and its highly advanced technology and its employees, who seemed to be the best of the best, at the top of their field from around the world in technological advances, biological studies, genetics, chemistry, and computer science in general. At this award-winning company where Gary worked many long hours, he had a much-coveted and very high-ranking position. Even though it was not directly involved in the actual biology, genetics, chemistry, and alchemy side of the company's operations, it was still a highly respected, integral position in the company. Dyna Corp was known to bring forth advances in genetic testing, biochemical testing, and a lot of other human and animal studies, advances Chantelle did not even grasp the full weight of, but what she did understand was that they were an important Fortune 500 company with many high-powered players, many of whom she met this day.

After leaving Dyna Corp, Gary's boss met them at his penthouse apartment, where he resided with just his wife, Joyce; they had no children. The penthouse was grand, seemed bigger than Karen's family home. There they enjoyed a leisurely dinner with Gary's boss and his wife, both of whom made Chantelle feel very welcome and at ease, even though inside, Chantelle was very nervous and scared about meeting and spending such intimate time with Gary's boss. Besides their high-class lifestyle that was very intimidating to Chantelle's mainly simple middle-class upbringing, she also knew and understood how important making a good impression on Gary's boss would be if she was to have a permanent, lasting relationship with Gary, as his work and position at the corporation, as well as his ability to move up the ladder in the company, meant the world to him. Chantelle was truly interested in this company because even though it had an outwardly award-winning reputation, it still had an air of secrecy, a covertness to it, something Chantelle wasn't quite able to figure out why. She would never tell Gary about such feelings about the company as she knew how he valued everything about it; but something in her psychic, intuitive, knowing, internal makeup was telling her something was not as it appeared with this company. Something was hidden about this company; it involved their testing and other things they were doing with genetics, harvesting cells, and it piqued feelings from Chantelle's childhood that weren't pleasant.

Maybe this was why it resonated so deeply and profoundly in Chantelle's mind, body, and being as it took her back to a memory when she was around eight years old. She remembered what looked like men in black coming to her home near Salem and visiting with her mom and dad, and also with her for some reason. Chantelle remembered that during their visit with these two men, she mostly played around them, but she also vividly remembered them showing her this weird green display of lights, advanced computer technology that they would scan and display on the white walls of their living room. Technology that was much too advanced for that time more than ten years ago; and even thinking back on it now, it was still advanced for the technology now, but it was shown to her by these unusual, unemotional to the point of direct and matter-of-fact men in black. The remainder of these two men's visit was a blur to Chantelle, but she remembered feeling it to be extremely odd and out of place with the people her family knew, and usually socialized with in the community; their visit, was never mentioned after this day. In fact, the whole visit just got forgotten, dismissed, so Chantelle never knew the meaning of and reason for their visit. What she did know was that her whole life growing up was a series of oddness and strangeness, with her seemingly at the center; and as she grew older, it became unsettlingly apparent that she was either being watched closely and/or monitored by people around her and around her community. She remembered at times being coerced to undergo certain mental and physical testing, and she was not quite sure why they were even doing it, like an experimental, investigative testing under the guise of health monitoring, and she could never figure out why her family would agree to subject her to such bizarre research.

The men in black and their weird advanced technology often came back into Chantelle's mind; and when that unusual day when she was about eight years old, was ever brought up to her parents, they would deny that such a visit ever occurred; and because her brothers were not around when these men visited (they had been conveniently taken out of the house on an "outing"), her parents would make her believe the whole day was a figment of her imagination. This denial further made Chantelle leery of her parents and the occurrence, as she knew without a doubt that it most definitely occurred.

*****

Back at Gary's boss's penthouse, Chantelle felt compelled to ask a few questions about his biochemical genetics lab. She figured, what better time than as a new person, just seemingly inquisitive and curious about this grand company, to ask detailed questions? David and Gary would proceed to tell Chantelle about the company's advances in gene testing, which included novel biochemical advances, brain wave monitoring and testing, and, admittedly, more, very advanced work that was still very hush-hush and kept a secret from the general population, and therefore they could not go into too much detail about it. But David and Gary must have sensed Chantelle's slight unease with the whole genetic, human, biochemical testing secrecy, as they seemed to go out of their way to try to make her feel okay with their many significant and highly regarded advances in biological science—advances they were convinced were all done for the good of humanity in general.

But David and his wife were quite interested in talking about more than just the corporation. David was very interested in things Gary had apparently told him of Chantelle's gifts and abilities. Gifts and abilities that she tried to limit discussing with even Gary, but which he always drew her into a discussion of as he was very intrigued and interested in her childhood tales and stories of all things she did that were influenced by the metaphysical. Gary went on and on about her psychic, intuitive ability, even inferring that she was able to conjure and talk with beings from other dimensions. Information that she did not feel comfortable sharing with virtual strangers, and she wasn't even completely sure she remembered talking to Gary about these very private, personal things as yet, and definitely not in such detail; but she thought maybe Karen had filled him in during the many talks she would have with him, like at the wedding reception or at the house, while he would be waiting for her to come down for their dates.

She's sure Karen was just giving Gary somewhat idle chatter to fill the time and to allow him to know more about her best friend through childhood tales, even if the tales are unusual and hard for most to believe.

Gary knew of times when Chantelle and Karen played in the forest near Salem, making potions, performing spells, and talking with otherworldly spirit beings like the djinn, fairies, and other unseen forces. Gary even knew about her secret portal, which he threw in for good measure; so David must think Gary was dating either a complete flake, or a very imaginative child, who knew. But instead, Gary, his boss, his friends, and, later, people at Gary's work seemed to think the opposite: they were intrigued and interested to know more, which felt a little good but also unsettling and uncomfortable for Chantelle at the same time.

Generally, the night went perfectly, and Chantelle had made a great impression on David and David's wife, as Gary knew she would.

CHAPTER 4

THE LOVE OF MY LIFE

An uneventful Tuesday in early September at the gift shop, with the busy season starting to slow down, and Chantelle had been enjoying almost three months of blissful dating with Gary, who was turning out to be not only the most devoted, generous boyfriend of a lifetime, but also the love of her life even though she was only nineteen years old and he was only the first boyfriend she had, but from watching shows on relationships and seeing other people over the years, even from watching her parents and other adults around her, she knew Gary was the One. He was everything a man should be: he was kind, giving, and caring, not only to her but to her friend and the people around him as well. Gary was very affectionate, and even though he was thirteen years older than her, he did not pressure her into a sexual relationship, knowing that this would be her first experience. They stayed very affectionate through a lot of kissing and touching; but like Gary, Chantelle yearned to take it deeper, farther with him, but she not only didn't want to rush the experience, she was a little scared of the experience. She knew Karen was also a virgin, so even though she was very understanding, comforting, and open on the subject, Karen could not share a different perspective in regard to Chantelle's most pressing questions. Should she wait—wait for a longer time of dating, six months or more? Should she wait for marriage? Chantelle was not sure, but she knew she wanted him, now, and it took a lot for both of them not to go there, but they did wait. Gary waited because when it would happen, he wanted it to be special for Chantelle; so even though he had a beautiful home in suburban New Orleans where it would be a nice experience, with the right preparation and ambience for her, Gary would rather take her somewhere special with a much more relaxed and romantic ambiance, like a vacation spot or at least a local five-star hotel, for her first time, he mused. So for now, until they figured out where and when they wanted *their* first experience and Chantelle's very first experience to occur, they were somewhat content with kissing and touching.

Chantelle was pleased to find out that Gary enjoyed her love of antiquing, and they had spent many a Saturday and Sunday combing New Orleans and other parts of Louisiana for great old artifacts and collectibles. Other interesting dates included an enjoyable weekend at Gary's family's lake house, which included his parents', both of Gary's two brothers' and their families' entertaining stories about Gary's Scottish American family roots. Similar to Chantelle, Gary was also a middle child. Both of Gary's brothers had been happily married for several years and had children of their own; both were wonderful husbands and fathers, and very attentive to their family's needs, which was a great, comforting reassurance of Gary's character for Chantelle. Gary's brothers were both sweet and kind like Gary, and it wasn't a surprise because their parents, who had been married for forty years at that point, were very nice people as well and welcomed Chantelle with open arms right from day one. Her being biracial did not seem to play any significance in them disliking or liking her, only her personality; and she seemed to fit into the family.

Chantelle's family, on the other hand, had not met Gary as yet; but Chantelle could already hear her mother's disapproving words, something negative she would find about him—Chantelle just knew it. Her father and her brothers might smile at him, be nice to his face, but who knew what they would really be saying behind his back— that was the kind of people they were, and how they did things so many times in the past. Chantelle thought it would be best to wait to tell her family that she had met someone and had fallen in love for later, way later, when she was sure what their plans were for the future. She reminded Karen not to mention anything about Gary, as

Karen did occasionally speak to Chantelle's family when they called from Massachusetts.

The days flew by due to the blissful, happy, euphoric state Chantelle was in while dating Gary. Now with Christmas and a solid six months into their relationship, things were heating up fast. They decided that they would spend Christmas Eve with each other, and Christmas Day Chantelle would spend half the day with Karen and her family and the latter half with Gary and his family. It worked out wonderfully. Before New Year's Eve, they could not take the sexual tension that was building from their affection and attraction for each other and six months of fondling and kissing anymore, so they decided that for New Year's weekend, they would fly out to Aspen, Colorado, that Friday evening and spend the whole New Year's weekend in blissful lovemaking. The flight from New Orleans Henry Armstrong Airport to the Pitkin County Airport in Aspen was uneventful and smooth, just over five hours. Chantelle not only bought and packed all the cold weather ski clothing she could find, including what she had from living in Massachusetts, she also went lingerie shopping with Karen before her weekend getaway. Their five-star hotel was amazing: the large living space, A+ room service, a Jacuzzi tub en suite, a fully stocked wet bar, a gym, and five-star restaurants all within a short distance. Chantelle was in heaven and enjoying this with the man she loved; she was in absolute nirvana. She daydreamed. How could life get any better? She was nervous for the upcoming intimacy, but she loved and trusted Gary, as he did her; and she knew he had her best interest in mind, and at all times, so she decided to relax and go with the flow, go with the mood, and "What will be, will be" was kind of her general motto in life. Gary felt the same way. They decided together. No pressure: if *it* happens, it happens; but if not, they still would have had an amazing New Year's weekend getaway and lots of fun.

Gary had been skiing before, including in Aspen, but Chantelle never skied before, but she was eager to learn, though. Gary paid for a few hours of a professional teacher to give Chantelle the basics of skiing and to help her feel good on skis; and then after that, he was the only teacher and assistant she needed to navigate the slopes. She wasn't anything close to good, especially on the bigger slopes, but she held her own and was having fun doing so, even when falling down, which she did often. Saturday, December 31, New Year's Eve, and they ended up skiing early and came in for an early dinner and some wine after a relaxing Jacuzzi tub bath together.

After dinner, Chantelle slipped into her newly bought passion-red lingerie, tasteful but sensual- and romantic-looking; and they sipped wine and laughed about the day's events. Then midway through a sentence, Gary laid a deep, lingering kiss on Chantelle's plump cherry lips. And as their kiss grew deeper and deeper, it led into touching, rubbing, and groping. They could barely keep their hands off each other. They moved to the bedroom, where they both passionately and quickly took off their clothes. Chantelle was enjoying rubbing Gary's fit, tanned, abdominal area and well-developed biceps as he was enjoying starting at the top, kissing her neck and moving down her body. As they enjoyed a passionate night of lovemaking, she could not ask for anything more in a first sexual experience. Gary was loving and attentive, gentle and strong all at the same time. And that morning, Chantelle awoke to hot coffee and a gourmet breakfast, all courtesy of the five-star room service but served to her by Gary right in bed. After another session of lovemaking that morning, they had to start packing for a late-afternoon flight back to New Orleans. It had been a perfect weekend, even though they realized they missed the official midnight transition into the New Year, that night had other, more significant memories, cumulating in the best New Year's celebration for both of them as they now returned to their homes in Louisiana—relaxed, contented, and emotionally closer than ever.

Chantelle had barely unpacked her bags when Karen appeared at her door. "Inquiring minds want to know—how was your weekend?" She knowingly beamed on.

Chantelle, half smirking and giggling, gestured to Karen with a thumbs-up and said casually, as though nothing out of the ordinary happened, "Fine." She wanted to tell Karen all the details of her first time with Gary, but a part of her felt protective not only of this most personal, private information but also of Gary's privacy. She did not want to kiss and tell, even though she knew that Gary would understand, since he knew how close and strong the bond was between her and Karen and respected that relationship.

"Don't give me the thumbs-up," quipped Karen. "Come on, details, details," she impatiently demanded. Chantelle still wanted to hold on to some of the private glow from being with Gary, but she wanted to honor the bond between her and her good friend, so she gave Karen some vague details of her night with Gary, just enough to confirm that they had sex, her first-time sex, that weekend, and that it was great but steered away from getting into too many intimate details as she still felt that it would be violating Gary's privacy and their relationship.

Karen didn't want to be an overbearing and noisy friend on such a personal topic, and therefore was quickly able to read her friend and know when it was time to let the subject drop and not pry any further for details of their intimate weekend.

As the cooler, darker Louisiana days and nights continued in January of the new year, the heat continued to stay turned up between Chantelle and Gary. Chantelle was so happy she was now even thinking about setting Karen up with one of Gary's single friends and going on a double date, but she wasn't sure which one of Gary's single friends would be perfect for Karen and fun to go on a double date with. Chantelle mulled over three great choices for her friend: There was Peter, who was a coworker of Gary's, a very smart, ambitious, college-educated young member of Dyna Corp who, despite his age, already held a high position at the company and was very close to the boss-owner, David Candice.

Then there was Frank, who was a childhood friend of Gary's since grade 8, when they were fourteen years old. Frank worked at a local car dealer's and was very good at selling, the "able to sell an igloo to an Eskimo" type of person. He was a smart guy, and a financially stable too—another potentially great match for Karen.

Then there was Shawn, who was a college friend of Gary's and who right away connected with Gary in their late teens as though they had known each other all their lives. He worked in real estate and finance, like Gary, and was an extremely successful real estate broker in the Louisiana area. He was a very driven, high-energy, bordering on hyper, personality, definitely a type A personality; but he had a very caring, down-to-earth side to him at times, which also made him a very good potential candidate for Karen.

So now they had to figure out which one of these guys Karen liked the best and which one wanted to date her. Karen was attractive, cute, and nice, had sandy-colored hair and a curvy figure, and also very intelligent, so finding someone to go on a first date wasn't really an issue. She had met all of them at other events and social interactions, so all parties knew of each other, but who did she prefer, and who was attracted to her? Chantelle asked Gary that Friday during their movie night if he was okay with setting up a double date with Karen and one of his friends, which he immediately thought was a great idea. Chantelle now needed to get his male prospective on who he felt liked Karen the best and would be a good match for her, personality-wise.

Gary chose his good friend Shawn, which wasn't a surprise, because of the three, he was closest to Shawn and would find it enjoyable going out on a night with his good college friend tagging along. But was he a good match for Karen or just a good buddy match for Gary? Did Gary pick him after considering the personalities of both Karen and Shawn and whether they were a true match? Chantelle trusted that Gary was a stable, sensible guy, and guys being guys, he would also not want to be responsible for hooking up his good friend with a *terrible* date, even for one night; so she knew he must be the right choice for Karen.

It was set. Karen and Shawn both agreed, and they were feeling good about their double date night that following Friday in late January. A cold date night, but a good opportunity to wear a wide variety of clothes, so Chantelle and Karen drank wine, dressed, and helped each other with accessories, hair, and makeup. Promptly at 7:00 p.m., the doorbell rang. It was Gary and Shawn at the door, both looking very handsome and perfectly coiffed for the night ahead. Appearing like perfect gentlemen, both Gary and Shawn had a beautiful bouquet of flowers for their respective dates. Shawn seemed taken aback, and pleasantly surprised, by Karen's appearance and told her unapologetically that she looked very beautiful, even better than he remembered. The night went off effortlessly as Karen and Shawn were getting on perfectly—laughing, drinking, and enjoying each other's company. Both couples had a fantastic time, and love was blossoming between Karen and Shawn, who really seemed to have a strong attraction for each other. They couldn't seem to stop kissing and take their hands off each other, making Gary and Chantelle a little uncomfortable; but they understood, because that was how they felt for each other right from the start. Definitely more of an attraction than Chantelle and Gary could have ever anticipated, because Karen and Shawn ended their first date night back at Shawn's apartment making love, Karen's first but not her last, as Shawn and her became official boyfriend and girlfriend, and inseparable, after that earth-shattering first date, as they described it.

That February 14, Valentine's Day, fell on a Friday; and after almost nine months of blissful dating, Gary decided Chantelle was the woman for him, the wife for him, and he didn't want her to get away. He arranged an elaborate dinner for the two of them at his exclusive country club—the Rock Wood, the country club where they had their first date. Dinner was perfect, and the ambience in the room was perfect—with just a few other people and just light chatter. After dinner, before dessert, Chantelle was in mid-conversation with Gary, but he could barely follow her as he knew that any minute he was going to ask Chantelle to marry him and was all of a sudden very nervous and sweating, not usual for his normal cool, calm exterior, something Chantelle right away noticed. Looking at him kind of puzzled her because her conversation was very light; hastily, she saw Gary down on one knee, holding a large ring box and nervously opening it, and then without further hesitation, he said, "Chantelle, my love, my beauty, my friend, would you do me the honor and be my wife?"

Chantelle was completely blindsided. Even though she knew things were moving quickly, and blissfully, between them, she was not expecting a marriage proposal so early in their relationship. Between her own nervousness of the moment and all the spectators looking on in awe of the situation, she managed to mutter a quiet but notable "Yes" in a half-tearful voice. Gary was elated, and seemingly surprised, at her response, even though he knew how much he loved her and she reciprocated that love toward him, so why wouldn't she say yes? Maybe her tender age of nineteen was vaguely in back of his mind as to why she might say no, but she didn't. She was extremely happy at the moment, and gave him a passionate hug and a deep, long kiss while the onlookers applauded, elated over the joyous event that just unfolded. Still stunned and on cloud nine all at the same time, Chantelle could not wait to get home and tell Karen about her blissful night. She was going to be Mrs. Gary Moore.

The news caught Karen off guard, but Chantelle's engagement news was still received with extreme happiness and joy by her best friend and, unknown to her yet, maid of honor. Karen and Chantelle spent the rest of that night, into the wee hours, laughing and musing about her perfect wedding—*when* and *where* it should be and the type of dresses she would consider. It was a night of girlish fun like when they were children. Chantelle couldn't wait to share the news with her family back in Massachusetts even though she felt apprehensive sharing such news with them as she knew they would be stunned by this unexpected engagement, seeing as not only did they know next to nothing about Gary, they had been dating for less than a year, and Chantelle wasn't even twenty years old yet. That Sunday, Chantelle phoned her childhood home and first spoke with her older brother, giving him the news and then each of the remaining family members came on the phone. They all seemed surprised and uncharacteristically elated by her good news.

Since Gary and Chantelle became engaged two days ago, they hadn't seen each other as Gary was knee deep in paperwork for his boss, so they were content to share a little quality time over the phone, and Chantelle was not bored as she had Karen to keep her entertained. They spent the rest of the weekend discussing boys and dating, but now it was Karen's turn to dish on how she felt about Shawn and all about her passionate nights with him. Because she and Karen were so busy over the last weeks, she found it a good time to now ask Karen all the questions she had on her mind since her blind date with Shawn and the subsequent passionate nights with him.

Chantelle was curious about what had changed. Karen had seen Shawn on several social occasions before their official *blind* date and never said too much about him except that he was cute and very nice, so what had changed? What had changed so much that they would sleep together on the first night? Whatever had changed, they both seemed to have felt it as Shawn was dating her and gushing about her to Gary every chance he got. Thank goodness for all involved, their date turned out the right way, as it could have ended up a bitter one-night-stand, snowballing into awkward social gatherings moving forward, for both their best friends, who would have to referee in the turbulence.

After a busy week at work for both Gary and Chantelle, they were finally afforded time to see each other that following Friday, a week after their engagement; and they had a hard time keeping their hands off each other. They spent a wonderful weekend lounging and making love at Gary's home, which Chantelle acknowledged would soon be her place. She thought about what cosmetic changes she would like to make to it. Or should they sell this house and buy something more to both their liking, and bigger, so they could add to their family, she further speculated in her mind while Gary was making intense phone calls to his boss, as things at his company could become quite stressful for Gary at times, and this was definitely one of those times, followed by Gary having a hard time relaxing the remainder of that weekend. Still, Gary made the best of it and used the weekend of lovemaking with Chantelle as his stress reliever. He would joke with her, as they managed to still enjoy a somewhat peaceful weekend with lots of one-on-one quality time. Chantelle helped Gary to relax, take his mind off his problems at work—problems he would never discuss with her—by telling him all about her week at work, her conversations with Karen, which included his best friend Shawn, and how *their* relationship was going, ideas the women came up with for the wedding and the engagement party, all very stress-free, distracting, and relaxing conversations for Gary.

Now was a perfect time, Chantelle thought, to see if they could agree on a wedding date. What date did Gary have in mind for their nuptials, and did he even tell his parents yet? Gary admitted, of course, his parents knew of their, possible, engagement as he had run the idea by them first; his mother even helped him pick out the engagement ring, he informed her. A ring that was a gorgeous Cartier Princess-cut diamond, over two carats in a platinum setting, with smaller diamonds around its complete thick band. It was grand, Chantelle thought as she admired it closely again and puzzled in her mind, what did she do to deserve such an engagement ring? It was fit for a *queen*, not a princess; and Gary made her feel like royalty every chance he got. Gary knew in his heart that this was to be his one and only marriage, the love of his life, and therefore, he didn't want to spare any expense in showing her that love, added to the fantastic position he achieved within Dyna Corp utilizing his vast talent, for which he was generously paid for his time and performance.

Gary was very generous himself with everyone around him, but he especially loved showering Chantelle with random gifts, gestures of his love; and Chantelle could never get accustomed to it because she was never treated this well in all her almost twenty years of life. She was madly in love with Gary and would not, could not, imagine her life without him—a very scary thought she would ponder, even at her young and carefree age. She got a feeling of slightly losing her independence for dependence, as she had always relied only on herself in life thus far; and now she found it too easy, and a bit scary, to release some of that power to someone else. She had always felt controlled by her parents, family, and, to some degree, her community back in Massachusetts, especially seeing as there was a part of her that always had to be hidden; but now that she had found a degree of freedom here in Louisiana, was she again giving away her power, her control on her life to Gary, she had to wonder. She would tell herself it would only feel like she was giving away her power, her control if they were not in sync, if they were not compatible, and that being in love with her, Gary too had relinquished some of his power and control over his life to join their lives together—thoughts that were true but still scary just the same with the upcoming nuptials in her mind.

Chantelle playfully, yet with serious overtones, asked Gary if he had a date in mind for them to become man and wife. Gary loved the sound of them becoming man and wife but never really thought of a date as he figured Chantelle would be like every other woman out there and want to be the one with the final say on the blessed date. "What date did you have in mind?" he asked Chantelle.

Chantelle and Karen had played with a spring wedding like May, a summer wedding like late July or August, and an early fall wedding like September; and seeing as it was already almost March, booking for spring was way too rushed and stressful to do even though it did not seem that between her friends, family, his friends and family, some coworkers, the wedding list would exceed one hundred—maybe one hundred and fifty, but she still wanted a wonderful and grand wedding regardless of the number in attendance.

"Well," she whispered in a sultry voice to Gary, "Karen and I looked over a few dates, and I really like July 1 for our wedding day."

Gary paused for a moment and then agreed emphatically, "Yes, yes, July 1 it is, then. Perfect. I love that date!" They both agreed, but even a summer wedding would not give them very much time to plan all that needed to get done—invitations, the gown, the hall, the church, the engagement party, and, of course, the honeymoon plans; but cost was not a factor, as Gary insisted on paying for everything. Chantelle had much to do and was excited, excited, and in love. They also agreed that it would be best, more meaningful, if they agreed to not have any sexual relations for at least two months before the wedding, so April 30 was C-Day, they joked, for Celibate Day. Chantelle decided to let Gary decide and make all the plans for their honeymoon. "Surprise me," she told him, and Gary happily took the challenge. And one more wedding matter for them to decide: who was going to be the maid of honor, which was obviously, Karen, but also the best man; and in light of Shawn and Karen now being a couple, it would make sense to have Shawn as the best man. It was decided then, but the only worry they had was, what if Karen and Shawn broke up before the wedding and would be forced to spend all that time together as maid of honor and best man? Chantelle and Gary decided it best to take their dating friends out for dinner and officially ask them to be part of their wedding party, while also gauging their relationship; discussing the what-if's would probably be in order with their respective best friends. Chantelle reassured herself that the good thing in that whole scenario was that the wedding was only a few short months away and not a year or more, where a lot more things could go wrong, like a breakup between her maid of honor and Gary's best man.

Chantelle started the planning that following Monday with Karen on board with the dates, the reception plans, the dress hunting, and more. It was stressful, but fun stress. Karen also agreed, along with Shawn, to have dinner with Chantelle and Gary that upcoming Friday night, Gary's treat. Karen knew she and Shawn would be maid of honor and best man but thought it was a lovely gesture, and a great idea, to go out to dinner and discuss their exciting plans some more. Karen, being the good friend she was and always had been to Chantelle since childhood, was just as excited for Chantelle getting married as she would be if it was her own wedding. She held no jealousy or resentment, just happiness for her friend, a friend she knew finally deserved some true happiness in her life.

News spread quickly around Dyna Corp of Gary's upcoming nuptials. Everyone was elated at the news, and most assumed they were invited to at least the wedding, if not the reception. But that elation quickly turned to stress at work as more and more pressure was on Gary to not only keep the financial end of Dyna Corp healthy with new and old investors, but he was also hired as a *finder*, they called it—a title and job he never mentioned to Chantelle, but for good reason. It was never to be discussed outside of the corporation. A finder was a special and secret appointed position, fit for a person who found the perfect human specimens for testing and investigations, much of which fell outside the lines of legal human testing. It was a position that Gary reluctantly accepted. He could barely bring himself to think about this part of his job because in the five years he had been at Dyna Corp, he had really only needed to do "finding" a handful of times, but in every case, the people were unwilling participants—participants he would never hear from again after they were handed over to the control of the powers within the company.

Gary, being a religious guy, couldn't believe what he had gotten himself into. He knew it was a sin, it was wrong; but he couldn't jeopardize such a coveted and lucrative position at this prestigious company by refusing to do this part of his job, but the guilt always wore heavy in his mind and heart. Lately, there seemed to be even more pressure to find their next specimen, as they had an important advanced genetic and biometric testing needed for their buyers and were looking for that special someone to basically, if the truth be told by Gary, abduct, drug, and keep at their private, secret lab facility out of state for these extensive tests.

How could I truly feel happy with my life, with Chantelle having this dark secret, Gary thought. To make matters worse, it seemed that he must find them their next specimen fast, as their interest in getting to know Chantelle and her abilities was intensifying. Gary had noted that all-too-familiar glimmer of excitement in his boss's eyes when talking about Chantelle. Unfortunately for Chantelle, David and Dyna Corp looked good on paper but underneath operated a dark underground world that Gary was too involved in now to get out. The company employed the best and brightest mad scientist–type minds who would stop at nothing to produce outcomes and genetically engineered advancements for their high-powered, wealthy clients from around the world. Gary found human specimens for his boss through the connections he had, *good friends* who worked at hospitals and labs in New Orleans and across the country; whenever someone would come through fitting the criteria, they would inform him. The criteria included very little family connections, the right age range, the right intelligence and profession, and, most importantly, a specialness, a uniqueness, and sometimes even blood work with unique qualities defying the norm—many qualities that Chantelle exhibited. Gary would receive these reports from those facilities, and then the arrangements would be made, the covert operation would be initiated. Even though Chantelle could never understand *how* or *why* Gary's position as a so-called financial advisor for Dyna Corp was so stressful, especially after all these years of doing the same job, Gary could never tell her the true nature of his stress, which was already putting extra added stress on him, and now on their relationship too. One of their labs attached to a hospital in Minnesota had found a perfect match and notified Gary, who let his boss know the details. It took the stress off for a little while, but the guilt was starting to really weigh on Gary.

*****

Chantelle and Karen had the Hall, a beautiful outdoor spot in the heart of the French Quarter, and the church, old, eclectic and near the hall, booked within a week. Now it was time to go dress hunting: they combed all the higher-priced shops, lower-priced shops, even secondhand stores, looking for the perfect dress; but they could not seem to find what Chantelle was looking for—simple but elegant, old but new, classic but modern. Chantelle admitted she was not easy to shop for. One would think it would be easy for Chantelle to find *her* dress with her perfectly proportioned figure at 120 pounds in a five-foot-five frame, but their task was not easy, even though they enjoyed the hunt. It was a great bonding experience for her and Karen. So while Chantelle pondered where to find the perfect wedding dress, they decided to plan the engagement party, who was going to be invited to it, and when they want to have it, the traditional night before the wedding or a few days before the wedding. They decided to have it the night before the wedding, June 30, as the venue was available, and Chantelle agreed it would be a great way to decrease wedding jitters, seeing all her friends, family, other loved ones, and coworkers the day before her wedding.

As Chantelle's birthday, March 23, approached, the wedding jitters seemed to increase and weigh heavily on her, but not Gary. He was calm now and without stress for the moment, as everything was calm and happy at work with his latest find. Gary was planning to throw a surprise birthday bash for Chantelle at his and her favorite country club restaurant, where he had invited all her friends from work, three or four of them, including Karen, as well as Karen's parents. Gary also flew in Chantelle's family from Massachusetts for the birthday festivities, giving himself a chance to meet them before the wedding as well. Her family all accepted the invitation and the free flight, along with hotel accommodations in Louisiana. They thought it was a very nice gesture by Gary to meet his fiancée's family and celebrate her birthday all at the same time. The festivities were to be on Saturday, March 21, as her actual birthday fell on a Monday that year, so Chantelle's family were flown in on Friday, March 20, unbeknownst to Chantelle.

Chantelle and Gary arrived at the country club at around 6:45 p.m. for a supposed 7:00 p.m. dinner reservation, according to Gary, but instead, she was greeted by a roomful of people screaming, "Happy birthday" when she opened the door to the private banquet room. Chantelle was shocked, to say the least, as there stood a roomful of coworkers, including many of Gary's coworkers, friends, and her family, whom she had not seen in over a year. Chantelle was fighting back tears not only from the feeling of love and caring coming from the room but also at the thought of the extensive planning Gary had gone through for her. As she opened her many gifts in front of family and friends, everyone was in awe of the grand display of the engagement ring, as well as at Chantelle and Gary's constant exchanges of affectionate glances; it was obvious that these two were madly in love and that they couldn't wait to be Mr. and Mrs. Gary Moore. The night went off smoothly and was a wonderful occasion for Gary and Chantelle's family to meet and get to know each other. It was also a wonderful reunion for Karen, her family, and Chantelle's family who had not seen one another in over five years.

Chantelle's family flew back to Massachusetts that Sunday, and Monday, work and everyday routines resumed, along with the detailed, finite planning for the wedding. Karen and Chantelle had planned another wedding dress search day, along with Karen's mother, for that coming Saturday. Wine and dress hunting would be in order, with Karen's mom as the designated driver. They went to a swanky bridal boutique in the heart of New Orleans that made a specialty niche of embracing the ambience and atmosphere around the whole bridal shopping experience. The bride and her attendees were pampered hand and foot, as well as supplied them with flowing complimentary champagne while they shopped and tried on dresses and accessories. Chantelle had an idea of what she wanted her wedding dress to look like even though she never really thought of it before her engagement. She was open-minded, though, and easygoing, with trying on different dresses, different looks, different styles of wedding dresses. Chantelle did finally find the perfect wedding dress—a princess-style, mermaid-cut dress that made her look like a young girl. She was elated. Her wedding dress featured, a slimming, figure-hugging cut, void of sleeves, and tastefully showing cleavage. It was a beautiful pure-white silken dress with some shimmery sequins, tastefully sewn throughout. With the perfect hairstyle and a gorgeous long veil train, they could easily envision how Chantelle was going to look on her wedding day—a showstopper.

The ladies spent approximately two and a half hours in the fancy boutique and accomplished all they needed to for the nuptials, including finding a dress for Karen's mother, the selection of maid of honor dresses, and a potential bridal party dress color and style. Chantelle wasn't 100 percent sold on having a bridal party, but she knew that if she did have one, it would only include two or three other girls, close coworkers basically. She was having an early summer wedding, but she still wanted darker colors for the bridal scheme, so she chose black and wine—wine meaning a deep berry red to be the color scheme throughout her day.

After the ladies finished taking care of all the important matters for the day, they decided to relax and end the wonderful day by going out to dinner, Karen mom's treat. They found a fun, sports bar–type place that was upbeat and bustling with single young people having fun on this Saturday night. Chantelle called Gary to let him know the additional plans and to see what he was doing with his extended time without her. He was at his home doing paperwork and bookwork for the company and was just going to sit down to a relaxing evening beer after a long day of work. He was happy to hear from her and all the details of her productive and pleasant day with her closest confidants, other than himself, and had no issue with her staying out even longer for dinner. "More time for girl talk with the ladies," he joked. Chantelle and Gary both agreed that it was a long, tiring day for both of them, and not seeing each other until the next day was fine. Chantelle promised to call him again the moment she returned home, so he knew she was safe and that all was well.

The ladies enjoyed a lovely meal at the sports bar, even though both Karen and Chantelle were already starting to watch what they ate so that they would look even more fantastic for the wedding events, and they did manage to find a light salad dish among the blue cheese, hot wings, nacho, and dip selections. After their nice, light dinner that included laugh-out-loud girl chitchat about boys, and even some boyfriend dish by Karen, stuff that her mother might not have wanted to know, the ladies retired to home for the night by 8:00 p.m. They were spent.

After Chantelle had washed off her makeup and gotten into her night attire, she managed to muster the last bit of energy she had to call Gary, as she promised, to assure him that she was home safe and would see him tomorrow by noon.

Chantelle slept soundly that night and woke up refreshed around 10:30 a.m., which was a late start but okay for a Sunday. She felt happy, calm, and refreshed and ready to have a peaceful Sunday afternoon and evening with Gary, even though she did not know what he had planned for them, if anything—maybe a quiet night in. They had postponed their double date, post–engagement dinner with Karen and Shawn to the following Saturday as this weekend ended up being too busy for all involved, including Shawn. Gary knew that Karen, being Chantelle's best friend, would be her maid of honor, and had basically already accepted the task; but Gary had not asked Shawn yet, and he and Chantelle still wanted to speak with their newly dating couple about the what-if's in relation to their upcoming wedding. They spent a quiet Sunday in his home and around the neighborhood. They sat outside in the warm early-springtime air. Chantelle started to do some planting for Gary, adding various seeds to pots in the yard; and then after dinner, close to twilight, they went for a long walk in the cool springtime night air of New Orleans. Gary lived in a very safe and upper-class area of the New Orleans suburbs. It was lined with many newly developed and fairly large houses, a comment on how well he was being paid at Dyna Corp at his, relatively, young age; it was an area that signaled growing wealth, and its desirability, was going up every year.

Aware that their C-Day was fast approaching, Gary and Chantelle decided to make the best of their quiet Sunday night together: Chantelle stayed overnight, and they enjoyed a playful, and lust filled night together. They were not sure how they would manage two months without intimacy of this level before the wedding as they found it hard to go a week without tearing each other's clothes off, literally; but they knew in the long run, it would add to the perfectness of their special day and the honeymoon that would follow—a honeymoon that Gary confirmed to Chantelle he had already decided on as far as where they would go; he had already booked their trip, and all he would tell her was that it was somewhere tropical, and they would be flying out the day after their wedding.

Chantelle was not worried, because not only was Gary worldly and had great taste in everything he did, she also remembered the elaborate five-star skiing trip he took her on for the New Year, and therefore had no thought or worry about his chosen destination, or about the itinerary for their honeymoon. That was one of the amazing qualities that made Chantelle fall even more in love with Gary— his ability to take charge, do a great job, his attention to details, and his general good taste in all things he did. Chantelle, like Gary, had fallen deeply in love. It was a very scary place for them both, but oddly comforting at the same time—a place neither of them had ever been before, not even Gary, who was thirteen years older than her. He had dated many women before, some for long periods of time, a year or more, but none had stuck, he admitted; none got deep into his heart and soul like Chantelle had, and so quickly.

Gary was up early for work the next day, Monday, and Chantelle went in at noon at the shop for an afternoon shift. As the week progressed, uneventfully, Chantelle reminded Karen to confirm that she and Shawn were having dinner with her and Gary Saturday, Gary's treat. Saturday came not a minute too early for Gary, as he was looking forward to a pleasant, mindless, easygoing, laughter-filled night with his fiancée and their good friends, seeing as he just had another brutally stressful week at Dyna Corp, which seemed to be becoming more and more frequent lately. Gary unpleasantly reviewed in his mind, while waiting for Chantelle to arrive at his house, how Dyna Corp would have him old looking and gray headed before his thirty-fifth birthday with the kind of stress he was being put under. He wasn't sure if the big paychecks and bonuses were worth the now daily stress and headaches. Plus, with every day that went by, Gary was feeling ever more uncomfortable with the frequent inquiry by David about Chantelle and, how special she was with the unique talents she had been born with, even hinting, or more like pushing, that they needed to start their family immediately after the wedding to bring forth "more special individuals in this world for us all to learn from," Gary recited, mimicking what he called David's creepiest Dyna Corp tone. David's cryptic messages and conversations were weighing just as heavily on Gary, as were the many unsettling tasks the company was asking him to do lately. It was as though they were preparing him for a really big task, a much bigger task; and the thought of who it might involve made Gary's stomach turn, as he was unexpectedly, truly, and deeply in love with Chantelle.

Just then, Gary heard a knock at the door. It was Chantelle, and Gary struggled to get back into a good mood, a saner mood than the one he was currently in. Thinking about his unscrupulous boss and his company was truly giving him a headache; in fact, he felt a migraine coming on and quickly took a couple of aspirins before it became worse. As he greeted Chantelle at the door with a big, tight hug and a long, deep kiss, she was flabbergasted,

"Wow! What did I do to inspire that greeting?" She was puzzled but didn't really care because she enjoyed the affection.

When they arrived at the classy black-tie-attire–type restaurant and saw his best friend and Karen waiting for them, he whispered into Chantelle's ear, "Did I tell you today how much I love you and how beautiful you look tonight?"

Chantelle giggled at the spontaneous and sexy whispers from Gary as they approached their seated friends and greeted them with excited hugs and kisses. It was obvious to Shawn and Karen that Chantelle and Gary were so much in love, they looked as though they might have been intimate just before arriving at the restaurant for their double date.

The evening proceeded with lots of wine, laughter, and good times, just like Gary had prescribed, intertwined, in a delicate way, were Gary and Chantelle, bringing up Karen and Shawn's relationship in the spirit of keeping it light, making sure to be not too invasive and to be sincere; but eventually, they confessed to Karen and Shawn what their concerns were in relation to their upcoming wedding. Karen and Shawn were not mad with the grilling into their relationship and what their feelings were for each other; instead, they completely understood how and why this would be a bit of a worry for them. They all understood and agreed that weddings could bring out either the best or the worst in people. They had all seen it before with friends and family. Karen and Shawn assured Chantelle and Gary that their relationship was solid, progressing slowly like they agreed on, and they were not putting any pressure on each other in that regard, and that they had strong feelings for each other and therefore did not feel that their concerns would come to fruition— at least not before their wedding, Shawn and Karen lightheartedly joked. The late night ended with Karen and Shawn going back to his place and Gary driving Chantelle home, as he had an early-morning business phone conference with a European investor at eight o'clock on Sunday morning. Gary needed to be alert, well rested, and clearheaded for this important meeting as all details would need to be relayed to David bright and early Monday morning. After a long kiss goodnight in the car, Chantelle ran in to the house. Karen's parents were fast asleep upstairs, leaving the house uncommonly quiet. Chantelle fell sound asleep that night.

For Gary, the time leading up to their engagement party, and their wedding the following day, flew by quickly. Between busy days at work and fitting in quality time with Chantelle, he barely had a moment to ponder that he would be a married man soon. The latter weeks of June came in with extremely hot days in New Orleans. All plans for their wedding had already been secured, paid for, and ready to roll out, including Chantelle having two bridesmaids to pair with Gary's two other good friends in the bridal party, Frank and Peter. And just as they reassured months earlier, Karen and Shawn were still happily dating, and their relationship was growing stronger and stronger, every day. Gary again insisted on paying for Chantelle's whole, immediate family to fly out to Louisiana for the engagement party and the wedding, and they would be arriving on June 29, the day before the engagement party. He also set them up in a five-star hotel near the venue of the festivities. The guys planned Gary's bachelor's party the Saturday before the wedding, the same day the women were hosting the bachelorette's party for Chantelle. The guys went to what they called classy, but still trashy in the women's eyes, strip club in the heart of New Orleans; and even though a lot could go wrong with that scenario, Chantelle completely trusted Gary and knew how much he loved her and how in control he was at all times, even when drinking, so she had no concerns. The women did not feel the need for male strippers at home or at a club and instead decided to fly to Vegas for a full twenty-four hours of drinking, gambling, and taking in shows and the crazy ambience of the Vegas Strip. They had a fantastic time.

Afterward, with the bachelor parties behind them, Chantelle and Gary were starting to feel a little more nervous as the engagement party and the wedding day loomed. Chantelle loved that Gary had flown her family in for the wedding and also booked a room for Chantelle and Karen together that was close to the rooms of Chantelle's family, so that she could have a quiet night with Karen and her family the night before the wedding. The engagement party was at the Four Season's Hotel's Banquet Room, and they had approximately sixty people there, including their dates and spouses. Chantelle got ready at Gary's place, wanting to make love before the event but couldn't as their C contract was in full effect. They were handling it quite well, considering they both painfully wanted to be with each other.

Chantelle wore a tight-fitting, low-cut black cocktail dress paired with expensive black platinum pumps, courtesy of her generous fiancée. Gary wore a custom-tailored black dress pants, with a tailored, almost-fuchsia dress shirt, which he had no issue wearing—in fact, he loved when he could wear bright colors for his attire, something he could not do too much of at Dyna Corp. The engagement party was a fun-loving event with family, friends, and coworkers, a perfect prelude to the following day's grand events. There were drinks, stories by Gary's family, friends, and coworkers of old lovers and good times, even vacations together. Chantelle's crew did not have as many colorful, good times to share for her tender years of only twenty, but her friends and family managed to impart unique Chantelle stories to the mix, so all could know the bride and the groom that much better. The party ended early, by 9:00 p.m., so all could get a good night's rest for wedding day ahead, which was promising to be a long and emotional, event.

Both Chantelle and Gary had a very hard time falling asleep the night before the wedding and staying asleep for more than an hour or two at a time, which did not make for great mental and emotional stability for the big day. Gary awoke to an empty house, which he fondly reviewed in his mind would be filled with the loving sounds of Chantelle after the honeymoon. Chantelle awoke with her mother and Karen in her room, both of whom she needed for emotional support that night. The wedding was to take place at 1:00 p.m. in the very large old medieval cathedral in the heart of New Orleans. It was a very old church, but well maintained and rich with history. They had a nondenominational pastor preside over the matrimony. Pastor Henry Everett was a kind and fun-loving ordained minister who had been making them feel at ease and calm about the whole vow taking and wedding procedure since yesterday, at the rehearsal segment of the engagement dinner.

All parties were on time, so the nuptials started promptly at 1:00 p.m. Chantelle was beyond nervous, and so was Gary. They weren't nervous because they didn't love each other or didn't want to be legally man and wife, but due to the elaborate importance society placed on this event, the significance of the whole day and the permanence of the vows. It made them feel that they were vowing and signing their life away to some unseen forces. Gary and Chantelle found it very hard to believe that everyone did not feel some level of nervousness when getting married; it was just that some people could handle the pressure and stress of the day better than others, they told themselves the night before while commiserating on the phone.

Gary looked so handsome waiting at the front of the church for Chantelle that it melted all the nervous energy from her and replaced it with immense love and passion and wanting to be his Mrs. As soon as the traditional wedding music started, Chantelle's father gripped her arm and started to escort her down the aisle with tears down his cheeks. He could not be prouder.

As Chantelle approached Gary, a knowing look, a look that conveyed, *You are beautiful*, came over his face and produced a tear in his eye. Chantelle approached in front of the pastor, who stood perfectly front and center of the church; and now as she also stood beside Gary, her father offered her hand in marriage to Gary. The wonderful marriage vows were exchanged, followed by tears, sealed with a kiss, and cheers by onlookers. They were finally Mr. and Mrs. Gary Moore, and neither one of them could be happier, more loving, or readier to spend their first night as man and wife. The reception was a real party; all the guests were dancing and having a grand time with the best music by a well-known local DJ and a live band, intermingled with lots of speeches, champagne, dancing, garter throwing, and, of course, the bouquet throwing. There was traditional fun with all the people whom Chantelle and Gary loved, and it helped make their special day a wonderful event, ending with them being escorted by their best man and their maid of honor to their bridal suite at the Four Seasons, cumulating in a long and intense night of lovemaking.

Early the following morning, Shawn and Karen came by the hotel to drive the newlyweds to the airport as they wanted everything to go effortlessly for this loving and happy couple. Now for the reveal: what flight were they going to take, where was Gary taking Chantelle for this wonderful surprise honeymoon? As they approached the various airline booths, Gary revealed that he was taking her to the Fiji Islands for their honeymoon, and Chantelle was delighted. It was a long flight from New Orleans over the Pacific Ocean to the Fiji Islands, but they eventually arrived; and with their energy on high from all the festivities, they managed to stay up after their arrival, have dinner, go swimming, and then head inside for a long and much-anticipated night of absolute bliss and happiness. Gary had booked two weeks in Fiji for him and Chantelle, and he had arranged with Karen beforehand to confirm it being okay with Chantelle's boss, the extended time away from work; and of course, Gary's boss, David, was okay with this extended honeymoon. It was a very relaxing and peaceful two-week honeymoon that was highlighted with several times of lovemaking in a day, unprotected lovemaking; but neither one of them really cared about those details anymore, and just basked in the deep love they felt for each other. Two weeks flew by, and even though Chantelle was feeling more than ready to head back to real life and begin life as Mrs. Gary Moore, Gary felt dread and apprehension at the thought of his boss and Dyna Corp. It all made that uneasy, sick feeling in his stomach resurface, and he knew why.

CHAPTER 5

TROUBLE IN PARADISE

Back in New Orleans and feeling confident and strong as Mrs. Moore, Chantelle returned to work refreshed, happy, and ready to find out how her friend's love life was going. Would there be another wedding, Karen and Shawn, soon. Karen confirmed that things were progressing, slowly but surely, between her and Shawn; and everything seemed stable and moving as it should. But Karen wanted to discuss babies, as in were she and Gary planning on starting a family right away? The topic was scary for Chantelle, but she did sense that Gary wanted to start a family right away, which she thought was okay;, she never really thought of the subject too much—she just figured it would happen when it happened.

On the home front, Chantelle and Gary both enjoyed Gary's bachelor's residence and were comfortable there for the time being; but they agreed to go looking for a new home. A house they both picked out as husband and wife would be not only fun but would be a better fit for their new life together. So they started house hunting every weekend they could, but they knew there was no huge rush to move; they would just like to find that perfect house that resonated with both of their spirits. Chantelle liked older, eclectic-style homes that had a bit of the haunted feel to it, personality to spare. Gary liked a house that was a little more modern or traditional, so they would have to find a happy medium, or one of them could compromise a little. Gary did enjoy older houses too, so he was open.

They enlisted Shawn to be their real estate agent, which was perfect because then Karen could tag along on many of the viewings of houses Shawn found for them. One thing they could agree on was that the right house would find them. Gary was superstitious and spiritual in this way, and like Chantelle, he believed that the perfect house would call out to them, call out to their soul, and they would just know. Gary believed in good and bad energy and following one's intuition. Being from New Orleans, he embraced this part of his nature, his being, and so did his family to a certain degree, even though they were very religious. Chantelle would spend many evenings telling Gary a little more about herself and her talents, even showing a bit of it as though he were Karen when they were young children playing together. She also liked reading tarot cards for herself, Gary, Karen, and Shawn; and much of what she told them would come true. But during some private readings, when no one was with Chantelle, some very dark cards, dark readings would come through around Gary and his work, and she could not wrap her mind around these readings. Much of what she saw and sensed from Gary's work, boss, and coworkers seemed positive and upbeat; yet very dark and ominous warning cards would come up surrounding them, and she was perplexed. Chantelle would not dare tell Gary about the darkness, and dread she felt from those tarot readings that she kept receiving about him, his work, and including his boss David. Gary would not believe her tarot readings anyway, not over his feelings for his work and his boss; and he had never said anything negative to Chantelle about Dyna Corp, so Chantelle thought it was best to keep the information to herself and just observe the situation. She was starting to feel an old and familiar uneasiness, but now with her new husband, his place of work, and his boss, she was not sure why. And she didn't even know if she should even mention it to Karen to see what she thought.

The second Saturday in August was Dyna Corp's annual black-tie summer party, and the second black-tie event Chantelle had gone to with Gary, the first as his wife. After an evening of lovemaking, they showered and were looking dazzling as a gorgeous newly married young couple ready for a night of socializing, drinks, expensive food, and pep talks from Dyna Corp's CEO. Chantelle was having a good time but was feeling like the center of attention, as though all eyes were on her, and she did not know why. Was her dark reading about the place fogging her judgment and making her see something that wasn't there, or was there something to her feelings? She had learned long ago that her intuition and natural knowing should never be ignored; but why would things be feeling this way now, when while she was dating Gary all seemed normal? Did her newfound love for Gary and their whirlwind romance block her from seeing what was going on around her? she asked herself. Chantelle tried hard to keep any dark thoughts and uneasiness out of her body language, and she tried hard to focus on positive things at the gathering. She convinced herself that the extra attention directed at her was just because she was the new wife of one of their top executives, and that what they had was love and admiring feelings toward her—that was all there was to this unwanted attention. Chantelle told herself that it would subside over time, or even by the time of the next black-tie event, which was usually in the fall.

The remainder of the night could not end quick enough for Chantelle, and try as she might, Gary still noted a change, a strangeness to her behavior, and asked her if everything was okay, while they were on the ride home from the company event. Chantelle did not want to lie to Gary, and her body language was obvious and spoke volumes. She couldn't seem to hide it—she was having an adverse reaction to Dyna Corp, and she hated herself for it, and more so because Gary picked up on her indifference.

"So what was wrong tonight?" he said to Chantelle in a stern, even angry, tone—a tone Chantelle never heard from him before. They barely ever disagreed, much less ever argued. Chantelle felt a sadness, a scare, in the pit of her stomach. She did not want to talk; she was almost feeling fear at conveying her feelings to Gary, and so she just shook her head to convey "Nothing" to him, as tears started to well up in her eyes, tears she fought to hold back as this would definitely demand an explanation to Gary, and she was not yet ready to share.

"What is wrong?" he asked.

She said, "Nothing. Nothing is the matter, Gary. Why would you think something was wrong?"

Gary was becoming more frustrated because now she was acting like his observations were wrong, and that he did not know her well. Yet he had never saw this side of Chantelle, or this type of reaction by her. Gary was even starting to think that maybe it was hormonal, maybe she was pregnant, which he was very excited about, and so he calmed down. The rest of the ride home, and the remainder of the night went on in silence as Chantelle tried to understand what she was feeling and Gary tried to figure Chantelle out.

Sunday proceeded in virtual silence between them, and the following day, Gary left early morning for meetings at Dyna Corp, leaving Chantelle sleeping in bed. He gave her a kiss on the forehead before leaving for work, and Chantelle pretended she was still sleeping, with eyes tightly closed, as she just needed time to think to herself.

At work David greeted Gary in an empty meeting room with coffee and talk of the weekend Gala, but it was mainly geared around Chantelle and his anticipated new family. David wanted to make sure Gary updated his work profile and added Chantelle to his company health plan—a health plan that was 100 percent free because they had an on-facility physician, and of course, a lab right there on the premises. All employees and their families used it for their yearly, semiyearly, even weekly medical needs and medications, which Dyna Corp also manufactured. David encouraged Gary to head down, today, add his new wife to his health plan, and schedule her for the, mandatory first health visit, as part of their policy was prevention, which helped to keep costs down. Dyna Corp believed, and policy was, that if a health profile is developed early and maintained, new problems could be dealt with in a timely manner before it became a costlier health issue, even preventing debilitating and deadly outcomes such as heart attacks, strokes, and similar issues due to early detection and treatment. Gary agreed to go down and update his family health profile, even booking an appointment for Chantelle, before checking with her if the date was all right, but he knew her work schedule. The appointment was in one week, which Gary reviewed in his mind on the drive home would give him enough time, a few days anyway, to broach the subject with Chantelle, very naturally and delicately, given her odd aversion to Dyna Corp all of a sudden.

He greeted Chantelle that evening with red roses and a planned, new attitude, like nothing was wrong, because he wanted to get her out of her head, out of the bad feelings she was having because he knew that Chantelle was able to sense things and did not want this bad feeling toward Dyna Corp to stick. Gary was hoping she was not picking up on the dark side of the company, which he knew quite well about. *Could she be actually picking up on this now?* he wondered out loud. And why now? Was it because Dyna Corp was getting more involved in activities, in testing, in experiments? Gary couldn't figure it out. He did not want to admit to himself how involved he was in Dyna Corp's dark side, corruption—the reason for all his increased stress over the last several months.

Chantelle was elated and visibly overjoyed with the beautiful roses Gary presented to her. She knew he was trying to calm the weird silence between them, and she appreciated the gesture. They ordered Chinese takeout that night and decided to talk about what Chantelle was feeling. Chantelle admitted to using tarot cards, which came up very negative in relation to Dyna Corp, but she opted to leave out the results about him. She agreed that it probably meant nothing and was a silly parlor game like Gary would describe them at times, in an effort to also keep the peace. Chantelle admitted that at the black-tie event, something had changed, and she couldn't place a finger on it; but it was there and real. She asked Gary if he noted any changes at Dyna Corp or felt any negativity there, seen any unusual activity at all, and Gary denied it, a denial that didn't resonate as 100 percent truthful even though Chantelle pretended to take it all in at face value. Gary thought it was a good time to mention, in an upbeat, positive way, how David wanted her to be added to his health plan right away as his new wife and family member. "Which is great," he said as he continued to sell her on it. "Because they pay for all appointments and lab work. The only thing a member pays for is their medication and even that is at a substantially reduced cost."

Chantelle tried to smile and told Gary, "That is great."

Then Gary told her, "You need to do the initial appointment right away, though, to get a file started to get any benefits enacted, so I booked you in for a week today for your first doctor's appointment at Dyna Corp."

Chantelle did not know if she should smile or cry. Something did not seem right, and she hated her intense feelings. As a newlywed, she was supposed to still be in the giddy honeymoon stage, but she couldn't bring herself to even fake it. She did manage to say, "Okay, that sounds fine" to Gary's appointment date for her, as what else was she to say? She had no real reason to object without sounding out of her mind and paranoid. It was a quiet evening, and they were both emotionally exhausted and decided to retire early that night.

Next day at the Mardi Gras shop, Chantelle could not turn her mood around enough to fool Karen, who could not understand what could possibly be wrong with her newlywed friend. Chantelle was visibly not present at work but did not appear to want to discuss what could possibly be wrong; Karen thought she should venture asking her anyway. Chantelle did not respond; it was as though she just could not generate the energy to speak about it, and just blankly looked past Karen as tears started to build in her eyes.

Karen did not want to pry any further, and knowing Chantelle like she did, she knew that either she would figure it out, or Chantelle would talk to her about it when the time was right, when she needed someone to confide in. The week flew by, and Chantelle's mood did lighten up a bit as her physical checkup at Dyna Corp was looming, which was shocking to her as she assumed by the date of her physical that she would be in even more of a terrible mood and emotional state.

Gary was way too busy at work during the week to really follow up on Chantelle's brooding mood, and he was exhausted when he came home at night, but he did remember the day of Chantelle's appointment, so he left work early to pick her up and take her to Dyna Corp for her appointment. It was a quiet ride in the car, but a longer-than-usual drive as the midafternoon traffic was starting to build. Gary did not have much to say to Chantelle before her appointment, and Chantelle was not offering up anything to him either. She was emotionally spent and a little confused. Gary and Chantelle agreed that she would go into her appointment on her own and Gary would stay in the waiting area. The Dyna Corp physician assigned to Chantelle was a gynecology specialist, and even though he was a male doctor, Chantelle was okay with him.

Dr. Winston was a young doctor, not much older than Gary. He was very nice, knowledgeable, and made Chantelle feel at ease. The physical was uneventful. He was assisted by his female nurse, and besides a full physical and an internal checkup, he also performed lots of blood work for many different things, most of which Chantelle did not understand, but she figured it must be necessary, especially for their initial documentation and files. During the ride home, Chantelle's mood seemed to be lifting, and she was returning to her usual pleasant self, Gary noted. Maybe the doctor's appointment, with the nonthreatening atmosphere, made her pleasant feelings toward Dyna Corp return, somewhat. That night, they felt connected again as they spent most of it making love; and the heaviness, the unexplained weirdness, between them had gone.

Gary decided that maybe if they ramped up their house-hunting efforts and found the perfect marital home, that would keep Chantelle's mind off of whatever was going on with her last week. Gary called Shawn and had him put their "finding the perfect home," at the top of his to-do list and triple the number of homes they saw in a week, if needed. Gary even wanted Shawn to include houses that might be a little out of their price range. He was adamant not to let Chantelle's dark mood and indifference return, so he would do anything. Chantelle and Gary were looking at homes two to three times a week, many times after a long day's work; but they were determined to find that perfect house. After a month of intense house hunting, a house came on the market on the outskirts of New Orleans, in Dyna Corp's hometown of Pendle, which made Gary very happy. It was a semi–remotely located house, and both Chantelle and Gary immediately fell in love with this large old Victorian *Gone with the Wind*–styled house. Besides being large and very old, which could present its own problems, they did not care, as they both fell in love with its feel immediately, its location, and it was also a steal for its sprawling, grand size—four bedrooms, two and a half bathrooms, which were all a welcome bonus, as they probably needed to devote money to take care of all the upkeep a house this *mature* would need. But they were up for the challenge.

Chantelle could not wait to tell Karen all about the house the next day even though she was pretty sure Karen already knew most of the details from Shawn, whom she was still dating. They were able to move into their home within three weeks, which was a week before Halloween, and they were very excited. Even though there weren't tons of kids in the immediate area of these old homes, she still felt that the fall and Halloween seasons would be a great celebration there; in fact, she had the wonderful idea of having an intimate housewarming party on Halloween, inviting Karen, Shawn, David, and his wife, Joyce. Chantelle wanted to include Gary's boss and wife not only because they were his boss and had them over for dinner but because she wanted to prove to herself that nothing was wrong with David and Dyna Corp, that it was just a weird mood, maybe post-wedding letdown or something that she was feeling a few weeks earlier. So it was set: the two couples would come over on Halloween night, and Chantelle was excited by the challenge of not only setting up the newly bought house, unpacking boxes, and making the home flow with their energy, their décor, but she was also ready to be a gracious, wonderful host and wife, the perfect complement to her husband.

Halloween was approaching fast, and Chantelle was ready because she had taken most of the last week off work to spend on organizing and decorating their new house, something she could afford to do as her work at Mardi Gras was not really necessary for their finances. Chantelle's employment at the Mardi Gras was now something she continued to do to keep her independence and give her something to do day in and day out, at least until they had children. The guest arrived at 6:00 p.m. sharp. Chantelle and Gary had red and white wine, cheese, and other appetizers awaiting them. Chantelle was not much of a cook, and admitted as much; so for now, while she was perfecting her cooking skills, dinner was being catered by a wonderful local Cajon company. The menu was a smorgasbord of all the New Orleans staple dishes. It was a wonderful dining experience, which nicely intertwined with the sprinkling of children who rang the doorbell and yelled "Halloween apples" and "Trick or treat" from the doorway as the night proceeded. After dinner, Chantelle and Gary gave their guest a complete tour of their mysterious old house, which they all enjoyed even if the house wasn't quite David's taste, which was their upscale penthouse; but they liked it for the newlywed couple just the same, mostly because Chantelle and Gary seemingly found contentment and happiness there.

After the tour of their home, the guests settled into the game room area, which featured a pool table, billiards, and a large vintage chest table set, and where they also set up a lovely very large Victorian-style couch. The couples drank wine, laughed, played games, and told new and old stories as the night was progressing wonderfully; and even though it was now ten o'clock on this Saturday Hallows night, everyone was still high-spirited and full of energy to carry on the night a little longer. Things abruptly took a darker edge as David, in a slightly intoxicated manner, started to bring up Dyna Corp and the secret projects they were developing down at the facility. David, without hesitation, started discussing Area 51 and how great it would be if humans could breed with aliens—what a special race that would be. As he went into details regarding such a project and the types of people it would, and seemingly did, involve and what types of things Dyna Corp would test on these people, the room took on a decidedly dead silence as at least three of them in the room—Chantelle, Karen, and Shawn—didn't know what to make of what they were hearing. Half-heartedly, they laughed and assumed it must have been a Halloween joke and Mr. Candice, David, was probably just pulling their leg, so to speak, as such activities and testing would be way too dark and inhuman.

But David would not let the subject go, and it was obvious from his continued line of questioning to Chantelle that he felt she would be the perfect "specimen" for their testing, and as much asked her if she would volunteer for even a few studies. Gary could not believe his boss had brought up such a sensitive topic without consulting him first to see if he was ready for his wife to participate in these experiments and tests, knowing what he knew of Dyna Corp's underground elements. Gary quickly ended the night, as it was getting late, his boss was inebriated, and at least one of them was confused and shocked, and rightfully so. Unfortunately, a wonderful housewarming, Halloween dinner party turned into a nightmare as some of those dark feelings and thoughts started to return to Chantelle, leaving her, again, emotionally immobilized and unable to voice her thoughts and feelings to Gary.

Gary could not begin to know what would have gotten into his boss to ask such a thing and blurt out such intrinsic details of Dyna Corp's operations to several unsuspecting people, and at a perfectly happy, pleasant dinner party. David was usually able to hold his liquor a little better than he did this night. As Chantelle and Gary both lay in bed wide awake until the early hours of the morning, Chantelle finally said to Gary, "Did you know of all that unusual- and inhuman-sounding activities that David was speaking of?" Gary was not sure how to answer; up to this point, he had never lied to Chantelle about anything, but the subject of his work never came up in such detail, so he decided right there that the truth might shine a bad light on him, and definitely on the company—the company he usually loved working at—so he denied any deep knowledge of what David was talking about.

"I'm in financing," he quipped back to Chantelle. "They don't divulge specifics to people in the finance department, usually, even though we do hear rumors and talk about things going on, but I never heard anything as in depth and unsettling as David was speaking of tonight. He was probably joking," he said, trying to convince Chantelle and ease her tortured mind. Chantelle knew she was very young and didn't understand a lot about life and worldly happenings, especially advances in science and business; but as with everything in her life, she went by how it made her feel, and Gary's explanation did not make her feel any relief.

Gary did not want to ask Chantelle at that moment regarding David asking her to be *the subject* of some limited testing for Dyna Corp, because at the moment, he was sure the answer would be no.

Gary was not sure how he felt about Chantelle, the woman he ended up truly loving, being part of Dyna Corp's experiments now anyway; and he also just wanted to speak to his boss first to find out what he was thinking blurting out that gruesome depiction of Dyna Corp, on Halloween, to Chantelle.

Gary dropped Chantelle off at work that following Monday morning on his way to Dyna Corp as she and Karen were going out to dinner after work, and Karen would drive her home after. When Gary entered the Dyna Corp offices, Chantelle's physician, Dr. Winston, approached him with news of her tests and blood work. Dr. Winston knew it was best to call Chantelle and have her come down to review her results with him personally but thought he would discuss a few things with her husband first. Dr. Winston started by saying that everything looked pretty good with Chantelle's physical, but her blood work came back a little puzzling.

"Puzzling?" Gary inquired.

Dr. Winston went on to ask, "Has Chantelle been tired or showing any unusual signs of fatigue?"

Gary did not know how to answer that question because before the wedding, Chantelle seemed fine, but as of lately, she had been a little depressed or something, but he was not sure if it was her or her new environment that was causing it, or a combination of the two. "Where are you going with this," he asked Dr. Winston.

"I'm not sure what the blood work means, but I do want to do more tests on her to find out what might be going on and prevent any further advances of anything adverse that might be there."

Gary could not help but think this had to do with his boss wanting to do testing on Chantelle and figured this would be a legitimate way to do so without being obvious. He took copies of Chantelle's file and told Dr. Winston that he would discuss the results with her and any further questions she might have, she would call him if needed. Shortly after 10:00 a.m., Gary had an opportunity to speak privately, one-on-one, with David. Gary did not want to jump down David's throat, as he was his boss after all, but he had so many questions on what David was thinking that Halloween night, and why did it have to be Chantelle for the full experimental phases, and now? Gary knew that David was intrigued by Chantelle, and by her unique birth numerology, and her abilities, but why he wouldn't at least consult him first before bringing up such a sensitive topic was what really puzzled Gary.

David apologized for his insensitive outburst at the housewarming party, but between the need and the deep desire to study a specimen like Chantelle, and knowing that Gary might find it hard to broach such a subject with his new wife, David felt the intense need to at least bring up the subject to Chantelle.

Gary asked David why he was so blunt and open with the exact biometrics and genetic human study part of the company's dealings. "Your explanation of tissue samples, tables with bright lights, and drugged participants didn't help the cause to get Chantelle to volunteer."

David again apologized and agreed that it could have been handled better and that maybe the Halloween atmosphere and many drinks did not help prevent his indiscretion, but he would talk to Chantelle again and try to clean up the offer; and hopefully, she would volunteer and there would be no need for a more forceful approach to the matter. As those words rang deep within Gary, he was now really wondering what type of monster he was working for, who couldn't calmly and patiently wait for him to speak with *his* wife to avoid fear and suspicion in her, making the whole transition to her being experimented on an easy and seamless progression. Gary felt his boss was overstepping his boundaries, acting as though he owned him and his wife. Gary knew that regardless of David's money and power, he refused to be pushed around and commanded to do anything, especially pertaining to his home life, and specifically his wife.

*****

After work, Chantelle and Karen decided to pick up some food and then go back to Karen's place to eat and also have some wine, and then have Gary pick Chantelle up when they were done. They picked up a gourmet meal from their favorite Italian restaurant, and now that the wedding was behind them, they decided to enjoy more than a salad; they enjoyed all their favorite comfort foods. As they sipped on red wine, Karen had to ask Chantelle if everything was all right, all right with her, and in her marriage. Chantelle finally had to break down and cry, but she wasn't completely sure why. She still had not figured out why she was feeling these intense, unsettling, bad feelings; but she knew better than to ignore those feelings. "What is eating Gilbert Grape?" was what she had been asking herself over and over for weeks now, as she knew there was something wrong, but what? Was she manifesting trouble in a perfect relationship between her and Gary, and inadvertently trying to destroy a great marriage as being truly happy had always been a struggle in her life, as she never really felt accepted and loved at home. It was definitely something she had been trying to dissect in her life, so at this time, she was not able to tell Karen yes, everything was all right, but she couldn't fully and correctly say no everything was not all right, so she told her she was not sure. Karen again accepted her friend's explanation and need to release her feelings even if she didn't know why, so she just sat there and consoled her friend and tried to put a lighthearted spin on everything.

Chantelle wanted to know what Karen made of the information Gary's boss shared on Halloween. Karen didn't want to feed into Chantelle's mood *and situation* any further, so she told Chantelle that she felt that David was just being silly, and that surely he and his company would never be able to get away with the things he described, so she shouldn't worry about such things. Karen then reassured Chantelle that Gary loved her and would not let anything bad happen to her, so she should not worry. "Trust your husband." This pep talk did help to ease Chantelle's alarms in her mind and body, temporarily; but as when she was a child, any dark intentions, dark attitudes, "off" energy in general rang through her body like a bolt of lightning; and there was nothing she could do to remove the feelings except remove the bad energy. But who or where was this dark, evil energy coming from, was her question. All Chantelle did know was that every time she was around Gary now, something felt wrong, like a lie, and this was also what she felt around David and Dyna Corp. Worse yet, she thought, this off energy or darkness she felt not only toward Gary, but it was starting to creep into their home life, as Gary's unstated intentions were becoming more and more palpable to her. It felt as though a heaviness, a darkness, a dark cloud was now hanging over their home.

Gary came to pick Chantelle up from Karen's house around 9:30 p.m., and with a big and tight hug from Karen, she was off, back to home in Pendle with Gary. Chantelle definitely knew something was wrong in the marriage when her thoughts, as Gary was driving home, went to her wanting to go back to the old days and return to living at Karen's house. Chantelle didn't want to leave the security of Karen's home; she was becoming scared of Gary, scared of the unknown, scared of his unspoken intentions. Despite their indifference, Gary wanted to show affection to his wife this night, and as he made love to her, he also told her he wanted to start a family, right away. Chantelle had nothing to say after her lack luster lovemaking session. She was not about to say no to wanting children with Gary, as she didn't know what she wanted any longer. What she did know was that Gary really wanted a baby girl. Chantelle half joked, in her mind of course, *Is he going to send her to the lab for that also, to guarantee that baby girl.* It was a joke that wasn't necessarily that funny or unbelievable, as Dyna Corp seemed to be able to do anything. Chantelle angrily kept thinking, *I'm sure they could figure out a way to do this without any test tubes or anything, just modify something in our bodies.* Both Chantelle and Gary fell asleep quickly after that long night. Both of them had an early day ahead.

That morning, before Chantelle left for work, Gary brought up the results of her physical with Dr. Winston, stating, "Here are the copies of your physical. He said all was well, but there was some unusual occurrences in your blood work. He would need to investigate into that with more tests. You can contact him if you would like to discuss it further—otherwise, he will contact you for your next appointment, shortly."

Chantelle didn't know what to believe. Did she really have something rare and different in her blood work that needed further investigation, or were they trying to trick her into being their guinea pig? She was scared of either prospect. Dr. Winston seemed like an honest and sincere doctor, so she thought maybe she should make an appointment to speak with him directly beforehand. On the drive home from work that night, Gary decided that enough was enough. It was almost Thanksgiving, and Christmas season was approaching, and since their marriage in the summer, nothing seemed to be going right—there was always tension, so tonight, with a case of beer and some wine in hand, he decided that he and Chantelle would talk out their feelings, the indifference, something they both had been avoiding up to this point.

When Gary arrived home, he saw that Chantelle had made a lovely-looking pot roast with a special seasoning she had learned to make in her cooking class, which she had been taking since the wedding. She was happy to see Gary, as he was to see her also. Gary showed Chantelle what he had bought and told her he wanted to talk about their relationship. Chantelle got a tight knot in her stomach because even though they were technically newlyweds, she knew she wasn't being the best wife, and she thought for a moment, could he be wanting a divorce already? The thought frightened her. Sure, she was having trust issues with Gary, but she realized she loved him very much still, and she would die, not knowing what to do if he left her. She was intimidated by his cryptic invitation. She looked deep into Gary's green eyes to try to figure out what he had on his mind. Did he not love her any longer? Had he had enough of her already? As she stood beside Gary in the kitchen opening bottles and placing dinner on plates, something came over the both of them; and the passion, the old passion, they felt overcame them, and they made love in the kitchen. After their lovemaking, they ate dinner, had cocktails, and Gary opened up the conversation.

Gary knew and understood that Chantelle was young and her emotions were all over the place, so he wanted to be delicate and understanding of her and not be judgmental, as he knew her feelings were not completely without justification. "Chantelle," he began, "I love you. What can I do to make our relationship better?" He continued, "I am so confused, Chantelle. We went from madly in love to cold and indifferent shortly after the honeymoon. What changed?"

Chantelle started spontaneously crying, gripping Gary's hand and sobbing at the same time. "Please, Gary," she said, "forgive me. I don't know what is wrong. I am so confused, but I do know I love you."

Gary was touched. He felt bad for Chantelle as he knew that with her *gifts and abilities*, dissecting information could be quite emotional and hard to figure out. He didn't want to add to her pain. "Chantelle," he started, "just know I love you also, with all my heart. And even though you have a hard time believing it at times, I would never do anything, purposefully, to hurt you."

His words were comforting to Chantelle, but she did note the *purposeful* part as meaning he might hurt her, but not intentionally, which wasn't as comforting. They did have a good opportunity to talk on this night, somewhat inhibited due to the alcohol, but still Gary was not admitting any dark dealings, any untoward activity within Dyna Corp. And Chantelle was not able to fully convey her feelings out of fear of Gary's reaction in trying to protect Dyna Corp, so not much was accomplished on this night, other than them agreeing to disagree really. And what was clear to them both was that regardless of what was happening, they were still deeply in love, and the idea of not being together was more than either one of them could handle; so they needed to compromise and make the marriage work.

CHAPTER 6

WHO CAN I TRUST?

That weekend, Karen and Shawn came over to Chantelle and Gary's house to discuss the holidays and a holiday vacation they wanted to take as couples. It would be fun. But they couldn't decide if they should make it a winter snow trip like to Aspen or Banff, or a hot weather vacation like to Hawaii, the Caribbean, or Mexico. Decisions, decisions. They decided on a hot weather vacation after Christmas, and Hawaii sounded like the perfect location, they all agreed. Chantelle was going to make the best of this vacation to reconnect with and understand Gary and their relationship with each other. Gary had one more point of discussion he wanted to make clear with Chantelle—he wanted to have a child right away, a girl preferably, but any offspring was welcomed, and he wanted to increase their efforts toward this as he felt she was not motivated to have a child with him right now, and this made him a little upset. Gary asked Chantelle outright if she wanted to have a child with him, hopefully becoming pregnant before the end of the year. She agreed as she knew that to disagree would lead to further discord in their marriage, and she wanted the marriage to work, so whatever it took.

*****

It was now mid-November, and Gary and Chantelle went shopping for their first tree and found a large and lovely blue fir for their first holiday season together as man and wife. They spent the weekend before Thanksgiving decorating their tree and drinking egg nog. Things were beginning to be blissful and light again. They spent Thanksgiving at Gary's parents' house with his brothers and their families. It was a pleasant, jovial time being with Gary's family who insisted on constantly asking when they were going to start a family even though Gary kept telling them, "We are trying."

Black Friday, the day after Thanksgiving, Chantelle and Karen decided to partake in the great deals and made a girls' shopping day while their men were at their respective houses doing paperwork for their companies. The women bought holiday gifts and decorations and spent a relaxing afternoon at a spa when they were done. Life seemed happy and carefree on the surface, but Chantelle knew it was because she had managed to suppress and push away any dark and bad thoughts that would resurface, if she truly focused her mind and energy on Dyna Corp, its owner, and her husband's involvement in this company. Chantelle thought that now, while she and Karen were peacefully soaking in the Jacuzzi tub at the spa, would be an appropriate time to ask her friend, again, her feelings on Dyna Corp, and David, and whether she felt there was anything unsettling, hidden, shady in the back scenes of this company, including its employees.

Karen admitted to Chantelle that she really hadn't given it too much thought since that Halloween night with David's weird behavior and Gary's nervous and decidedly angry response to his behavior; but she suggested to Chantelle to just ask Gary outright, "Ask him if your suspicions on Dyna Corp has any merit, to see his response."

Chantelle actually liked that suggestion, even though it was a little scary and could end in a fight, or revisiting bad feelings between her and Gary; but she agreed that trying to just figure it out was not enough. She needed to ask Gary again, plus tell Gary her concerns and feelings about Dyna Corp and David.

*****

By early December, Chantelle finally had her follow-up appointment with Dr. Winston of Dyna Corp to recheck her blood work which was so very unusual with very low white blood counts and other immune system markers, yet Chantelle was not exhibiting any signs of sickness, tiredness, nothing—she was the perfect picture of health on the outside. She and her company-known *gifts*, along with her unusual blood work, made for some interesting tests moving forward; and all involved hoped she would be open to and on board with any and all testing they wanted to conduct. But they knew she had suspicions and doubt on the company's ethics and true motives. Chantelle was not even sure her blood work was what they said it was. It could have been altered for justification, allowing them to do more testing on her, as she was starting to realize that they wanted her, and they seemed to be wanting her bad, and her husband would not stand in the way of them getting what they wanted.

Dr. Winston had always been very nice during her doctor's appointments and, uncharacteristically, did not give off the same bizarre and dark feelings she felt with all the other parts of this company. As she walked around the facility, it was as though everyone—employees, managers, and higher-ups—was watching her but trying not to be obvious while watching her. This feeling of being watched and the people acting bizarre she would never mention to the *good* doctor regardless of how friendly and caring he acted because in the long run, he was still working for Dyna Corp, which meant he was part of whatever agenda they had; and he would probably love the agenda to include a psychological assessment, or even committing Chantelle to an institution so they could have full control of her activities. This was apparent.

Chantelle knew she was starting to sound very paranoid, but until she knew the nature of their full agenda and what secrets this company had, she knew she had to stay vigilant of all things going on around her; and she was not liking what she was seeing. Chantelle was becoming more and more sad as she thought she had finally broken free of her family's controls when she moved to Louisiana, and definitely when she married Gary; but now she felt more controlled and confined than ever before, and Karen was her only real friend and confidant. At this point, Chantelle was not even sure of Karen, even though she seemed as consoling as possible. She was never ready to say anything bad, or even admit that anything was unusual in any way about Dyna Corp and David, not even with David's behavior on Halloween night. Would Chantelle also need to keep her guard up with her best friend, along with Gary, David, his wife, and Dyna Corp's employees there. Who else knew of this agenda? she rightfully wondered. Chantelle felt that she must be truly living in an alternate universe because this stuff just didn't happen, like a horror-spy-alien movie one does not want to be featured in, and one whose plot was unbelievable, yet true.

Chantelle decided that she had to find out the true agenda and activities of Dyna Corp before it was too late, but how? Who could she trust, as she needed someone in the know, most likely someone on the inside, or at least, used to work at Dyna Corp. Karen did have a somewhat good idea, which was to just ask Gary outright; but she knew the most she would get from her husband would be to read his reaction, she was pretty sure, now, that he would not give up Dyna Corp's secrets. His Halloween cover-up and reaction was evidence enough. Chantelle decided to first start with searching on the Internet for information on the aliens that David mentioned, as this was almost fifty years before her birth. Chantelle found out that Area 51 was in Nevada, where supposedly they were still testing UFOs, and other such activities. But the original aliens were found in New Mexico in the 1940s. Also, regarding aliens and Area 51, it was suspected that the military encountered real aliens since then, and had information about these otherworldly beings, about what had really happened to those original aliens' bodies, the possible extensive research on its genetics and more—information that was being hidden from the general population.

Just as Chantelle was finishing her online search, Gary returned from work; and she decided then would be a good time to talk about Dyna Corp and how she felt about it, if he was open to this conversation. Gary was tired but agreed to talk to Chantelle after dinner and a shower, but his agenda was to convince her to participate in the testing. Chantelle had made Gary a wonderful beef stir fry that night, with rice, and they enjoyed some wine and beer with it—a perfect, unencumbered married couple night. After they ate and were sitting on the couch with drinks in tow, Chantelle thought she would dive directly into the topic in mind.

"Gary," she started, "tell me about Dyna Corp—the real Dyna Corp. What type of human testing do they do?" She asked this question confidently.

Gary was taken aback by her immediate candidness but responded with, "What real Dyna Corp, real testing, Chantelle?" Already, Gary had built a barrier between himself, Dyna Corp, and Chantelle; and Chantelle knew she would not be getting any true information from him. His response also told her that he was more involved than she previously thought, which was sad and frightening all at the same time. But Chantelle was slightly mad because she felt he was treating her like a stupid child—a stupid, blind child who couldn't obviously see there was something very peculiar and hidden with Dyna Corp.

Gary was starting to get irritated, as he had no intention to tell Chantelle anything and found her badgering him about a company that did so much in her life to be ungrateful and unnecessary.

Chantelle did not want to fight with Gary on this night as she never won on this topic anyway, so she decided to drop the subject; but now, more than ever, she was convinced her marriage was not what it appeared to be; was that fateful day at the gift shop really fate or a planned first meeting? She was now starting to wonder about when she first dated Gary. And now she had to figure out what to do about it. She was vulnerable and overwhelmed by the task ahead. She went over in her mind that if this situation was not dealt with correctly, as in knowing who to trust and who not to trust, it could mean severe consequences for her—her existence, her safety. That night, as Gary slept, she started to mull over information and things in her mind—things like, could she trust Karen? Who else in the community was involved? Should she allow Dyna Corp to do limited testing on her until she figured out what to do next, or should she make an escape? And if she escaped, where to? She had a lot to figure out, a lot to do, and in a cool, and calculated manner so that those involved did not suspect that she was aware of their activities and that she was, therefore, trying to get away.

That morning, Chantelle tried her best to act like everything was all right, outwardly, in Gary's presence and that she had already forgotten their conversation from the night before. Gary seemed to have bought into this act; he kissed Chantelle before leaving for work and talked in a normal manner about seeing her after work. Chantelle knew Gary thought she was too young and not mentally prepared to properly process all that was going on, and that she might even be in some denial, and therefore probably did just "let it go," as she appeared to have done so. As soon as Gary left, Chantelle was on the phone to the city's Business Bureau. She wanted to know if there was any more information, or complains filed on Dyna Corp's activities, and then she decided that what she needed to do was hire a private investigator to find the answers she needed. Chantelle refused to speak to the investigator on the phone and insisted on coming down to his office, because she had good reason to suspect that possibly the home phone, maybe the computers, and very possibly the home in general, was being watched, monitored, and surveilled by Gary and Dyna Corp, to some degree.

At the private investigator's office, Chantelle found it very hard to push back tears as this was the first seemingly normal person, a person without an agenda, she had spoken to in months, mainly because he was not located in New Orleans but in neighboring Baton Rouge, which was approximately a one-hour-and-thirty-minute drive away from the New Orleans area; but Chantelle felt this would be for the best, hopefully insuring that the investigator was unbiased, untampered, and unaffected by Dyna Corp and its cult minions. Mark was young, in his late twenties, very good looking with dark hair and ocean-blue eyes, was six feet one, rugged, and strong. He looked like a walking dark-haired Ken doll, yet he was also a very friendly, knowledgeable, easygoing guy who owned and operated his investigative company, P.I. Spy, it was called, and had been doing a successful business for almost seven years now. Mark's fee was reasonable, but still expensive on her budget; her pay from the gift shop could not pay for these services, and she knew she would need to get the money from her and Gary's joint account.

Chantelle had not planned an excuse, yet, on how she would explain these ongoing cash withdrawals as she paid Mark's weekly or monthly fees, depending on how long it took for Mark to do his surveillance of Gary and the Dyna Corp organization, but she had to figure out something. She definitely had to pay by cash, as all bills went to Gary, and a charge from a private detective firm would be a major red flag, a possibly unforgiveable red flag, and unimaginable, on how she would explain it. Chantelle set up her PI surveillance account with Mark, gave him the initial payment she brought with her in cash from New Orleans as she also could not use an ATM in Baton Rouge. Mark was to start the following day and give Chantelle daily and/or weekly updates as necessary. Chantelle felt terrible that she couldn't trust her husband and had to go to these lengths to find out what was going on; but she needed to for her own peace of mind. And if she was to feel secure and comfortable in their marriage, she needed to know exactly what their secret was. She was praying there was nothing to find.

It was now the second week in December, and Christmas was fast approaching; but Chantelle had all her gifts bought and wrapped for not only Gary but also for Karen, Karen's family, Shawn, and Gary's family. She had even already mailed off gifts to her family in Massachusetts. The first set of updates was ready for Chantelle from her investigator, Mark; and she decided she should drive down to his office in Baton Rouge to discuss the matter with him. December 20, Chantelle had her meeting with Mark, and the investigation was turning out to be "quite a secret, and unusual," Mark agreed. He continued to tell Chantelle that he was having a lot of trouble getting much information from locals, even ex-employees from Dyna Corp; and many seemed either scared or apprehensive to talk to him, an outsider. When he managed to get into Dyna Corp on one of their company facility tours, his natural senses did register that there was definitely more than meets the eye there but that it would take some deep surveillance and monitoring of its players. He did confirm that he was able to leave some listening devices in key rooms and hall-ways. He wished he had more information to give her, especially see-ing as she insisted on coming all the way down to his office to discuss his findings, but he was willing to confirm that Dyna Corp gave him the creeps, including their robotic-looking workers; and their explanation on what was being tested, and how, did not seem complete. Chantelle did not mind that she came all the way to Baton Rouge to hear this information; she was just elated that he sensed what she knew were unsavory activities going on there and was eager to find out what. He did mention that he saw Gary going to and from work, even picking her up from work once. There was nobody unusual he met with, but he did manage to place a listening device right at his office as well. Chantelle did not know if she should be happy or sad. She felt sad about the violation of trust she was displaying toward her husband by having him monitored by a private investigator, and the lack of trust in general in their marriage; but what were her options? This was the only way to find out what she needed to know. Maybe if her suspicions were wrong and this was just a big mistake, it would save her marriage. But she knew in her heart the likelihood of this being nothing was slim to none.

*****

Christmas Day had finally arrived. Gary and Chantelle went to Gary's parents' house, where his brothers with their wives and family would also be going. Chantelle and Gary were the first ones there, arriving just before 11:00 a.m., as they had no kids to get dressed and organized, after their gift-opening session at home; therefore decided to head down and start the eating and drinking festivities early, which his parents didn't mind—the company and the help with getting everything ready. Chantelle and Gary bought each other only a couple of expensive gifts and some smaller ones such as the beautiful expensive matching watches they bought as a joint gift to each other. Because, they already had the upcoming trip to Hawaii with their friends after Christmas, Karen and Shawn, where they were booked into a five-star resort with adjoining rooms for Karen and Shawn. Gary's parents, brothers, and their families loved the gifts from them, and they received expensive coffeemakers, sweaters, and other cute household items, the type they would never really buy for themselves, like mugs with their names on it, matching his and hers socks; Chantelle and Gary loved and appreciated everything, as did his family. The Christmas dinner was elaborate, including every traditional American dish possible, and Gary's mom who was not only a fantastic cook, could bake nearly anything, made the highest-calorie but extremely delicious cookies, cakes, and pastries. Everyone was stuffed. After dinner, Chantelle was introduced to many of the traditional Moore family Christmas games. She enjoyed the family festivities and warmth very much, and the day extended to almost 10:30 p.m. when everyone agreed that the party should wrap up as the kids were starting to fall asleep on the couches and the floor. It had been a wonderful family Christmas at the Moore home again, and everyone was happy.

Monday, December 27, Gary, Chantelle, Karen, and Shawn had a 1:00 a.m. flight from Louis Armstrong New Orleans International Airport to the Honolulu International Airport. They arrived at their Waikiki Beach Front Hotel by 1:00 p.m. They were exhausted, but excited to be in beautiful, warm Hawaii, especially after the hustle, bustle, and stress the holiday season always seems to bring out. They all had a full two weeks in Hawaii to enjoy all the swimming, sunbathing, lavish food and drinks and shopping they could, including ringing in the New Year in Hawaiian style. The days were progressing painlessly, full of laughter and good times, for the friends. Shawn and Karen even decided to take their relationship one step farther, with Shawn proposing on New Year's Eve to Karen, and Karen excitedly accepting. Chantelle and Gary could not have been more delighted for their friends and the newly engaged couple, right away letting them know they were to be the maid of honor and the best man, if they would be so kind as to accept, which Chantelle and Gary graciously did. They were honored. The happy, content couples left Waikiki and all its lovely, warm, inviting ambience on Monday, January 10, on an early-morning flight, arriving back in New Orleans by midafternoon. They were all tired from their trip and jetlagged and retired to their respective homes for an early night's rest.

Gary did decide to go in to work that following day even though he was not expected at Dyna Corp. He wanted to catch up on the mounting paperwork he knew he would have on his desk and office mailbox that only he could take care of. Chantelle stayed home and was happy to not have work scheduled, as she was still feeling quite jetlagged, tired, and even a bit nauseated. She spent the day bundled up in bed with chicken soup until Gary arrived back home around 4:00 p.m. That night, Gary agreed, Chinese takeout, was in order, and ordered enough to feed an army, or at least good for several days ahead. Dead of the winter season, the end of January, an uneventful, movie-watching Saturday night between Gary and Chantelle turned to a night of symptoms mimicking food poisoning for Chantelle. As Gary tried to nurse her back to health, Chantelle realized she had not had her period in more than four weeks, six weeks now, and nothing.

As she voiced this information out loud to Gary, he said, "You do look a little thick in the middle, dear. Could it finally be possible?" he said very excitedly. Chantelle continued to vomit in the toilet more and more as Gary kept talking. She was thinking, *Oh no, it couldn't be possible. I'm not quite ready for this.* Gary wanted to go down to the pharmacy, right away, to buy a pregnancy test because he had been waiting and wanting this since their wedding night six months ago. As Chantelle waited for Gary's return, she was trying to gauge how she felt, other than shock. As she lay there silent, she knew what the test results would show. She knew it would be positive. Gary returned, and as suspected, he was finally going to be a dad. Gary celebrated with beer while Chantelle tried to keep down flat ginger ale. February 14, Chantelle was seen by Dr. Winston, who confirmed she was approximately eight weeks pregnant, and everything looked healthy and as it should for that week of pregnancy, which meant she conceived a couple of weeks before Christmas. As Gary took Chantelle around to all his coworkers, including, of course, David to tell them of his good news, Chantelle could not help but think, what had she gotten herself into? If she thought she was helpless and trapped before, she was really stuck now. This was the best Valentine's gift ever, Gary chimed, pretty much yelling it down the halls of Dyna Corp. That Valentine's night, they did not go out. Chantelle was too sick to be out for too long, especially around food smells that would cause her vomiting outburst, so they ordered in Italian food as Gary spent much of the night on the phone to his parents, brothers, and his friends Shawn, Peter, and Frank, telling them of his wonderful news. Chantelle decided she should call Karen then and tell her, as Shawn was sure to tell her, and she wanted to tell her best friend. She also called her family back in Massachusetts and gave them the news.

Next day at work, Chantelle was greeted with a huge hug by Karen and her other coworkers. Karen was extremely happy for the couple as she knew how badly Gary wanted to start a family. But she couldn't help but wonder about her own wedding in August and how far along her appointed maid of honor would be. Would she be able to, or want to, still be in the bridal party? For only being eight weeks along, Chantelle was already showing a fair-sized paunch, and her extreme nausea and inability to keep food down continued for several weeks more. By ten weeks, she was feeling a little better, though still quite nauseated. But she was enjoying the extensive pampering and coddling she was receiving from Gary; it was feeling like the days when they were still dating. By twelve weeks, at around the middle of March, Chantelle was ready for another wellness appointment with her doctor; she was still feeling nauseated often and just wanted reassurance that everything was progressing all right. Now that she was starting to get used to being pregnant, Gary's excitement was starting to rub off on her. She was finally starting to feel comfortable with the idea of having a child with Gary at this point of their marriage. She was starting to already feel a bond with this child and wanted to do everything to ensure a healthy pregnancy, including taking yoga classes, meditating, and remaining stress free.

Everything was looking good with the pregnancy, Dr. Winston told Chantelle and Gary. And because they did want to know the sex of the baby, he scheduled them for another appointment in two weeks. It would be a solid fourteen weeks' gestation; and a few days after Chantelle's twenty-first birthday, they were a happy couple once again. On a beautiful Tuesday morning in March, with Chantelle's fourteen-week prenatal appointment in a couple of days, life was moving along in a fairly predictable, easy way. Her nausea had even started to subside. She had planned a quiet day of laundry, meditation, and music when suddenly she felt a sharp cramp in the lower part of her abdomen as blood started to run down her leg. She knew something was very wrong. She quickly used her cell phone to call Gary, who could not have been more than twenty minutes away as he abruptly hung up and said, "I'll be right there!"

By the time Gary returned home, Chantelle was cramping more, with more pain associated with the cramps and blood, clots. They both knew something was very wrong as they rushed to the emergency room at the local hospital where Dr. Winston had privileges and said he would be standing by awaiting their arrival. As Gary pulled up to the emergency entrance where the ambulance bay was, Dr. Winston came running out with a nurse and a wheelchair, and they rushed Chantelle inside as Gary checked her into the hospital with the triage nurse. Gary waited anxiously in the waiting room, wondering what was going on, as it had been forty-five minutes since the medical team took Chantelle inside to the maternity surgical unit. Then Karen and Shawn came rushing in. They were as frantic looking as Gary was; and everyone sensed that this was very serious and might not end in a good way, even though no one was saying much. Karen sensed Gary could use something hot, something to take the edge off the cold, the emptiness he must be feeling inside, and brought him a cup of coffee in an attempt to console him a little and show that they were there for him. Gary graciously accepted the offering and started to tell Karen and Shawn what had happened, as far as he knew. Gary felt shaky, faint, not sure of the future, which were foreign feelings for him.

As forty-five minutes turned to one hour and fifteen minutes, Dr. Winston finally appeared in the waiting room to speak to Gary and his friends. Dr. Winston's face alone spoke of the terrible news he had for them this morning. "Chantelle lost the baby, and we had to do an emergency dilation and curettage to prevent her from bleeding to death, and we completely removed anything left from the pregnancy."

As those words rang through Gary, his legs literally buckled. He felt faint, and Shawn and the doctor eased him to a sitting position. Gary felt bad not only for himself but for the fear his young bride must have had as these quick decisions and events unfolded—so quickly the doctor did not even have time to tell her husband what was going on before proceeding. As tears started to trickle down Karen's face, she asked the doctor if it was okay to go in and see Chantelle. Gary stayed back for a few more minutes with Dr. Winston to find out what he thought caused this abrupt loss of the fetus at such an advanced stage of the pregnancy, since usually, by fourteen weeks, the chances of spontaneous abortion is greatly reduced, as they were told. Dr. Winston gave Gary some possibilities, the most plausible being that it just wasn't meant to be, but they did tell Gary that tissue testing would be done on the aborted fetus to see if any abnormalities or other causes could be detected. Chantelle was sobbing, devastated, when Karen and Shawn entered her hospital room. Karen ran over and gave her a big hug and offered her condolences on the loss. Chantelle was shaking and wanted to know how Gary was taking the news. She had barely finished the sentence when Gary walked in, in a somber, stunned demeanor.

Karen and Shawn agreed to give the couple some privacy but let them know they would be waiting in the waiting room in case they needed anything. Chantelle and Gary just held each other, sobbing, with words unspoken. When Gary was able to compose himself, he asked Chantelle how she was feeling, physically, if she was still having any pain. Chantelle assured him that the pain was under control as she received strong pain medication through her intravenous; but the emptiness inside and the emotional numbness would not go away. Chantelle spent three days in the hospital before Gary could take her home, and then another six weeks at home. Dr. Winston wanted her to physically and emotionally heal, which included no sexual relations with her husband, something that was farthest from both Gary's and Chantelle's minds. They were still struggling to come to terms with what had occurred.

It was now nearing the end of May; spring was in full force, and Gary and Chantelle were starting to feel a little more like their old selves. They were finally coming to terms with what had happened and not blaming themselves for what occurred. They had planned for a date night the last Saturday in May and decided to dress up to go to their favorite restaurant, the Rock Wood Country Club, where they had their first date and where Gary had proposed to her. After an enjoyable light dinner, Chantelle and Gary finally felt ready for a night of passion, a real night of connection that was long overdue and much needed after almost eight weeks of feeling slightly withdrawn and disconnected from each other. They agreed to try again for a pregnancy as Dr. Winston said the report back from the tissue sample of the fetus did not show any abnormalities needing further testing, just a natural unexplained event. And even though Gary and Chantelle were trying to work on their relationship, their marriage, something felt different between them: Chantelle felt that Gary still seemed a little withdrawn, even cold and angry, toward her.

As she had promised to both Gary and Dr. Winston, Chantelle agreed to some limited testing. Before her pregnancy, she had been scheduled for testing for Dyna Corp to study her blood peculiarities and her general special, and unusual abilities; but it was put off due to the fast-paced times during her short fourteen-week pregnancy. As Dr. Winston entered his clinic at Dyna Corp where Chantelle was waiting for him, he greeted her with a warm, consoling, smile. "How are you feeling, Chantelle?" he began.

Chantelle was feeling better, a little less cold and empty inside, but she was still somewhat emotionally detached and withdrawn, the same as her husband had been, she told Dr. Winston.

The doctor assured her that these emotions were normal for both her and Gary, and that they would get better over time, so he was not alarmed or worried about these very normal reactions to such a tragic event. He had Chantelle put on a sterile hospital-type gown and then lie on the gurney, as he needed to not only take several blood samples from her, but also, *they* needed to, and wanted to, add some low-level gene study material to her body as part of the testing she agreed to. Chantelle felt scared and apprehensive about this gene being added to her blood, her body, but she was tired of continuously fighting with her true feelings on the subject. Chantelle knew her participating in this testing would make Gary happy, which was definitely what she wanted to keep the peace in her now bipolar, fleeting happiness of a marriage. The blood withdrawal was easy, the gene induction was painful and made Chantelle feel flushed, slightly nauseated to the point of being sick, which the doctor and the nurse said were natural reactions to this experimentation.

Dr. Winston would not tell Chantelle what foreign genes were injected into her body, but he did not want to overly test, and stress, Chantelle this day either, and make it a bad experience in any way, as there was much more testing, and hopefully more in depth, to come. The doctor did need Chantelle back in two weeks to analyze the gene therapy results, and her body's reaction to it. Chantelle agreed to comply. Gary left work early that day so that he could drive Chantelle home after her day at the Dyna Corp medical lab, her first testing day, which did make him very happy that she was being such as good sport in regard to the testing.

Back at work at the Mardi Gras shop, Chantelle was feeling an odd energy, a negative energy, a negative attitude coming from Karen toward her; and she couldn't figure out why. Karen and she rarely disagreed, so this was an unfamiliar feeling she was getting from Karen, yet very real. Was it her, or was Karen mad about something in her own life? Maybe she and Shawn had a disagreement, or worse, they had broken up. Chantelle wasn't sure, but she knew she needed to get to the cause, to the root of her best friend's cold behavior. Chantelle decided to go to the local coffee shop and bring back coffee and doughnuts for all, including several of Karen's favorite doughnuts, the cake doughnuts with sprinkles, in hopes of buttering her up and warming that icy disposition.

Karen was still not saying too much to Chantelle, and it was now noon, so Chantelle decided to confront her as soon as possible at lunch break as to what was troubling her. As the two women sat down together for lunch, Chantelle blurted out, "Is everything okay, Karen? You seem mad at me or something today. You barely said two words to me all day, and giving me the cold shoulder."

Karen admitted that she did feel somewhat slighted or pushed to second importance, yet she had her big day coming, her wedding, a mere two months away, and no maid of honor assistance had been offered thus far, even after Chantelle had recovered from her loss of the baby. Chantelle felt terrible and did apologize to Karen and agreed that this weekend, they should get together with the other bridal party women, to discuss some concrete activities, and her needs for her upcoming nuptials in August. And even though during their conversation at lunch it felt like an "uh-huh" moment and she had gotten to the root of Karen's mood and attitude toward her; but she still couldn't shake off the feeling that something more was going on, that something had changed between her and Karen—but *what*, and *why*? It was a feeling that seemed to extend from Gary to Karen and the coworkers at the gift shop, to even in the community, as she was feeling a weird watching and a weird indifference from even the usual people she interacted with at the local shops near her home. Chantelle was beginning to question, was it her just being overly sensitive to all the people around her, or was there something going on? Chantelle could not imagine that she would be just feeling overly sensitive toward people as she was always good at using her intuition, her knowing, her abilities to read people, even things, objects, and knew in her heart that it wasn't her imagination, so what was it and why was still to be answered.

That Saturday, with Gary at home doing the usual paperwork for Dyna Corp, Chantelle headed over to Karen's house to meet with the other women in the bridal party for the collaboration and close to final plan making night before the wedding. The night was seemingly proceeding as usual, with appetizers, wine, and laughter; but Chantelle could still sense that Karen was directing her pleasant attitude to all her guests and that something still did not seem right between her and her childhood friend.

After the other guests had gone, Chantelle stayed back to help Karen with cleanup and, hopefully, an opportunity to talk with her deeper and maybe figure out what was bothering her friend. "So that was a productive bridal party meeting. Things seem to be on track and going smoothly," Chantelle said to Karen as they washed and dried the dishes. Karen started to nod her head and was able to utter a "Yes, things seem to be in place" response. Chantelle again asked her friend if everything was okay as she felt a wall between them, a change, but Karen denied any such feelings; and with that, the women ended the night, and Chantelle headed back home where Gary was still awake and feverishly working on *stuff* for Dyna Corp. As Gary wrapped up his paperwork, his attention went to Chantelle and when she was to go in for further testing, gene placement, and genetic experiments with Dr. Winston. His cold and robotic approach to this questioning was startling and further upsetting on an already-upsetting night with her friend Karen. Chantelle did not like to be suspicious; for one thing, these were the only family and friends, she really knew and thought she trusted, but things were starting to make her feel very uncomfortable, again, and many red flags were going up in her mind. Chantelle, in a matter-of-fact tone, did let Gary know that she did already have an appointment with Dr. Winston at Dyna Corp in two weeks, but she wanted him to know how uncomfortable all this testing was making her. Gary did not seem to care, more than ever now since losing the baby; he seemed increasingly bitter toward Chantelle, like she did something to lose the baby. Was Gary's anger clouding his judgment and feelings for Chantelle? Did he say something to Karen, and the others, that caused them to act so cold and indifferent toward her?

Chantelle had not heard anything from her private investigator in weeks, but he told her he wanted to concentrate on getting a bunch of information together to present to her and get back to her when it was ready, which he did say could be some weeks due to the activities deep inside Dyna Corp being quite hidden. She did still need to touch base with him in the face of her ongoing, and seemingly never-ending, testing and the peculiar shift of attitude toward her from those closest to her. She knew something dark and sinister was going on at Dyna Corp, including with her husband. She needed to know what—if not for anything, for her safety moving forward. As she suspected when she called Mark, he was working solely on her investigation case, as this was not only intriguing and fascinating to him, but he was highly curious about what Dyna Corp could be doing in that lab and in the other facilities they owned across the country. Mark knew that with all of Dyna Corp's and Gary's secrecy, her case needed the best covert expertise to get the information needed, and much time needed to devote to doing so. Many hours he was not even fully billing Chantelle for, partly because he liked her but also because this was so fascinating, what he was learning, what he was hearing through his surveillance devices. Mark never knew of a lab existing that was so futuristic sounding and bizarre; it was his pleasure to find out more, better than a TV horror movie he was thinking, but he wouldn't say those words to Chantelle out of respect for her rightful fear of these people. Mark promised to call Chantelle within another couple of weeks, for sure, and they would meet for a follow-up on whatever he had found thus far, as he could sense her progressing fear, anxiety, and need for a friendly, reassuring voice.

*****

It was now the third week in June and time for Chantelle's second testing at Dyna Corp, a session that Gary insisted on sitting in on. As Chantelle got into the hospital gown and lay on top of the gurney again, she couldn't help but feel an overwhelming amount of dread and helplessness at her plight. Gary's cool demeanor continued toward her but only toward her because she noticed that when Karen was around, or even talking with Dr. Winston, he seemed warm and back to the old Gary somewhat. What she had done to inspire such contempt she was really trying to figure out, and then she was mad at herself for blaming and taking on this attitude toward her like she had done something wrong when she knew she had not. Dr. Winston proceeded to take more blood samples and again withdraw some substance from a petri dish that he painfully injected into her arm. The site of the injection was more painful than when it coursed through her body, all reactions Dr. Winston described as normal but very uncomfortable nevertheless. Chantelle couldn't take it any longer. She insisted on knowing what it was that was being injected into her arm, whose cells. As she started to get a little upset and agitated, and with the bright lights blinding her view, all she could hear was Gary okaying something with Dr. Winston, and the next thing she knew, she was extremely drowsy and very relaxed, to the point where she could not stay awake.

When Chantelle awoke, she was already sitting in Gary's car, being driven home by him, and it was very late for them to be going home. It was now 7:00 p.m, a full four hours after her appointment with Dr. Winston. Chantelle was panicked but did not want to fully let on to Gary. "What happened in the doctor's office?" she said to Gary in the most unshaken and forced nonfrightened voice she could drum up.

"Why, what do you remember, Chantelle?" Gary asked.

If she wasn't frightened enough and untrusting of her husband before, this response did not help her feel at ease. "Well, that's just it. I don't remember anything after the point where you okayed something to Dr. Winston very early in the procedure, and then I awoke up in the car four hours later. What happened?" she asked again.

Gary seemed to be becoming frustrated with Chantelle, as if asking a basic question on testing that was being done on her was uncalled for and was disturbing to him, or shocking, that she did not trust him, Dr. Winston, and Dyna Corp.

After dinner, Chantelle decided a hot bath in their Jacuzzi tub was in order and settled in with a nice cup of chamomile tea and candles to do so. As she relaxed, and settled into a slightly meditative state while bathing, her mind went blank, as it should; but then she started to see flashes of unexplained shadows that seemed to be hovering above her. These waking dream sequences were very vivid, but she couldn't quite place all who were in them. But she knew it made her feel scared and uneasy, and she didn't know why. Why was she having these fearful reactions to these waking dreams, and who were the people, shadows, in the dream sequence seemingly hovering over her? Chantelle became panicked. Was she starting to remember something that happened earlier, that afternoon, in Dr. Winston's office-slash-experiment lab? And why was the memory not a pleasant one? And who were all those shadows or people in attendance when it should have only been the doctor, her husband, and maybe the nurse? Many unanswered questions, but she did not feel that telling Gary that she was having flashbacks of the events would be a good idea, partly because this might make them increase the dose of whatever drug they used to put her to sleep, and she wanted to, hopefully, be more lucid to remember what was going on.

Later, Chantelle woke up around 3:00 a.m. in a sweat, and again with much the same vivid dream yet vague idea of who the participants were; but she knew she was there, in the dream, and she knew it was at Dyna Corp. What were those weird dreams she was now experiencing, and why could she not answer any of these things? Chantelle studied the situation; she had to admit to herself that no one around her would tell her the truth even if they did know. Even worse, she now knew that Gary definitely knew what went on at Dyna Corp; her being drugged proved that to her. The only person she could trust to tell these things to and to help her figure out what was happening was her new private detective and friend, Mark; and even though; seemingly single, and without a family to take up his free time, he was busy doing surveillance overtime for Chantelle, so she did not want to disturb him at the moment.

As testing continued, more often now, the experiments were causing Chantelle increasing sadness and uneasiness when done. She did broach the conversation with Gary again to see if he would offer any more information, seeing as she had been such a cooperative, compliant specimen. Gary would not offer any more information, as in the first time the experiments and the testing occurred, but he did try to reassure Chantelle that he was there for her, that he would not let anything bad happen to her, and that everything was legal and safe. "Not to worry. Pretty soon we will inform you on its details, but for now, we need you as a placebo-type specimen, unknowing, so that we can properly test the end results." Gary's explanation did register as being truthful, from what Chantelle remembered in science and psychology classes, with experiments using placebos, but the only problem she had was, who else would allow you—and she used the word *allow* very loosely—to test on them not only in a drugged state but also without knowing the exact details and nature of the experiments? Were there unknowing participants, illegally being drugged? Other women and men being subjected to their testing that they would never remember later, or only vaguely remember, like with Chantelle but not enough to piece together the events? Chantelle was now panicked again with these thoughts. Was Dyna Corp paying people to participate in these tests or in something darker? All very good questions, and ones that Chantelle hoped Mark would have some insight into by now.

Chantelle scheduled an appointment with Mark at his office in Baton Rouge, also to bring him the next cash payment for his services. They met later that week on Thursday. Chantelle was happy, more like ecstatic, to see Mark that week, as not only was he a friendly and trusting face who was on her side, but he possibly had some insight into what was going on at Dyna Corp, with David, and with her husband Gary. Mark too was surprisingly happier to see Chantelle than he thought he would be. He actually never thought of it too much, as she was a client like any other; but for some reason, she struck a sympathetic cord in his heart. Mark couldn't help but give Chantelle a huge hug and a kiss on the cheek upon seeing her and asked her to be seated in his office for their private conversation, telling his secretary to hold all calls and not to disturb them. Mark started with asking Chantelle how she was doing as he knew of her miscarriage, and with the stress from this situation, he could only imagine what she was going through. Chantelle confirmed that she was physically okay from the miscarriage but that indeed, her emotions and the not knowing anything of this situation were taking a toll on her.

Chantelle confessed that she needed his expertise and insight to help her, hopefully, ease the unease she was feeling. Mark let her know, right up front and on the phone, that he had not even touched the tip of the iceberg of what was truly going on at Dyna Corp and with her husband, but he did have some insight. Mark continued to say that he absolutely agreed that something was covertly happening and was very mysterious at Dyna Corp, and not in a good way. Like her, he did not want to sound like he was crazy or out of his mind, but he did feel it had a very futuristic, cloning, genetics feeling to it, activity unknown to the average person. He continued, "I feel what is going on—the genetic testing, genetic cloning, and much more—has a very *out-of-this-world* feeling. Secrets are being kept at Dyna Corp." Mark cringed to even say such preposterous and crazy things, but he had to. This was what he was finding in his limited surveillance, audio, and some videotaping of workers and the heads of the company; but many times, it was a very cryptic half conversations, he admitted. "It was obviously being done to keep their operations an utmost secret." Mark finished by saying, "What I do know is that the people in the know keep this information very close to the vest and secret, and those that aren't on the front lines of this seem to suspect, but no one dares to discuss or question what's going on."

Chantelle wanted Mark to elaborate on what he saw and heard, and when he said *out of this world*, did he mean aliens? Mark did not want to elaborate too much at this time out of not wanting to unduly frighten Chantelle, plus he wanted more concrete evidence before making such hard-to-believe claims. What he did definitively find out was that "not only do they have very elaborate pharmaceutical labs and similar such departments at each facility, but their *specially made* medications have components embedded into a person's prescription. Microchipping components," Mark carried on, "Microchips, in one or more pills of any given bottle, that once digested, unbeknownst to its recipient, lodges these microscopic chip particles that migrate mainly to the person's eyes, for eye microchipping tracking, and to the brain cells for brain microchipping, monitoring, and controlling of the person's activities. That alone, Chantelle," he continued, "was sinister and illegal, as many people do not know they have received these tainted pills. When ingesting the microchip pill, most have no unusual taste, texture, or identifying factor that would cause that person to suspect anything was happening or was unusual with their medicine. And because these microchips are so tiny, ground almost to a powder form, they easily lodge into the appropriate tissue, all through the way these pharmaceutical labs manufacture, the density, and accompanying substances in these medications. Once embedded into these vital tracking, monitoring, controlling, organs of the body, it is there permanently, barely, if ever, really detected at any significant level when scanned by airport customs and such, and are permanent. They don't need to continue to give you these pills. One pill will do. Two in a bottle is just a backup for them, a guarantee. I'm surprised you have not received such a pill yet from your pain meds or during your semivoluntary lab testing, as it seems they eventually want everyone with these microchips as it allows them to monitor, control, and track a person—and you would be a prime candidate, especially now."

Chantelle wanted to know how Mark was so sure she hadn't been given the microchips.

Mark continued, "Because you coming here and hiring me to investigate them would not be a secret. They would not only be able to tap into all your thoughts at any given time, but they can follow and track you remotely. You would have absolutely no secrets from them, and definitely no privacy; and as I could sense right now, they are not on to me. So my advice to you, Chantelle, especially if you want to continue this investigation and know what is going on before it is too late, is to delay, refuse any further voluntary testing, and, most definitely, do not take any pills from them or get any medications, intravenous or otherwise, as pill form is not the only way they can get these microchips into your body. Your living with Gary is danger enough, as he could add it to your food. There are a million ways they can get these painless, tasteless, odorless particles into your body. You need to be careful and aware."

Now Chantelle was really scared. Mark was right to hold back all that he needed to tell her. What she had to figure out now was how she would be able to get out of any further testing, and how she could continuously monitor Gary to ensure he was not spiking her drinks and her food. Chantelle agreed that this information, including her husband's involvement in it, was very unsettling. She had no one to trust or turn to except Mark now. Because she had no one to trust but Mark, inadvertently exposing Gary, Karen, Dyna Corp employees, and the community to Mark would surely spell her doom. Chantelle knew she had to muster her strength and do all she could do to prevent being microchipped, even if it meant never eating food from the house, never leaving food and drinks unattended. Whatever it took, she needed to do it. Before ending their meeting, Chantelle asked Mark, "Is there any other important need-to-know leads or information I *should* know about what is going on at Dyna Corp and with my husband specifically?"

Mark shook his head no, but he did confirm, "There are a lot of secrets at Dyna Corp, and I in no way think that the information I divulged to you, as bad as they are already, is all there is. I suspect—I know there are a lot more deep secrets to Dyna Corp. Just take care of yourself and call me from a secure, safe place if you find out anything you think I should know, and most importantly, trust no one."

As Chantelle ran out of his office into her car for the long drive back to Pendle, she was visibly shaken, to the point of nausea. She could not imagine how or why this was happening again, and worse than ever, why her? Did Gary ever love her? she pondered, half watching the now-rainy road. Was Karen ever a real friend, or was she placed as a setup too? Was anything in her life a real decision, or was everything just a well-coordinated trick and façade? Would she get out of this alive and unharmed, and who could she trust if she did. And where would she go? Chantelle was very grateful to have found Mark and hired him when she did. Intuition, she thought as things seemed to be falling apart at an accelerated rate now, and she would have been trapped with no one on the outside to save her, help her save herself, or at least know what happened to her.

*****

July 1 was Gary and Chantelle's first wedding anniversary, but neither one of them was in a happily-ever-after marriage mood to celebrate; they did manage to defrost the saved cake from their wedding day and enjoy a nice candlelight dinner, including a beautiful bouquet of flowers courtesy of Gary, who didn't forget the day. As July proceeded at a hastened pace, Karen and Shawn's wedding was fast approaching, with all its activities. The two couples decided to go out for a pre-wedding night dinner to reconnect before Karen and Shawn's big day in August. As Chantelle was getting ready with Gary to go meet their friends in town for a night out, she had to remind herself to keep calm, to not let out what she knew, or that she even suspected anything, not to trust anyone, and, more importantly, to stay focused, to not ruin their looming wedding event, including no bickering and fighting with Gary. Chantelle figured maybe she would just drink a consistent amount of wine, therefore avoiding having to think deeply, and she would appear relaxed; but on the other hand, she thought she would have to make sure she didn't get too relaxed, end up saying something she would regret, something that would be detrimental to her well-being. As they drove to the restaurant, Chantelle, even though it was against her best judgment, still thought it a good, safe time to tell Gary that she would not be participating in any further testing.

As Chantelle started to talk, she was very mindful of her body language. She wanted to present herself as unassuming, unaware, to the point of being a silly little girl, which was how she felt Gary viewed her many times anyway. Thank goodness Gary had a beer while they were getting ready as his mood had improved much, and he seemed less perturbed and less demanding of her.

"Gary, I'm not going to do any more testing. I'm going to cancel the one for next week with Dr. Winston, as it makes me too tired and sick, and I just don't like it, or care to assist in these experiments any longer," she said as sweetly and naively as possible.

Gary paused for a moment and then looked directly at her, even though he was driving. "You will do no such thing. You can't just quit an experiment partway through. Those tests and experiments cost a lot of money. How would it look if my wife just abandons it?" he barked.

Chantelle was stunned. Her eyes started to well up with tears as she was not sure what to say as a comeback, but if she didn't say something at this moment and try, it looked as though she would be going for testing next week, something Mark warned her not to do. She was thinking that if she even had her friend Karen, or even Shawn, on her side and she was able to trust them, she would have been able to recruit them to go to battle for her, gang up on Gary on why she didn't want these tests and experiments done. But she had no such person to go to bat for her; not even her family back home could she definitively trust. The one person who would speak up for her, who she could trust, was Mark; but no one could know about their association. For now, Chantelle knew it was best to let the subject drop and try to come up with a more concrete reason later, except now, Gary knew that she was not a willing participant and any other excuse, regardless of how good, he would probably not believe it; but she would have to worry about that another day.

Chantelle did not want to ruin the nice night out, hopefully a relaxing night, with Gary and their friends; so she casually and very easily changed the subject to something more pleasant. They arrived at valet parking and headed into the restaurant where Karen and Shawn were already seated and started cocktails. In fact, Karen and Shawn had appeared to have already enjoyed two or three strong drinks as they were having a really good time, including dancing on the dance floor, laughing, joking, along with a fair share of affection, something lacking from Chantelle and Gary for some months now. When Karen and Shawn spotted them approaching the table, they stood up in over-excitement to see their friends, and they immediately called the waiter over to order them drinks as they wanted Gary and Chantelle to have as good of a time, as they were already having. They wanted Gary and Chantelle to catch up to them. They spent most of the night talking about the wedding plans for Karen and Shawn and their announce-ment that they were going to Tahiti for their honeymoon for two weeks and then coming back to start house hunting. All exciting and fun information. Chantelle and Gary were not bored, not even for a minute, with the constant wedding chatter and honeymoon plans. It made them remember their nuptials and how excited they were to plan their wedding a mere year ago. The night wrapped up very late as they had migrated to the restaurant's outdoor covered area. Then off Karen and Shawn went in their cab, and Gary, who always controlled his alcohol intake, drove Chantelle and himself home.

Gary was feeling calm and felt Chantelle was also receptive to him after many weeks of no marital relations. Tonight was a night they both felt a little like their old selves toward each other. After their lovemaking, Chantelle thought it might be a good time to bring up the experimental testing and her not wanting to do them any lon-ger. As she began to talk about it again, Gary abruptly turned over, facing away from her in an obvious response to her attempting this subject again. He did not want to discuss this right now, so Chantelle immediately stopped as it was apparent she was pretty much talking to herself anyway.

Next workday at the shop, Chantelle was with Karen and very few other staff that day as everyone seemed to have called in sick. Karen was being nice again, like her old self, toward Chantelle, which Chantelle took as a sign to let down her guard, a bit, and maybe ask Karen a few things about Dyna Corp, Gary, and the community in general. Karen was puzzled by what exactly Chantelle wanted to know about these people; she said she knew nothing more than *she* did about Dyna Corp, and as for Gary, she denied Shawn mentioning or telling her anything that Chantelle would not already know about her own husband. And Karen's response about the community was that she acted very confused about the line of questioning, puzzled, as though she wanted Chantelle to expand on the line of questioning. Was Karen lying, brainwashed, or did she truly not know? Chantelle could not decide, but what she did know was that she had to have Karen swear that she would not tell anyone, not even Shawn, that she had asked her those questions. Karen agreed to keep Chantelle's unsettling inquisition and vague accusations a secret, even from Shawn, who would most definitely take the information right back to Gary. Chantelle was not 100 percent sure that Karen would not mention it eventually; she was just hoping that by then she would have figured out what was going on, with the help of Mark, and be far away and safe from any repercussions. Chantelle figured since she mentioned a taboo subject already with Karen she might as well bring up the experiments, the testing they did at Dyna Corp, how she felt about them, including that she was trying to get out of these experiments; but Gary would not let her. Karen first wanted to know why Chantelle wanted to stop doing the experiments, a question Chantelle immediately flagged as suspicious. *Why didn't Karen ask? What are they doing to me during the testing and experimentation?* she contemplated. Chantelle thought she should try to play it smart with Karen, her equal, try to get the most out of this potentially revealing conversation.

"Karen, have you ever participated in any of their experiments, or know why and what they do during these experiments?" Chantelle inquired.

Karen, though denying participating in the tests, did acknowledge knowing of the experimental genetic testing going on at the Dyna Corp facilities; but other than that confirmation, she did not seem too intrigued or interested in information on what was happening to Chantelle during her sessions.

Chantelle now impassioned and outraged at her friend's lack of empathy, said, "Let me tell you, Karen, about the scary, hellish experience I have had so far. I have been used as a guinea pig, to put it mildly. They have taken many vials of blood from me, injected me with cells and other serums, substances that they wouldn't even tell me what they were, drugged me to the point that I wake up hours later in Gary's car, and no one will tell me what happened in those missing hours. But I keep getting weird flashbacks of mysterious-figured shadow people hovering over me. Could you explain any of these occurrences to me?" she angrily asked Karen.

Karen just looked at Chantelle blankly, as though she was not shocked at what her best friend had just divulged to her but more as if to say, *Stop complaining. This isn't all about you.* Which was very upsetting, and now it made Chantelle very angry. What kind of best friend was this? she was contemplating.

The rest of their time at the gift shop that day went on virtually in silence as both Karen and Chantelle were angry at each other. Chantelle was furious and was now, more than ever, sure that Karen would be telling Shawn about the conversation they had and Chantelle's line of questioning; so she knew, it was just a matter of time before it got back to Gary.

On the way home from work, Chantelle kept playing back in her head the heated and strained conversation she and Karen had, wondering what she was going to say to Gary once he confronted her about it. The way Chantelle was feeling, she was hoping she would be long gone when, *that* day came—not that she knew where she would be going if she left New Orleans.

CHAPTER 7

WHAT DO THEY WANT?

Before Karen's wedding, which was the third week in August, Chantelle was scheduled for another session of blood tests, injections, and, basically, drugging, because ever since the first appointment, every experimental day thereafter, her husband had come along like a thug, a bodyguard, making sure she arrived at the appointment. Also, Gary was needed at her appointments to drive her home from the now-guaranteed drug-induced experiment sessions. Regardless of how much Chantelle protests, no one, not even Dr. Winston, would stop these procedures. Chantelle was in tears after awakening, every time. Even more upsetting during *this* experiment day, Gary's boss, David, had the audacity to make an appearance in the testing room. He acted very happy, like nothing strange was going on. David was on top of the world, which Chantelle was sure he was from whatever high-stakes money system he had going on there.

Chantelle had not heard from Mark in weeks; she needed to know if he found any further information on Dyna Corp, Gary, the community. All she knew, as she started to slowly drift into another unexplained, unremembered testing day was that Mark would not be happy that she allowed herself to be tested again, as if she had a choice. Chantelle thought, how would she know if she was micro-chipped this time, jeopardizing not only their investigation but both of their safety? Such covert operations would have a high price to pay for those who were found out, inadvertently or advertently, spying.

Chantelle didn't know for sure if any microchip had been implanted this time, and she didn't want to jeopardize their purpose and expose Mark and their mission, so she was going to first research the subject a bit to see if she could tell if a person was being tracked, learn any information on how a person acts when microchipped with this type of technology, if such information was even available on the world wide web. Chantelle also wanted to know who monitored these microchipped, implanted people, where. She even reflected that this might be a good time to do some snooping around Gary's home office for this information, and any other information she might find that would be helpful to Mark in their undercover investigation.

*****

It was early Wednesday morning, and Gary had just left for work. Chantelle thought this would be a perfect day to do her office snooping as Gary usually worked late on Wednesdays. Gary had always locked his office door, and even though Chantelle knew where the key was, that wasn't a secret, she always wondered, why he had to lock this room in their home, maybe today she will figure it out. Chantelle was fairly confident that Gary would not suspect she would even contemplate combing through his office, out of fear of being caught, and because she was too naïve, and unknowing, to figure out what she was looking for. Even with that, Chantelle knew she couldn't be obvious. Things needed to be put back properly; the room needed to look undisturbed by the time Gary returned from work. Chantelle even remembered Gary's computer access code, she had all she needed to tackle his office, and hopefully get some answers, but she was very nervous, nervous at what she might find, nervous at being found out, nervous about the plight of their marriage. As Chantelle unlocked the door to the office and crept in, as if someone else was there who would hear her, she noticed a lot of little pieces of paper with notes and reminders written to himself and to David as well.

As Chantelle sat down at Gary's computer to unlock it and see what popped up, her stomach started to hurt terribly. A tight knot had formed, and she started shaking. She wasn't sure if she would be able to do this today, but she knew she had to. Gary's computer opened up right to the Dyna Corp webpage where he had his company account login. Chantelle was hoping it was the same login info as the one for his home computer, and it was. Chantelle was happy, shocked, shaking, and scared, all at the same time. Scared to see what might pop up or what information would be available on opening his computer. As she combed through Dyna Corp accounts, she found Gary's accounts, and she started to read through e-mails between David and Gary. The e-mails between the two men were explicit and shocking to Chantelle as it gave the details of what they called "classified testing," which involved humans being injected with unknown substances that were extracted from beings—*alien* beings—that were secretly being tested on, some alive, some dead that were just being studied. This classified testing file continued on to name the hundreds of people who had been unwillingly subjected to these tests through abduction or "whatever means possible" as she read further, in shock. The e-mails and the files, Chantelle found, detailed the various types of tests they performed on people and their outcomes, classified in different categories: Manufactured People, Zombie People (also known as Microchipped, some of those with or without alien being gene induction), Cloned People, and the highest tier, the *New Breed.*

A New Breed was taking preferably a human female to mate with these, Beings, willingly or unwillingly, through a drug-induced state and impregnating them. This newly formed embryo was taken out of the female several hours later after joining—sometimes even a week later, before she knew she was pregnant—and grown and incubated in their controlled Dome facility.

Dome facility? Chantelle deliberated. *Where is that, and what is that?* She was admittedly in shock. This was worse than she could have ever imagined; and it was obvious that Gary was not only aware of all these illegal activities but he was actively participating in their execution.

It was 1:00 p.m., and Chantelle had been in Gary's office for four hours already. There was so much to read, all so intriguing, so shocking that when her phone rang, she almost jumped right out of her skin. It was Gary calling her, as usual, to see how her day was going. Chantelle knew she had to compose herself and build up the strength and courage to talk to him, to act extremely normal, like her day involved hot tea and a bath, a normal routine.

"Hi, Gary," she answered. She talked to him and, more importantly, tried to find out how late he might be working that night.

He said, "Today was actually a light day, so I will be leaving shortly. Do you want me to pick up something for dinner?"

Chantelle responded, "Yes, definitely." She knew she had to quickly clean up his office and make it look undisturbed as usual. Gary's ride back home was only around thirty-five minutes, so she had to hurry. "Okay, see you shortly," she said in the most, unshaken voice she could drum up.

Chantelle tried to print out as much of the information she found as possible, so she could show it to Mark. She also quickly tried to look through Dyna Corp's site, to see if it explained the microchipping they did, what signs and symptoms people had, but she was becoming increasingly unnerved by her husband's imminent arrival, so she decided to wrap it up. Chantelle hoped she was not microchipped as she wanted to contact Mark in the morning the following day, as soon as Gary headed out to work. She could not process and dissect what she had obtained from his computer without Mark. He was becoming her rock, her safe place now in this crazy existence she was living.

As Gary drove up their driveway, Chantelle felt pretty sure that she had everything back where it should be, thawing any suspicion by Gary. She had cleared his history of her activity, returned papers in their previous place, or very close, pushed the chair back to its previous angle, locked the door, and put the key away. Chantelle waited for Gary to enter the house from her spot at the entranceway. She gave him the usual greeting kiss, took the takeout food from his arms while he descended to the bedroom to get into comfortable clothes.

Chantelle decided to dim the lights and have dinner by candlelight, portraying a romantic husband-and-wife interaction. Chantelle did not want the stress, worry, and possible evidence of her lying to

Gary visible on her face; so she figured a darkened room would be calming to her extremely frazzled nerves as she tried to act normal during dinner. Chantelle was grateful Gary brought home an extra bottle of red wine this night, as she knew she needed several glasses to get through the night with him. Plus, she was extremely anxious to touch base with Mark early the following day, before he made other plans. She urgently needed to show him what she had found. Chantelle needed Mark's investigative, concrete mind to unravel what her mind was saying was unbelievable, unheard-of information—information that she couldn't have really read. She needed confirmation of her sanity, as she was sure she was now living in an alternative reality. As Gary nonchalantly chattered on about his day at Dyna Corp, Chantelle started to think about her investigation with Mark, what direction it would take, what about this Dome place that was mentioned, and maybe she should invite Mark to her home to look at Gary's files himself. With all the constant crazy thoughts going through her mind, she was also wondering about her testing. What had, or hadn't, been done to her? Was she herself being injected with these alien genes while drugged? Were they extracting impregnated embryos from her body? If so, where are these children? And therefore, was she being subjected to the alien being sexual encounters?

She had to stop her thoughts right there, as she was now starting to become nauseated, and faint all at once. Chantelle needed to rest her mind for the day, not think any further until she had spoken with Mark. She let the wine take full effect, and hoped to fall to sleep until the crack of dawn, shortly after Gary left for work. In some ways, she was hoping that when Mark saw the information he would say, "No, not possible" and this was not what *he* saw or knew to be true from his investigation. But Chantelle knew that this was not to be the case as he had already alluded to "out of this world beings." Mark did not want to elaborate on this information to Chantelle due to not wanting to unnecessarily frighten her, before he knew for sure what was going on, information Chantelle now, had written proof of, all available in black and white, to read.

Chantelle got Mark on his cell phone right at 8:00 a.m. the following day, as soon as Gary had left for work. She was obviously jumbled, upset, speaking very fast, and wild; Mark could barely get all the information she had to share. Mark agreed to meet with Chantelle as soon as she could drive down to his Baton Rouge office, which was at least one hour and twenty minutes away, longer if traffic was bad. Chantelle did not mind the drive as it gave her time to focus, relax, think, and review all the important points she wanted to cover with Mark, such as what they were going to do with this information. Chantelle now wanted to become actively involved in the investigations and hoped Mark would be okay with this as things were too unreal and close to home for her not to be. Chantelle needed to make sense of this information, understand fully not only what was being done to her but what all exactly Dyna Corp was involved in, and what her husband's role was in her and others' tests. Did Gary directly participate in, the alien gene therapy being injected into others, possibly her, and genes being withdrawn and added between the species? Did Gary see these incubated children, the embryos, being exacted from women? Did he authorize all these activities, help with funding, find investors? Chantelle had so many questions, many of which Mark probably couldn't answer; but she wanted to discuss everything with him anyway.

As she pulled into Mark's office's driveway, she was praying she was not microchipped—at least not yet. Which would be shocking as this seemed to be the basic part of the human testing they did. Maybe they had a reason not to do so as yet. As far as she could tell, Gary did not seem to expect her to engage in any dubious activities, or of prying into Dyna Corp's activities. She assumed that if they microchipped her, they would be tracking all her activities and would be aware of Mark and his investigative practice. Chantelle felt it was safe to meet with Mark today, but it was just a matter of time. They needed to use their time wisely and thoroughly; it was of the utmost importance. Chantelle reflected that if she wanted to assist Mark with the onsite investigation and live monitoring, she had to keep herself from being microchipped and being tracked, or for sure, she would not be able to join Mark on this part of his investigation into her life; and she really needed and wanted to.

Mark was wrapping up on the phone with another client when his secretary escorted Chantelle into his office. She sat at the comfy big office chair centered in front of his desk, in front of him on the other side of his, large dark-wood desk. As he hung up the phone, he stood up with a sympathetic look on his face and opened his arms wide, wanting to give Chantelle a big hug. "How are you doing?" he said in a kind, empathetic tone. He must have sensed the panicked, upset, and distraught tone in her voice earlier, coupled with whatever he already knew of Dyna Corp and the terrible situation she had found herself in.

Mark was trying to ease her mind, that everything was going to be all right, even if he didn't fully believe it himself, yet. "This sounds serious," he said. "What did you find out, and how?"

Chantelle grabbed her thick files out of her tote bag and handed it to Mark. "Mark," she began, "you will not believe the bizarre and unsettling things I found out from Gary's Dyna Corp account on his home office computer while Gary was at work," she said, halfheartedly proud of her investigative work and halfheartedly scared of her investigative work. As she sat down and let Mark take his time and read through the files, she made commentaries on additional things she found. Things that Chantelle admitted she had no time to print out, plus there were so many detailed files available; it would have taken all of Gary's ink and paper to do so. Using all of Gary's ink and paper would have been a dead giveaway that I was fishing around in his office, his computer files," she confirmed to Mark, who already understood her dilemma.

Mark read through the files, mostly skimming, hitting the flagged important and very specific details Chantelle neatly had ready for him, which shocked even her herself as she had been too nervous this morning to do much more than shower and come down to see him ASAP. It was all very important, lots more to read from Gary's Dyna Corp account and e-mails, but Chantelle highlighted the highest of importance so he could read all the dark, sinister, and unbelievable information that would never have been believed unless found directly from Dyna Corp's company server. Mark's jaw looked like it literally hit the ground; he could not fathom what he was reading, what he was trying to mentally absorb.

"Do you know what you have got here, Chantelle? This information is so potentially dangerous for us to have. Legally, it spells out violations of civil rights and illegal criminal justice activities, a fire storm, *no* more like a bomb." Mark was proud of Chantelle's courage in obtaining this information—information that affected herself and others, troubling information. Information that Mark, agreed he would probably have had a very hard time obtaining, if ever due to its extremely highly classified nature, guaranteed devastating company information if it got out to the masses and the authorities. Chantelle was again starting to become shaken, nauseated, and faint during their discussion. Mark brought her a cup of tea. Chantelle wanted to know, "Now what, Mark? What do you do? What do we do."

Mark paused. "We, Chantelle? I don't want you endangering yourself any further assisting with retrieving information. You have done enough to jeopardize your safety. Let me take it from here and figure out a plan of action. If anything, I need to gather more concrete information, pictures. Where do these people go? Who are they with, find out who's buying all these experiments or helping to finance them—all very important information needed for criminal charges, or any other charges," Mark attested.

In the meanwhile, he wanted Chantelle to play along as normally as possible and not let on about what she knew but keep her ears and eyes open for additional information and, most important, try not to be part of these tests any further, which Mark knew was virtually impossible with the controls they, and Gary, had on her. He, like Chantelle, was wondering what parts of this diabolical, futuristic, sick plot she was being subjected to. All of it was bad enough, but certain parts were truly sad and unsettling. He felt bad for Chantelle.

Chantelle too was wondering which part, if not all parts, of this company's experimental agenda she was already part of or scheduled to be part of in the near future. And why her and not Karen? Or was Karen an experimental subject too but not aware? "So much unknown still; it's so confusing, but that is probably how these sick high-powered companies set it up," Chantelle said to Mark, who listened patiently.

Chantelle wanted Mark to know that she did want to, eventually, directly help with the investigation, that she wanted him to find out where this Dome city or facility was located so they both could go together and check out what was inside. Mark felt it would be highly dangerous for her, to want to come along with him to this Dome facility and gain access with him in order to investigate it, but he knew disputing this with her would be pointless, so he agreed to take her with him once he found out where it was located. He was hoping to locate its whereabouts sooner than later. Mark reminded Chantelle to enjoy her friend's wedding next week, act unaware of everyone's potential involvement, including this weird town's activities, and, of the utmost importance, say nothing to no one about what she knew. Chantelle agreed.

*****

The third Saturday in a very hot and long August in Louisiana, and it was finally Karen and Shawn's wedding day. Chantelle and the whole bridal party were ready for all events, and activities that were to unfold. It was a beautiful outdoor wedding, with almost five hundred guests. Shawn had a pretty big extended family. Lots of laughter, food, and good times with people coming from all parts of the country to join in Karen and Shawn's festivities. Chantelle had forgotten, for a night, the crazy existence she was really, living. Even Gary was happy and having a good time on this night; and because Shawn knew Dyna Corps owner, David, and his wife, Joyce, well, through Gary, they were also at the nuptials and the reception that followed. David and Joyce were seated at the table with Chantelle and Gary, of course, which allowed the men to talk business, "shop talk," leaving Joyce to make small talk with Chantelle and get to know her better.

Chantelle felt a little uncomfortable with Joyce's line of questioning, as she wanted specific, detailed information on Chantelle and her childhood back in Massachusetts—her relationship with her mom, dad, and brothers; any other close family members she had; and whether she still had any ties to that community. Chantelle knew exactly why Joyce wanted to know all this information. She had read the Dyna Corp protocol of *the perfect specimen*, the perfect abductee, really, for their scientific experiments and testing. The perfect human specimen that would bring few to none of the police and not cause federal investigations, looking for that person, and Chantelle fit many of their criteria.

Chantelle was again feeling sick to her stomach. Joyce asked her if everything was okay, as she was looking unwell, and the color had drained from her face. Chantelle managed to tap Gary on the shoulder, signaling the bathroom as she ran toward there, short of breath and in a full panic attack. How brazen, she thought, for Joyce to ask her those pointed, obvious questions. But she had to remember that no one there knew that she knew, so to them, she was just an unassuming specimen they were sizing up. She had to carry that act out. It was becoming very clear to Chantelle that a lot of people in and around the community, and Dyna Corp workers, were in on these experiments and were very much aware of what was going on at Dyna Corp.

Dyna Corp and the people who paid for these tests and experiments had a lot of money that was not only going into these projects but also into keeping its secrets. This was all extremely nerve wracking for Chantelle, as a very young woman who was barely out of her teens; and though she had an unusual relationship with her family back in Massachusetts, she still believed the majority of the people in the world were good and to be trusted—something she was quickly learning to not believe, especially if she wanted to survive this. As she returned to the table, Gary and everyone at the table were looking at her puzzled and alarmed. "Are you all right, dear?" Gary piped up as all eyes were on Chantelle.

Chantelle nodded, indicating she was fine, but her face and her color did not indicate she was fine, something she, unfortunately, was not able to control. But she reassured Gary that she was fine. "Just digested something that didn't agree with me," she tried to convey to all concerned. As the night proceeded to the dances, bouquet catching, garter throwing, and drunkenness. Chantelle had a chance to study her friend Karen, the way she interacted with Shawn, with her family, with friends, with others from the community, and then their relationship of lately, and knew, without a doubt, her friend was not only, not part of being tested like she was, her friend was not who she thought she was. Karen was definitely not the childhood friend Chantelle knew from Massachusetts. A lot had changed, and a lot of truths were being hidden. It was also becoming clear that the whole community was one big religious cult, a brainwashed cult who were convinced in their warped way of thinking that they were doing God's work, and Chantelle was not part of that group, not part of the cult. Not that Chantelle would ever want to be part of this weird, mind-controlled cult; but she wondered, when did they meet, and where was this organization located other than the Dyna Corp headquarters? She had so many unanswered questions her mind was ready to explode. Thank goodness everything was winding down. People were starting to leave, and Chantelle was more than spent, mentally and physically, and couldn't wait to go home to bed.

On the ride home, Gary and Chantelle barely talked. Both were very tired from a long day; therefore, no conversation would be adequate and worth the little energy they had to devote to it. Instead of getting into anything in depth, they both decided it was best to avoid everything. At home, they both fell asleep quickly and woke up very late Sunday morning, almost at twelve noon, which was very late for them. Gary got up quickly, showered, ate, and went to his home office for an afternoon of Dyna Corp paperwork. With Karen and Shawn on their honeymoon and Gary working, Chantelle found herself bored with nothing to do, no one to speak to. She wished she could call Mark, but she could not. She decided to call her family back in Massachusetts to see how they were doing. Her mother answered the phone, as her dad was at the shop and her brothers were out.

"How you doing, Chantelle?" her mother asked sweetly.

Chantelle knew she was just calling for light chitchat and not to divulge any truths and, more importantly, not to blow her cover, a cover for a plot, a situation in which she would not be surprised if her mother and her family in Massachusetts didn't already know all about. Chantelle replied, "I'm doing very well, Mom. And you?."

Chantelle's mom did note the strain in her voice and followed up with "And married life—married life treating you well? Gary seems like a great guy." Chantelle almost broke out in a delirious laugh that for sure would have resonated negatively, and may even be held against her in the future, as a crazy cackle; but she couldn't help but think of the irony of the question between the words, implying *Gary was a great guy and therefore must be treating you well.*

Less than two minutes into her conversation with her mother, Chantelle was already feeling stressed. She could read her mother's thoughts, innuendos, things her mother wasn't saying but meant; and it drove Chantelle crazy—the dishonesty, the betrayal. She had to go and sit quietly somewhere. This was one of Chantelle's gifts, and also her curse—the knowing.

"Well, it was nice talking with you, Mom. I just wanted to touch base and say hi. Say hello to dad and the brothers, and I'll talk to all of you again soon." As she hung up, she couldn't help but break into tears—tears for the family she was born into, tears for the world with people like this, and tears for the predicament she found herself in, again. Tears and anger for it all.

Chantelle pondered, how did she keep attracting these people into her life and not find good people like Mark first? Chantelle was starting to feel mentally drained again, and went to lie down in a darkened room, falling asleep until Gary woke her for dinner. Gary was done with all his paperwork for Dyna Corp and decided to cook this night his specialty barbecue meats of all kinds—steak, chicken, pork with a side of potatoes and asparagus, both their favorites.

Chantelle and Gary retired early as they had to work in the morning, and even though Chantelle slept most of the day, she was still feeling drained and tired. She was starting to think that maybe she was depressed as it wasn't normal to sleep this much, wanting to spend extended time in darkened rooms; but she thought, could anyone blame her? That diagnosis wouldn't be shocking with the situation she was living in—the lies, the deception, the tricks, the unsafety; and this was from her family and friends who were sup-posed to have her back.

Monday morning, Chantelle was at the shop working with two other coworkers, none of whom were Karen, as she was on her hon-eymoon in Tahiti. Work was actually a relaxing place for Chantelle right now as it was the closest thing to a, *safe house* at this time. She enjoyed many of the items they sold there at the Mardi Gras; there weren't antiques and collectibles, but it had the haunted aura, Louisiana vibe, including many items with the infamous Voodoo Queen, Marie Laveau, on it, which Chantelle loved. Chantelle worked with very nice coworkers, at least on the surface. She wasn't terribly close to any of them, except Karen; but they never seemed to act odd around her like in a conspiracy or a setup. Chantelle didn't know if her coworkers knew anything, but she thought it might be a good day, seeing as the owner wasn't in today either to ask them questions about the community and about Dyna Corp, and to see what vibes they gave off. Her coworkers, Candy and Sarah, were the same age as Karen and her but they, unlike Karen, had always lived in Louisiana, born in the town of Pendle, where Chantelle now lived with Gary in their old Victorian home. As Chantelle started asking the girls questions in between customers coming in, she started to get puzzled and lingering stares from them, as they were obviously wondering where Chantelle was going with this line of questioning and what she thought might be going on. It was Chantelle's cue to halt the questioning before it got back to Gary.

Bright and early on a Tuesday morning, Chantelle called Mark. She thought it was time, regardless of what more Mark had found out to this point about Dyna Corp. They needed to make plans to break into the Dome, Dyna Corp's holding facility for their experimental projects, to find out exactly what went on in there. Mark was happy to hear from Chantelle and relieved to know that all was okay with her, physically and mentally, knowing what he knew of Dyna Corp and her husband. He was becoming worried for her safety when he had not heard from her in a number of weeks.

Chantelle whispered, even though Gary was at work, "Could we meet today to discuss plans on going to the Dome?" she asked Mark.

Mark was hesitant as he wasn't quite sure if he had enough information to securely break into the Dome as yet, and also, he wasn't sure regarding the safety of both of them in bringing the emotionally fragile Chantelle along with, and rightfully so, as it might spell a suicide mission, in many ways, for both of them if he did, he thought to himself. But Mark knew there was no way he would be able to convince Chantelle that it would be better for her to stay behind, so he thought he better not try chancing upsetting her further and straining the bond and trust he had built with her, as he only wanted to help her.

Mark agreed to meet with Chantelle as soon as she was able to come down to Baton Rouge, so she immediately jumped into her car after hanging up the phone. Plus, she needed to be back before Gary arrived home from work, and it was approximately an hour and a half's drive each way, so time was of the essence. Chantelle did not want to have to lie and figure out an excuse to tell Gary every time she met with Mark, triggering possible suspicion and causing him to track, monitor, and surveil her activities; so she was being discreet and not sloppy with her evidence like evidence of hiring Mark, who was absolutely important to her. On arrival at Mark's office, his secretary was off sick this day, and so he greeted her himself and escorted her into his office, after locking the main doors and putting out a sign: "Gone for lunch, back in one hour." Which was perfect, as no one could be trusted with the information obtained from overhearing the conversation, from what they were going to discuss that today.

Mark gave Chantelle a big hug. Before proceeding, he asked how she was doing and what the weeks had been like since he last saw her, last spoke with her. Chantelle could not help but to break down and start crying, not only because Mark showed some real concern for her well-being (something no one had done in months—not her best friend Karen, not her husband Gary, no one), but also because she had been holding in the intense emotions, fears, regarding her situation for weeks, in the attempt to be brave and strong. And now it was just too much to hold back any longer.

Mark let Chantelle let it out and just consoled her. He knew she needed this outlet and did not want to stop her justified emotions. After approximately five minutes of complete silence, only Chantelle made a sound, quietly crying as he rubbed her back. She gathered her voice to express what had been going on. She told Mark about the drug research experiments that continued on her, which she was powerless to stop from happening; but she didn't feel that any microchipping or tracking had occurred as yet. That she did see a further decline in her relationships with Gary; her supposed, best friend, Karen; her coworkers at the gift shop and at the community at large, all of whom she suspected had eyes on all her activities when Gary or Karen was not with her. Chantelle did mention having a fairly good and relaxing time at the wedding of Karen and Shawn; and the last week or so had been rather uneventful, just spent with her processing and trying to figure out what is going on, and why, and who all were involved.

As Chantelle pulled herself together, she turned to Mark. "So down to business at hand. Did you find out anything more about the Dome?"

Mark got straight to the point. "No, I'm having a very hard time getting any additional information about this secret, not-well-known place, but what I can tell you is that it is a highly evolved, mystical, out-of-this-world place. It's like stepping into Narnia." The only thing I was able to get was its location. It is located out in the New Mexico desert, so the question is, how do we get in? We will be going at it virtually blind as I have no information on its security setup, codes, nothing. The Dome is bound to be a highly evolved, electronically and technologically. A place such as this would definitely pose its challenges to being infiltrated blindly. What I do have and the only thing we have to work with unless some more information comes to light before our D-day for Dome day is this specialized handheld scanner, which is not sold in the general market. I've used this scanner to access door codes, recognition needs such as for a face or a finger for all devices, including doors and other scanners.

"Perfect," Chantelle added. "That sounds like something better than nothing, and a fairly good something, so when should we go?"

That, Mark wasn't too sure of. Plus, he knew Chantelle wouldn't agree not to come, so he wanted to wait to figure out that part of the plan together, as she had to find the perfect time to get away from Gary without being obvious; and he preferred to do this on a weekend, and during the night, as there would be less people, higher-ups and management-type people, around. They made a plan for Mark to call Chantelle in a few days. Sunday evening, at 4:00 p.m., she needed to be away from the house, of course, to take the call, and they would discuss the details of when they were going to initiate D-night. Chantelle agreed, and as she was driving back, she was not only figuring out where to tell Gary she was going this Sunday just before 4:00 p.m., so she was away from the house for the call coming in from Mark, but also she was figuring out how to explain an overnight trip to New Mexico, which she knew was going to be much more complicated to figure out an explanation for. Chantelle was starting to get a headache just thinking about it now as she pulled into the driveway of the beautiful old Victorian house she shared with Gary. She thought of how she would miss it if she had to flee and leave Gary. She wondered, if she mysteriously took off, would Gary come looking for her? Her mind started to go wild with thoughts. She knew she was tired and needed to rest.

Just as Chantelle was coming out of the car, Gary pulled up in the driveway beside her. "There you are," he said. "I was trying to get a hold of you on your phone, but it was going straight to voice. Where were you?"

Startled by Gary's early arrival home, Chantelle had to think quick of a plausible excuse. "I needed to clear my head, and I thought a drive in the countryside would be the perfect remedy, so I turned off my phone from all distractions and headed out."

Gary seemed to buy this excuse, as he gave her a big hug on the driveway and escorted her into their home. He was in a good mood this afternoon, and he told Chantelle it was because he got a promotion at work, which included substantially more money.

"Wow, more money," Chantelle congratulated him, all the while thinking, *I wonder what he had to do to receive this promotion, this substantial money. Everything has a price, especially in the corporate world.'*

Gary had picked up enough Chinese takeout to feed an army, again, and several bottles of wine—white, red, and rosé—and they settled in for a night of feasting and celebration. As they enjoyed a semi-romantic and joyous night, including lots of talk about Dyna Corp by Gary, something Chantelle was taking all in with a new enlightened ear now, he said that due to his new position as CEO of the company, he needed to go to Atlantic City the following weekend for a briefing and the company corporate update; a brainstorming, and seminars, weekend. This was absolute music to Chantelle's ears, as she immediately thought, *How fortunate.* This would be the perfect weekend for her and Mark to tackle the Dome. Now Chantelle didn't have to come up with any story to tell Gary on her whereabouts overnight, which would have been suspicious and would raise red flags with him at best. Thrilled over her own good fortune, she stood up and said, "Wonderful, Gary. I'm proud of you." She planted a big kiss on him, which led to an unexpected ending to the night of lovemaking, which, for a newlywed couple, was happening more and more infrequently.

The week flew by with the routines of life, which included work, and more work, for Chantelle and Gary. On Sunday afternoon, Chantelle needed a reason to leave the house for about an hour in order to receive the call from Mark. Gary was paper deep in work in his home office when Chantelle appeared at the doorway to his den, "Gary, I need to go to the grocery store for some toiletries for myself and some grocery items. Anything you need from there?" She knew he wouldn't question her needing to go to the store to pick up some of her personal care products, and she made a matter-of-fact statement, not asking him, as if she urgently needed to go, so it was a smooth, unquestionable, unalarming request, which he bought.

"No," he said, "I have all the toiletries I need for now and any food or snacks. Whatever you pick up will be fine." Chantelle abruptly turned while saying as she was leaving, "Okay, I will be back in about an hour. See you later. 'Love you." She tried to keep her composure and hoped her angst didn't reveal itself in her voice. Chantelle arrived at the grocery store parking lot at 3:55 p.m. and aware that she very possibly was being monitored, watched by every and anyone around, she was very careful with where she parked and who was within earshot of her conversation. Mark called at 4:00 p.m. sharp, as promised. *Thank goodness*, Chantelle thought as she did not want any time wasted that would build suspicion with Gary on where she was. And because she still had to go into the store to actually shop like she told Gary.

"Hi, Mark," she enthusiastically answered. "How are you doing?"

Mark didn't want to waste her time with any idle chitchat, either. He got right to the point. "Can you arrange to be away from Gary next weekend?" he asked.

Chantelle was elated he chose next weekend, as she proceeded to tell him about the wonderful and fortunate news of Gary's promotion that called for him to be in Atlantic City all next weekend from Friday and returning on Monday, so she was absolutely free and ready to dive into this investigation.

"Excellent," Mark said. "That is extremely fortunate. And lucky for you something is working on your side, besides me, of course." He chuckled lightly even though he was trying not to make light of this serious situation and be insensitive to her feelings during this decidedly upsetting and difficult time in her life. Mark agreed to call her back on Friday around 3:00 p.m. so they could finalize the details. He now needed to make arrangements for their stay in New Mexico and to write out an itinerary, a plan of action for the days they were going to be there on their overnight break-in investigation. Chantelle ran into the store giddily but also being very aware of her surroundings and trying to ascertain if anyone looked as though they were watching her while on the phone, surveilling her activities. Chantelle ripped through the grocery store aisles, quickly throwing in some toiletries she uses, picking up some food items including snacks, and heading to the checkout. Then she proceeded home to Gary, arriving back at 4:50 p.m., meaning she had been gone for something shy of an hour.

Gary was waiting in the kitchen when Chantelle came in with the grocery items. "Wow, you weren't kidding when you said you would be shopping for an hour." *You women can turn any shopping expedition into a full-day affair*, he mused.

Chantelle gave a light and relieved laugh at the obvious nonsuspicious nature of his teasing. "I bought some great snacks we can eat while watching a movie tonight, Gary," she gushed.

"Sure, I have an early-morning meeting at Dyna Corp tomorrow, but we can watch an early evening movie together." Gary wanted to make the marriage work by trying to keep the pleasant, open communication between them going. He knew he needed to work on balancing his work obligations, which took nearly everything out of him and his time and obligation to Chantelle and the marriage, so he agreed.

Gary left for work early Monday morning as promised; and soon after leaving, Chantelle wanted to see if there was any additional information she could retrieve from his computer and the Dyna Corp account that would help her and Mark with their break-in and investigation at the Dome this weekend. Chantelle did manage to find information on a secret backup master key that could be found at Dyna Corp, that would open the doors; and one other big find was the override passcode to disarm all alarms in the facility upon entering, but more importantly, she found information also on the correct entrance that *must* be used, to enter into the facility, to use this passcode. Chantelle did luck into one final vital piece of information, the master key for the Dome, where its exact location was at Dyna Corp's large facility. Chantelle found the exact room number, and building, where the key was located, so she could sneak in and get this key while there for her experimental testing, but she had to plan it carefully.

Chantelle decided that she would call Dr. Winston today and set up and appointment for Friday, as she didn't want to remove the key too early, and she would get it back before the following Monday so that no one knew it was missing. Second, she needed to figure out when she was to take it—before, or after her appointment, she knew she needed to take the key beforehand, due to her being drugged; afterward would not work. Gary would not be with her this Friday, as he would be out of town, Dr. Winston might forgo the drugging part because there would be no one to take her home and to watch her after such testing procedures. Regardless, she didn't want to rely on what Dr. Winston might, or might not do. She agreed, in her mind, that getting to her appointment early, finding the room she mapped out from Gary's computer, getting the key, and even quickly hiding it in the trunk of her car before her appointment would be the safest, least nerve-wracking approach. This way, the stolen key would not be on her during the whole appointment, chancing someone finding it on her, or if by chance it was reported missing while she was there, it would not be in her possession. Dr. Winston did fit her into a Friday appointment even though he was a little apprehensive due to her husband being out of town and not available during the testing and experiment. He agreed that it would be a varied appointment than the usual to accommodate for the lack of needed assistance in her care after the experiment by her husband. Dr. Winston did offer for Chantelle to stay at the facility for an extended time, allowing the staff nurses to see to her care immediately after a full testing after the experimenting period. Chantelle flatly refused; she knew not only would she never allow that, as these tests were being forced on her as it was, but she also had an evening, and night, that was fully needed to prepare for the next day's adventure with Mark.

Chantelle had to call Mark that Thursday instead of awaiting his call on Friday, as normally planned. She called him on her way home from work. She pulled into a parking lot and made the call. She updated him on what she found on Gary's computer earlier in the week—an extremely important find, the key and the added information on the code and the setup of the Dome. Mark was proud of Chantelle's hard and dedicated work on this investigation, "Like a real PI," he joked with her. Chantelle told Mark that she had to make the appointment for tomorrow, Friday, to try to get this master key from Dyna Corp, so she couldn't receive his call at 3:00 p.m. This was why she called him early. Also, because she was excited to tell him what she had found out, so he could add it to his itinerary, his planned outline of events. Mark warned her to be very careful. "Don't display any suspicious behavior, and keep yourself safe," he reminded her. Mark also reminded her to "never forget the inherent danger in this investigation of them, and of snooping around in general." Mark said he would call her Friday night to make sure she was all right, around 8:00 p.m., giving her enough time to get back home after the testing, and that if she wasn't answering, he was coming out to the house to look for her as he was driving into the New Orleans area after work, staying close by her home, overnight Friday so that they would be ready, bright and early, for their road trip to New Mexico during the wee hours of Saturday morning.

Even though the road trip to Corona, New Mexico, where the Dome was located in the desert, would be more than a sixteen-hour drive, Mark thought they would leave less of a trail later on, when someone was bound to start snooping into their activity, their relationship, and why she hired him. Two plane tickets on the same flight, and especially side-by-side seating heading to the barren destination of one of Dyna Corp's facilities, would be a major red flag, a major got-you find for Gary and his cronies. Mark was presently an unknown to them, and he wanted to keep it that way; therefore, the less evidence, the better. Mark also rented a car for the weekend drive, from his hometown of Baton Rouge to New Orleans and then New Mexico, not using his own, as another way of leaving less paper trail than them flying out to New Mexico. So they were to leave at the crack of dawn on Saturday, around 3:00 a.m., getting into Corona around 7:00 p.m. or 8:00 p.m., which was perfect, Mark thought. Mark planned for them to rest up in their separate but adjoining motel rooms that evening before heading out for part 1 of their two-part expedition to the Dome later that night. An adventure that made both of their stomachs nervous and unsettled, with a varying amount of fright and panic. Chantelle thought of inviting Mark to stay in one of their extra rooms at her home but knew he would not accept for the same reason she would not ask: it would be extremely dangerous with her being watched by the community to have Mark, a private investigator and a man who wasn't her husband and didn't look to be family, staying overnight in her home while Gary was away.

Friday morning, Chantelle drove Gary to the Louis Armstrong International Airport, kissed him good-bye, and wished him a safe trip. All the while, butterflies were in her stomach at the thought of her long, stressful, and tedious day ahead. Gary reminded her he would call her later that day after her testing, around 7:00 p.m., and then kissed her good-bye. Chantelle drove straight to Dyna Corp for testing, as her appointment was at 11:00 a.m. and she wanted to get that key and hide it in her car before starting any testing. To get to the key, according to the map and room number taken from Gary's home computer Dyna Corp account, she had to get to the opposite end of the facility from her usual appointment spot with Dr. Winston. She wasn't quite sure how she would explain what she was doing way down there if she was found, but she didn't care. She was desperate to get to that key. She kept Mark in her mind and how proud he would be of her when the key was obtained, to keep her strength and nerves up. As she snuck into the hallway, in a full sweat now, partly from rushing and running and partly from fear, she entered the room with the key, and it was exactly where it was said to be from the information in Gary's online account. She quickly grabbed it, threw it into her bag, and then headed out in a hurry. As she scurried back to her car to securely hide the key and get it out of her possession, she knew she had only about ten minutes before her appointment with Dr. Winston began. Chantelle hastily freshened up and tried to calm down, as she looked and acted like someone on the run from the authorities or running for their life. She needed a few minutes to compose herself and act normal.

Dr. Winston greeted Chantelle with his usual friendliness and agreed that seeing as she was unwilling to stay for further nursing care after the testing session, and since Gary was out of town, only basic testing would be done today. "Blood work, some memory work, and cross matching your gene cells," he said.

Chantelle had a feeling Gary's boss, David, would pop in and make an appearance during her testing, which he did. "How is it going, dear?" he asked.

"Pretty good', she replied from her mentally drained state, which the beaming bright lights and the excess stimuli testing caused in general. "And thank you for promoting Gary. He cherishes working at Dyna Corp and works tireless hours at home on projects for the company," she graciously added.

"My pleasure," David said with a sheepish smile. "He is one of my most valued employees, and making him CEO in my company was a no-brainer. You and he will have to come over for dinner when he returns from his weekend seminar," he said before being interrupted by an important call from another part of Dyna Corp and abruptly leaving.

On the way home from her testing, Chantelle pondered her life—what it had become, where it was going, good or bad, and decided she was going to fight again. She would not let this sinister plot, or whatever it was they were cooking up, define her or destroy her. She was hoping that with Mark's help, she would find proof of these illegal activities so it could be presented to law enforcement and stopped. Chantelle arrived home to a big empty house around 5:30 p.m. She decided instead on bringing in takeout. She should eat some leftovers from the fridge so that when Gary returned on Monday, he wouldn't wonder why none of the food had been eaten all weekend. As she was warming up some food in the microwave, the phone rang, and it was Gary calling as promised, but over an hour early,

"Hi, Gary, how was your flight?" Chantelle asked at once so that he would get the impression that she was concerned about him and his safety on the flight, like a loving, not-up-to-something wife would do. Even though Chantelle wasn't quite sure how she truly felt about Gray, knowing what she knew of his involvement at Dyna Corp and that there was so much more she didn't know yet, she had a hard time not being cold to him.

Gary inquired about how her testing went with Dr. Winston and what she had planned for the weekend, seeing as Karen was still on her honeymoon. Chantelle thought she should set the stage for her being absent for long periods of time, not answering her phone, so she said, "Well, I'm thinking about meeting up with a few coworkers from the shop for drinks tonight, or tomorrow night, and they were even joking we should head to Vegas for a couple of nights for some gambling like we did for my bachelorette's party seeing Monday is the Labor Day long weekend."

Gary replied with a little puzzled apprehension, "Oh wow, you never mentioned anything about going to Vegas. That's kind of short notice for such a weekend excursion, don't you think?"

Chantelle got nervous, thinking, *Oh great.* Now she had piqued his concern and interest in her plans for the weekend due to such outrageous initial plan ideas. She better change her idea for plans before Gary spends the weekend wondering, worrying, and obsessing on her whereabouts. Chantelle reassured Gary, "Yes, I told the girls that it might be too much activity for me on such short notice, and that I wanted a quieter weekend, like maybe at a spa for the day, shopping, a movie theater, or something like that, so that is probably what I will end up doing."

Gary seemed much more relieved and at ease with these alternate plans of Chantelle's, as he agreed strongly, saying, "Las Vegas should wait for another time."

Knowing that Chantelle always obeyed what he told her to do, Gary quickly moved on to another topic, telling Chantelle about Dyna Corp's planned outline for their weekend, an almost-minute-by-minute itinerary for the entire weekend. Still, Gary promised to connect with her every night around 10:00 p.m., Louisiana time, to touch base with her; and if she missed his call or he got too busy with Dyna Corp dinner networking sessions, he would be sure to get a hold of her in the morning.

Chantelle agreed and, again, assured him she was going to be fine with him away, not to worry, to enjoy himself with his colleagues, even do some gambling, seeing as he was in Atlantic City.

After Chantelle hung up the phone with Gary, she decided she needed to take a notepad for herself to write down and keep track of when Gary would be calling and any other pertinent information she needed to remember so as not to miss anything that would cause doubt and suspicion from Gary. Chantelle also made an important note to remind herself to have the electronically advanced Mark doctor her iPhone so that calls would not show where it was coming from. Chantelle calling Gary from New Mexico, a place that correlated with Dyna Corp's major laboratory, with the futuristic Dome being located there, would spark major red flags with him.

Chantelle opened a bottle of wine, which she decided she was going to finish that night, regardless of how early Mark would be picking her up for their trek to New Mexico. Mark called right at 8:00 p.m. as promised. He was already in New Orleans at his motel, and also enjoying dinner and some beer to relax after a long day at his private investigator's office in Baton Rouge. They kept the conversation short and sweet, talking a little about her day, her modified experimental testing at Dyna Corp, but as they couldn't be 100 percent sure the house or the phone wasn't bugged, they agreed to put off the full conversation until their drive into New Mexico; Chantelle was to be ready at 3:00 a.m.

Mark, true to form, was pulling into Chantelle's driveway right at 3:00 a.m., a perfect time, in that the neighbors were not awake yet and she could avoid having them see her getting into a stranger's car at an unusual time of the day, and with Gary out of town. Mark approached the walkway with the old Victorian iron gates and walked up to the big Victorian antique door with the old knocker, Chantelle answered immediately, he was surprised, she was ready to go on their adventure right at 3:00 a.m. Quite a feat, seeing as Chantelle had finished the full bottle of red wine just hours before Mark showed up at the door. "Come in", she said as Mark stood at the entrance to this huge old Victorian home that was well maintained and perfectly decorated. Mark said without hesitation, "Nice home. I love it.'

"Thank you." Chantelle grinned back. "I decorated it myself. We moved in here less than a year ago."

"Very nice," Mark said. With the formalities aside, Mark and Chantelle were more than anxious and ready for their adventure.

Chantelle grabbed her suitcase and her tote bag. She locked the doors to the house and jumped into Mark's rental car. She was obviously happy to be going on this elaborate, yet dangerous, adventure with Mark. "Mark'" Chantelle started, "If I had to pick anyone to go on such an excursion with, endanger my life, and save it all at the same time, I'm glad it was you. You are a sweet, down-to-earth, and solid guy."

Mark didn't know what to say from that gushing endorsement by Chantelle, but he knew she did just finish a bottle of wine a few hours earlier, so it could be the alcohol partly talking. Take it with a grain of salt, and don't read too much into it, thinking she was falling for him, or something of that nature, would be ludicrous, seeing as she was still a married woman—a newlywed woman. Mark had to admit to himself that he did find Chantelle to be extremely attractive and smart, and her exotic dark features intrigued him. Mark's usual pick for a girlfriend had always been fair skinned and mostly blondes, but growing up in Louisiana, he had developed an appreciation for the many diverse cultures. He had no type, just whoever he was attracted to and was available, which she wasn't. Mark let Chantelle sleep for the first several hours of their road trip, and she started to come alive around 9:00 a.m., when she was starting to feel an intense hunger. Mark did manage to pack some chips, trail nuts, drinks, and other snacks, as he was always a prepared investigator, who never left anything to chance. He knew better, especially seeing as they would be driving partly in the desert. There was a town coming up, and Mark promised to turn off at the highway and treat Chantelle to a drive-through breakfast, so they filled up with hash browns and hot coffee and headed back on their way as they had another solid ten hours of driving ahead of them.

Now that the both of them were wide awake, fed, and freshened up in the bathroom, as well as stretched their legs, Mark wanted to know more about Chantelle, starting with her childhood. Chantelle agreed to tell Mark everything he wanted to know about her life in Massachusetts, and then coming to New Orleans, after high school graduation; but first, she wanted to know all about Mark and his dating life, his love life, as she assumed it would probably be a less complicated, less drawn-out story than hers.

"Gentlemen first," she said to Mark.

"What did you want to know," he asked.

"Well," Chantelle blurted out, "how could such an attractive guy such as yourself still be single?"

"Who said I was single, Chantelle?" he questioned back as she stared deep into his beautiful and thoughtful eyes.

She said, "Well, aren't you?"

"Yes, I happen to be single. You're right, I broke up with my long-term girlfriend of five years approximately six months ago, and I have been keeping myself busy with work and friends, because I just did not want to think about dating and all its issues at this time."

Chantelle guiltily felt happy he was single as she felt she would have all his attention if he didn't have a girlfriend or a wife, back at home he needed to check in with or make sure was okay. On the other hand, Chantelle, felt selfish for feeling this as she could feel, sense, absorb the pain he gave off when discussing his ex and the relationship that once was. Even though this line of discussion was painful and still raw, a fresh wound for Mark, Chantelle had a few more questions she wanted to basically pry into Mark's life with: "Were the two of you planning to get married? Do you have kids with her, or with anyone else?" Chantelle shocked herself at how open and free she was being with questioning Mark. Something about him, about them together made her feel at ease with him, like she had known him before. She could tell he felt at ease with her as well, as there was never an uncomfortable, awkward moment between them; from day one, they had always been at ease in each other's company. Hence the road trip that neither one of them gave a moment's thought to, never thought twice about being together and in such close proximity for extended time periods, it was uncanny and cosmic all at the same time, as though they had known each other in a previous life. Soul mates, karmic connections, twin flames, all things Chantelle very much believed in but was not sure if Mark shared such an ideology. Mark admitted that he did think of marrying. Laura was her name, and they lived together for several years; but he believed that because he was indecisive, after five years of dating and still had not proposed to her—that was what, ultimately, ended their relationship, and no, he had no children with her or anyone else.

Chantelle again felt bad for feeling happy over his obvious grief, but she knew it wasn't his pain she was happy over—in fact, quite the opposite. If it wouldn't come off as inappropriate coming from a married woman, she would have grabbed his hand, while driving, to comfort him, maybe even gave him a kiss, all of which she couldn't do. Being an empath, in addition to her other sixth sense abilities, Chantelle had to admit to herself that his answers did make her feel that much closer to him. There was a bond between them, a bond from knowing his heart, knowing and feeling his true character. Chantelle was not going to lie—his controlled temperament, and sweet and down-to-earth disposition made her feel giddy, intoxicated, and extremely safe, in his presence, like everything was going to be all right. Not to worry, and if everything wasn't going to be all right, then they would then run off together, making everything all right.

Chantelle was daydreaming now, Mark could sense this, he said impatiently, "Now tell me about yourself."

Chantelle gasped, "Oh my, where do I start?"

"Start from the beginning," he said emphatically. "Tell me everything: where were you born, where did you grow up, how did you grow up? I want to know everything about you. I want to know and understand you better, and try to figure out how a beautiful girl like yourself could get herself in such a predicament."

He was right, she thought. *What he really meant was how could someone as seemingly smart as you are, be so stupid as to be fooled and tricked in such a dark and unbelievable plot?* If Mark knew the oddness of my life in general, Chantelle reviewed in her mind, he would better understand, but should she tell him about all the mystical stuff, all the nonsecular religious stuff? She wasn't even sure what his beliefs were on all those things—not that it really mattered as his client, but it would matter if she was more than a client.

"You really want to hear this? You really want to know this?" she said to Mark as she paused for a moment and cleared her throat, unintentionally, building the drama, the suspense.

"First, tell me something: what are your religious beliefs, your spiritual beliefs?" Mark wanted to know, "Why? Why would that matter? What does it have to do with your life story?" he insisted.

"It has *everything* to do with my life story. Just tell me, Mark," Chantelle replied in a half-begging tone.

Mark carried on that his family wasn't very big into religion, that they never really went to church, even when he was a child, but they did believe in a higher power, a creator.

"And now you have really intrigued me. Tell me about yourself," he demanded.

Where do I start, Chantelle thought. She proceeded to tell Mark about the significance of her birth date; her two brothers; the town near Salem, Massachusetts, where she grew up; the antiques shop her family owned in Salem; and how religious, conventionally religious, her family and the community around them were. She told him of the wonderful day when she met her best friend, Karen, as a young child, how they were inseparable from that day they met until she moved away the summer before high school began. Chantelle also touched on the weird "men in black" who visited her parents when she was a very young child, the cryptic conversation that transpired, the bright lights flashing on the wall, the advanced technology, high-tech computers, advances and capabilities. They showed her parents from that time period, how it had something to do with her but she was never directly told what. The information piqued Mark's interest; there were many things he wanted to talk about more, at a later date.

Chantelle then went into, and very carefully, her abilities—what things she had been able to do that defied the norm as we knew it here on earth; her spirit, and interdimensional friends; and the knowledge, a knowing she had had since she was young. Chantelle also touched on the woman who told her father and her brothers of her being a natural-born witch. Chantelle had a hard time getting out the latter part of her story due to the connotations surrounding the word *witch*, and with all the interdimension and spirit talk, but she wanted to be completely open and truthful with Mark. She ada-mantly wanted Mark to know that regardless of what those ladies or anyone else considered her to be, or wanted to label her as, all she knew was that, it is, what it is, nothing less, nothing more. She was not here to prove anything to them or anyone else, and she did not care what they labeled her as. "I am what I am," was her motto, her mantra in life.

With all that information to digest, there was a long pause as Mark stared at the road. And then he would stare at and study Chantelle. After he had sufficiently digested what he had heard thus far, he continued, "So how and when did you come to Louisiana?"

Chantelle couldn't help but laugh out loud at Mark's follow-up question after what she had just told him. Once they had composed themselves after having had a hardy chuckle, Chantelle answered his question, telling him how she desperately needed to get out of Massachusetts as the control from her family and the community's obvious monitoring of her every move left her intensely unhappy at her stifled life, which became absolutely unbearable when her friend Karen left, as she no longer had an outlet for happiness. No new friend to spend happy times with.

Chantelle admitted that she could never find a new best friend, someone she connected with, as no one really understood her. Everyone saw her as different, as strange. Chantelle said she decided that as soon as she graduated grade 12, she would go live near Karen, who lived here in Louisiana. And that was exactly what she did—she moved to Louisiana immediately after graduation, leaving the only thing she really loved about Massachusetts, the family's antiques and collectibles shop. "I loved that shop and it's ambience. Reading all the old items, its energy gave me immense joy and contentment an inner peace. My friend Karen was elated for me to come and stay with her and her family in Louisiana, and even got me a great job at the spooky and amazing New Orleans shop Mardi Gras, which gave me a small but pleasant memory of my family's shop back in Massachusetts."

As Mark concentrated mostly on the road ahead and driving, Chantelle could tell he was still very much interested in her every word. He found it all intriguing, and he was mentally involved in her story; he wanted to hear more. Chantelle then continued with the chance meeting, that fateful day when she met Gary—a day that she was now contemplating whether it was truly chance, fate, or whether it was all a setup. She paused while thinking to herself, *I guess that is what I and Mark were trying to figure out with this investigation this weekend.* She went on to talk about how it seemed to be, possibly, love at first sight for her and Gary, that it was definitely an intense attraction at first sight for both of them. Chantelle went into the details of their whirlwind romance, how he was her first sexual encounter, the quick marriage pro-posal approximately nine months into them dating, and then the wedding that followed that summer. Lastly she did want Mark to know a little about Gary's boss, David, the owner of Dyna Corp, and his wife, Joyce; their dynamics; and the dynamics of Dyna Corp and its employees. Chantelle knew she could not leave out the Halloween story, with David's most puzzling, weird, cryptic, drunken confession.

Chantelle concluded, "And then I contacted you, Mark, and it has turned out to be the best decision so far."

Mark reminded her that he was happy she contacted him, as he had a true desire to help her but that he had not done much for her yet. "I can't take all that credit. I'm hoping we can get down to all the truths and release you of these obvious dark attachments and bonds and people in your life, but we are not there as yet, not even close."

Chantelle agreed, but she did want Mark to know how much she appreciated his friendship in these tough and often lonely times, and how having someone she could trust meant more than he would ever understand right now. With all those emotional things coming up, Chantelle decided to go for another nap.

Mark continued to drive so they could get to Corona on time, and now he had a lot to ponder while driving, so he knew the time would go quickly. He was glad that Chantelle told him all this information; he felt he knew and understood her that much better. This whole odd situation could be better understood as well; it made a little more sense—the experimentation, the gene testing, cloning, the talk of otherworldly beings, and more.

As they pulled up to their motel in Corona, New Mexico, it was still very hot outside; but the sun was starting to recede. Mark paid for both of their motel rooms, as he didn't want a trace leading to Chantelle. He booked them adjoining rooms as promised, in case Chantelle needed him or he needed to speak with her. He did not want Chantelle unnecessarily going outside, chancing being seen and recorded. Mark helped Chantelle with taking her luggage inside her room; he made sure everything looked good and safe and then told her to sleep for a few hours as they had a big night ahead of them that would begin at about nine o'clock. Mark instructed Chantelle to meet him back in his room at nine to discuss the specifics of the first night's break-in. Chantelle agreed, went into her motel room, and took a hot, relaxing, bath. Luckily, she remembered to have her phone on as Gary called with his daily check-in shortly after she had settled into her room. After her conversation with Gary, Chantelle remembered to highlight and star in her notebook the written information by Mark on how to call out, if needed, to Gary or others, as a private caller, therefore not revealing her current, true location. But she was hoping she would not have to use this information.

Mark agreed to wake Chantelle if she slept through her alarm. She then easily settled into an uninterrupted catnap after her bath. The night was going to be long, stressful, and possibly a dangerous one, something they hadn't talked too much about but needed to keep in the forefront of their minds—the danger of their investigation. Chantelle woke up at 8:30 p.m. and felt quite rested, maybe because she took several naps during the ride down to New Mexico. When she called into Mark's room, he was already awake as well. Chantelle told Mark she was going to get herself together, put the needed documents together, and then she would be over to his room shortly, within thirty minutes. Mark reminded Chantelle to use the adjoining door. It was unlocked on his side, so she was to come right in.

When Chantelle got to Mark's room, he gave her a big hug and a kiss on the cheek, which surprised and startled her slightly; but she did welcome it. "Come in, Chantelle," he half demanded. "We have a lot to go over before heading out to the Dome tonight, so no time to waste."

Chantelle agreed, admitting to Mark that she was very nervous about this investigation tonight, and tomorrow, but she would not let that deter her from participating as it meant too much to her life, to her well-being, and she needed to see what was going on inside that dome with her own eyes. Mark and Chantelle reviewed all the break-in locations she pulled from Gary's computer, including securely packing the override key that she had managed to take from Dyna Corp during her appointment with Dr. Winston the day before. They now wanted to prepare themselves a little for what might be seen when they got inside the Dome. According to the blueprints, there was a room where they had people sedated called the Manufactured Room, an Incubator room, which according to the documents was the harvested human species embryos being incubated to viability and birth. There was a day care type of room that they were very interested in to see whether it meant there were children inside 24/7, as implied in the documents. There was a microchipping room and more. They knew it would take them probably more than the two days to fully comb through these rooms, take pictures for evidence, take any documents they safely could without it being noticed missing, or at least, take photos of them. There were many rooms to go through while keeping mindful not to be seen on videos, and without tripping any secret alarms. Hard, delicate, technologically advanced knowledge work, but work that Mark felt comfortable with as he had extensive training in cybersecurity and cyber technology and had done similar things, even though not quite so unusual, of a surveillance and information gathering before. If Mark had any concerns, it would be in worrying about keeping Chantelle safe, physically and emotionally, and keeping her from leaving a trail or any evidence behind, like a fingerprint, on tables, phones, files, and specimens, as she was not a professional investigator. Any and all wrong moves by them could be all Dyna Corp and the Dome corporations, needed to have them arrested before they had a chance to prove that a crime was occurring there. They drove in silence to the Dome facility in the dead of night as Chantelle reviewed in her mind what the plan was for accessing the facility. Her hands were in a cold sweat all the way down.

CHAPTER 8

THE DOME

Mark parked his rental car two blocks down from the Dome's entrance as they would not obviously pass nighttime security check-in. They managed to go through the bush to an obscure back area of the facility where they were going to gain access at a back door. With paperwork, facility map, and blueprints in hand, they were able to find the appropriate door to use the auxiliary key on to access the facility with, as documented in Gary's files and as they planned. So far so good, they thought. Mark immediately headed to the backdoor alarm system to deactivate any sensor or tracking alarm to that door and hallway; they were in and ready for their investigation of the facility. They were dressed in all black, which according to Gary's files they read, was the attire of many of the nighttime staff and facility attendees. They were also wearing black leather gloves so that their fingerprints could not be found at a later date.

The first room on their agenda was Manufactured People Room #1. As they peered into this room, they immediately noticed the intense bright lights and people on tables, sedated, just as noted in the documentation they had printed out. A glass dome covered each "specimen" with various flashing lights and other visual stimuli, found in and around them. At times their eyes were closed, and at times their eyes were open; but they didn't seem to be mentally present at the time. There were approximately twelve tables in this room.

As Mark and Chantelle advanced farther into this room, they were both shocked at what they were seeing, and they had just begun. Mark let out a "What the f——k," preceded by, "Tell me I'm not truly seeing what I think I am seeing." He was very shaken, and he started to snap several pictures of everything possible in that room while these Manufactured People opened and closed their eyes at various times, seemingly without noticing they were in the room, even when they were right beside a person in a dome.

According to the information from Gary's account, the Manufactured People were basically the apprehended everyday people that still needed to be microchipped, and now they also had the Special Species genes added to their blood via continuous intravenous infusion for a set, protocolled, and outlined time period. The Special Species genes, or SS as they coded it in their text throughout was their code for being from an alien species or alien gene, as it was further documented that they didn't want to use the term *alien* in case of unauthorized acquisition of any of the files, so SS, or Special Species, was a preferred term.

As Mark snapped photos and tried to assess these people's cognitive awareness when their eyes opened, Chantelle was looking for other files or information, they didn't already have, in order to get photos of it for later review. They were quite confident, though, that much, if not all, of what was observed in this facility would be noted and detailed somewhere in Gary's files as he was overseeing this project. Gary was assisting with finding the perfect specimen, according to documents, along with acquiring of financing for the company's endeavors and other tasks as David needed. He was indispensable to the company, hence his latest promotion. As they left that room to go up the hall to the next room, they noted that in the Manufactured People's Room, the human specimens' vital signs, biometrics, and other life signs parameters, including what light treatments they received, were all being controlled by a central control board, known as, an A.I., Artificial Intelligence, or Smart Box.

The room immediately adjoining was another Manufactured People Room, #2, another twelve-room lab completely encumbered with more human specimens. As Mark and Chantelle scurried into this room, they took some more photos for their investigation and tried to note any other important information they could take with them. Next was the Incubation Room. Chantelle was again very nervous at what might be found in this room, and with good cause. On entering this room, their first impression was how sterile the atmosphere was. It was an extremely large room where some stations had petri dishes marked with an embryo called Human A, B, C, and so forth, joined with Special Species, A, B, C, etc. There was a protocol on the wall of how long these New Breed babies were developed in their embryotic state and then frozen if not used right away or went directly to the incubator to be brought to viability like a human mother would do. The incubator baby growing machine, as it was called, was a fascinating, high-tech piece of equipment like never seen before by Mark or Chantelle. There were some women, in a sleep state found on examination tables in this room, presumably the women they extracted the egg from to impregnate with the Special Species to make the New Breed embryo that was, according to the documents found, left in the women to naturally incubate while they continued drugging her and maintaining her nutrition and other vital needs until the New Breed baby was viable. Or if it was a woman they needed to release as people would come looking for her, they would extract the embryo and grow it in the artificial, robotic incubator or use a willing Manufactured woman as a surrogate. This room was extremely disturbing to Chantelle as it elicited so many questions about her own experimentation, even her supposed, lost child at fourteen weeks' gestation. Chantelle was wondering, with all these Zombie-type people, Manufactured, New Breed, and Microchipped, where did Gary fit in? Was he any of these things already? After taking pictures of this room, they were off to the next room, Chantelle was hoping her stomach could take the remaining rooms, especially with all the new and disturbing thoughts starting to form in her head regarding all that she had seen at the Dome thus far.

They started down the hallway again, this time approaching a room where they could hear a lot of children playing and the sound of older, adult supervision as well. They knew they must be approaching what they called the Daycare Room. As described by

Gary's chronicles, the Daycare Room housed the full-term children, the New Breed children, that were either too young to integrate into society as yet, or just could not due to observed, different and unusual behavior from human children, or even Manufactured children. So these children were schooled there, lived there, taken care of by other Manufactured people, pure Special Species, and other such voluntarily Dome People. The children in there were of every race, various ages, and seemed happy—a naive, unknowing kind of happy, as they had no idea there was a life and a world beyond the Dome.

Mark and Chantelle were very visibly saddened by what they saw, and also a bit frightened, because these children, even though visibly attractive, seemed void of something, or maybe it was just their peculiarity showing through. Chantelle had to leave. She could not watch any longer; she was becoming very sick to her stomach by this point. Mark asked if she wanted to continue or stop for the night. Chantelle wanted to continue, knowing that with the robotics technology, coupled with the uneasiness she was feeling from being there presently, there was no guarantee they would have access again on another night, or want access on another night. Chantelle sensed that after that night, the people, the things, whatever you want to call them, would be aware that something was amiss, that someone was in the facility who wasn't supposed to be there, and they would have better surveillance ready. Chantelle wasn't sure she wanted to return anyway. Her stomach and her mind couldn't take this place for two nights in a row; it was too much to digest already. Chantelle and Mark carried on, quietly moving up, deeper into hallways, being very aware of their surroundings. Mark was looking for any alarms or cameras that looked active, and they were both being mindful of the presence of any nonsedated adult, or even children, be it human, alien, or both, as being seen by them would spell doom for their operation. As they walked through, following their map, they came across the Robotic Room. They carefully peered in but could not see any moving robots. They did see some inactive, full human-sized robots, but either out of commission or sleeping, as they weren't moving—just lined up against the walls. According to the documentation, these robots, when active, were highly intelligent, beyond any single human's capacity; they could do every task a human could, and much quicker. Mark and Chantelle quickly and quietly took pictures in this room so as not to awaken or disturb these robots; and then they scurried to another room as both were now becoming very tired after having been there for over two hours now, and were more than ready to leave this creepy facility. Chantelle was starting to panic, Mark noted, as she was worrying about being captured by someone, or something, there and being subjected, against their will, to the gene testing, alien interactions, and more. She was starting to lose her cool, and Mark could sense this.

They decided on one more room, and then they would leave. And it was a doozy of a room they chose to end up in—the Alien Room, or the Special Species, SS, Room. They carefully peered into a window of the Alien Room, and as the door was closed in, they peer through a slightly frost tinted window, and saw that the room had women and men on hospital lab–type tables, along with other beings who looked like humans but must have been male and female aliens as they were quite tall and perfectly proportioned. They were pacing around the room. At first, Mark and Chantelle did not know for sure if the ones walking around were full Aliens, Manufactured People, or one of the New Breeds, until one male being, obviously a full Alien, went onto the table over one of the women specimens. It had a weird probe part—a genitalia, they did not know for sure, but it penetrated her as in a sexual act as the unconscious specimen, the woman, lay there. Chantelle almost let out a scream. Mark quickly covered her mouth, and with that, they ran; but with the terror, they started running in the wrong direction. They were running more into the Dome, accidentally coming upon an outdoor atrium, a Utopia-looking city. A city inside this dome city where both taller beings and shorter beings were walking around, and medium-sized circular cars, mostly white with silver trim, were zipping through the air effort-lessly at the speed of light. Yet no one flinched. As this Utopia city stopped them in their tracks, Mark let out a "What the hell," and with that, they hurriedly exited back the way they came in and made their way to their vehicle waiting two blocks down the street. They ran so fast; not only did they not know how they got the stamina to get to their car so quickly, but they barely remembered doing it. They were so frightened by what they had seen, terrified by what would have happened if either one or both of them had been caught snooping around those halls. All they knew was that Chantelle needed to get away from Gary, Dyna Corp, the experimentation and testing being done on her, and that community in general, and fast.

As they drove off, extremely winded but happy to be going back to the motel, neither one could put into words something appropriate to say at the moment, even though they knew what the other was thinking. As Mark was driving, Chantelle started the first of their conversations since leaving the Dome. "Now what, Mark?" was all she could think of to ask Mark, but a very important question all the same.

Mark pondered the question for a few moments, as it was the same question he was asking himself, over and over in his mind, since leaving the Dome. He managed to utter, while emphatically shaking his head, "I don't know, Chantelle. I really don't know. I mean, it wasn't like we weren't expecting something weird, unusual, and basically illegal and secretive going on, but to see it up close, real, live is a whole different type of reality."

"I'm now worried about you—your immediate safety, knowing what we know, and your inevitable future." With that comment, Mark held Chantelle with one hand as he drove down the straight and dark road. They arrived at their motel in the very wee hours of Sunday morning. "We're here. You must be hungry and exhausted. Is there anything I can get you to eat from my stash or the vending machine, Chantelle?" Mark offered, with very little physical, and mental energy left himself.

Chantelle was too scared to sleep alone in her motel and did not feel shy or uncomfortable telling Mark so. She begged him to let her stay in the bed beside his for the night as she was way too frightened to be alone. Mark agreed, and they went into his room. Mark promised "to be a gentleman." He grinned with the last bit of energy while saying it, even though Chantelle knew he didn't need to say that. She knew him, and therefore knew he would be nothing less. Mark made them a deli sandwich each and some hot tea, and they immediately fell sound asleep, awaking Sunday morning close to noon. When Chantelle awoke, she quickly went to her motel, grabbed her personal effects, and brought them into Mark's motel. There was no way she was going to be alone, even in the daylight, in her motel, especially seeing as it wasn't that far from the Dome facility. While she was getting her personal effects together, she noticed that Gary had called her three times already that morning. In all the craziness and chaos, she had already forgotten about keeping a normal schedule with Gary so he didn't panic or become suspicious and start calling all her friends and coworkers wondering where she was.

"Shoot," she said out loud while walking back into Mark's room. As Chantelle listened to the messages, with Gary pleading and wondering where she was, Mark asked her what was wrong. "Gary! In all the mania of our night and exhaustion that followed, he had placed at least three calls this morning trying to locate me, not including the ones he must have made to the house, and he is wondering where I am. Now I need a darn good excuse detailing what I have been doing, and with whom, or else suspicion will start to set in, for sure."

"Okay," Mark began, "I will help you come up with a stellar alibi—airtight, at least for now. Tell him you decided to go for an early Sunday morning drive by yourself, seeing as Karen is out of town, to the countryside, to meditate, relax your mind, and get away from the hustle and bustle of the city life."

"You are a genius, Mark," Chantelle beamed. "And you barely know me, but that would be a perfect excuse. It is believable, and it explains why I haven't answered my phone before this, and would also explain the blocked unknown number I will be calling from. He will assume it registered this way because I was in the country."

Chantelle immediately blocked-called Gary, and he immediately answered his cell phone. It was now almost 3:00 p.m. Atlantic City time, and he hadn't gone for the nightly corporate dinner as yet. "Hi, Gary," she said slightly nervously.

"Chantelle, where have you been?" he said, with worry and panic in his tone. "I called everyone possible, and no one knew where you where, not even our neighbors. They said the car is there, but you're not answering the door, and the lights aren't on." Chantelle took a heavy swallow, realizing Mark forgot one detail in his perfect plan—her car. She had to think quick. "I rented a car for the day, Gary, because I wanted to go for a nice, long, relaxing drive to the countryside to meditate and enjoy nature, so I rented a car, as you know my car can give me trouble at times."

Gary paused for a few moments to think about the scenario she just painted. He thought, *Wow, that is kind of unusual for her to go off into the countryside by herself, but she probably needed the solitude and retreat.* "Well, good," he said. "I'm glad you're keeping busy. Just let me know next time in advance. I was ready to hop on a plane back to see if you were kidnapped, injured, or something."

The irony in his concerns were too much for Chantelle to take in at this moment. The entire last twenty-four hours were already giving her a headache, major anxiety, panic attacks, and nightmares rolled into one. "Well, I won't keep you from dinner, Gary. I miss you and love you, and I can't wait for your return tomorrow," she said sweetly. As she hung up the phone with Gary, she fell onto the extra bed in Mark's room and began to sob. She felt bad for lying, she felt bad for her life, she felt bad because she felt bad. Mark sat beside her and began to rub her back to console her. He knew why she was so upset and wanted to figure out how to fix it for her.

Chantelle and Mark needed to brainstorm; they needed to figure out how to stop the experimentation not only on her but also on the many unsuspecting innocent people, before this whole new world domination and new breed of people became a reality and became the norm in society. They needed to figure out how long this had been going on, how many years, how many people had been affected, made, bred, and where these people or beings were.

"Are they living among us and we don't know it? Obviously, the manufactured people are, and where are they? Can they be identified? Is there information on Gary's home computer Dyna Corp account with all the details and specifics on what we saw and experienced at the Dome?"

Mark told Chantelle that when they returned, he would spend a couple days more in New Orleans, seeing as it was a short week with the Labor Day holiday. But he was positive Gary would still go in to work next week. This would give him a good opportunity to access his home computer with her and find all the information possible from his Dyna Corp account regarding the Dome facility. Chantelle agreed, and now they were getting very hungry and needed to go out somewhere to eat, as the snacks Mark had brought were dwindling and were becoming tiresome.

They picked a quiet local mom-and-pop spot and went to the far back corner booth so they could talk in private about everything they saw and experienced without being seen or heard. Chantelle and Mark were both dying for some pancakes, eggs, and bacon, breakfast food, even though it was now nearing dinnertime, but they missed breakfast, so they had those anyway. As they soothed their souls with mounds of thick maple syrup and bacon to dip in it, they did manage to laugh once or twice in between the serious and intense conversation about the Dome. After they finished their meal and their plates had been cleared, they continued to drink coffee; but now they were talking seriously about what occurred over the last night. "Okay, Chantelle," Mark began, "we need to talk about what we saw last night. I think we should start with the most shocking—the fact that what people suspected about aliens being real is real, and that there is a small fraction of people that know this and are keeping it from the general population."

"Yes," Chantelle interjected. "I mean, dealing with the mystical side of life, my whole life, and interacting with otherworldly beings, as I told you, I knew of passed-on entities who came through as alien beings, so in some ways, I'm not too shocked. I think I'm more shocked that so many are here. Some people are aware and interacting with them. And most upsetting is that humans are being drugged and basically forced to have sexual interactions with these beings and producing offspring they don't know they have and never okayed having."

Mark asked, "Do you think it is possible they have bred you with one of these aliens, or special species, without your knowledge, Chantelle?"

A flashback of images and visions came flooding back into her mind, in bits and pieces, causing her to need to force back tears. Half embarrassed, she said, "Very possibly, if not yet, it is coming." As they paused to reflect on that sad admission, Chantelle yelled out, "I just don't know how someone who says they love you can do such things to you. Yet that seems to be the theme throughout my life, both in Massachusetts and in Louisiana."

Mark grabbed Chantelle's hand. "I'm sorry, Chantelle. Sorry you have been subjected to such terrible things already in your young life, but hopefully, we can stop it from doing any further damage to you, to your life."

"How can we stop them, Mark? And more importantly, right now, how can I save myself, remove myself from this danger? I'm basically married to the danger."

Mark was trying to reassure her, while not lying to her and giving her false hope. "I do agree, Chantelle. Before we can do anything further regarding exposing the corrupt activities of Dyna Corp and its facilities, we must first get you out of that environment, out of the control of your husband and that community, which won't be an easy task because you are married to him, not just dating him. If you were just dating, it would be easier to disappear without a trace, and you wouldn't really owe his evil self an explanation, but because you are married, there are legal issues. I mean you could still just leave and try to hide, but anytime you try to change your name or make any move, it could, and would, more readily get back to him, as he is your legal husband, therefore giving away your location and whereabouts. You need to divorce him if you truly feel you are endangered, that your life and your well-being is endangered, and you want to get away for good."

"Wow," Chantelle gasped as she broke out in a deep, heartfelt cry, causing Mark to naturally come around to her side of the booth to hold and console her, as obviously, the events of the last twenty-four hours, along with his grim diagnosis and solution for the problem, was way too much for Chantelle to bear, even though she knew he was right and was only saying the inevitable, the obvious solution to this terrible predicament she had been involuntarily thrust into.

Mark started rambling on while Chantelle let out her emotions. "We can't even fully deal with the children we saw—the half-human and half-alien people we saw—and figure out where they go in society. Are they among us even though we will comb through everything we can this week and gather all the information possible on that place so that once we have you in a safe location, away from Gary and all of them, we can then study the information and figure out what to do about it, or at least what further investigation is needed, including *when* and *how* to bring the authorities in? Right now, I don't think they would believe a word we are saying, and without cause, they would have no reason to get a search warrant for the Dome, especially seeing as we have gained access there illegally ourselves, and then we would be telling them to go check out the aliens. Aliens that, other than being mostly very tall, six feet tall, don't look like aliens at first glance. Another thing we will need to look into from the files and additional information we find on Gary's computer: where are the big-headed aliens, the bulgy-eyed aliens we were told about and see in movies? Even the Roswell alien pictures showed an alien with a saucer-shaped head lying on the table back in 1947. Are there different species of aliens? Maybe there is more than one kind, like people. We all look different and have different races. Or maybe they can transform themselves into any shape they want temporarily, who knows? But I want to know," Mark demanded. "This is why these types of findings and information should not be kept secret for only a small few to know—and the most powerful few at that, which usually equals the most corrupt 1 percent of our society. The power-hungry, wealthy part of society who can use this knowledge against others and the unsuspecting masses. Fortunately, the printouts and documentation on the Dome's activities from Gary's Dyna Corp account should provide helpful and vital information on all its intricate activities—*when, why, how,* seeing as Gary is so deeply involved. Depending on how deeply we must dig on the limited time we will have, we should get many of these answers," Mark concluded.

Chantelle slowly started to pull herself together, as she was listening to Mark talk with surety, strength, and confidence in his voice. She wanted to know what he honestly felt. "Do you think I will be okay, Mark? Do you think I will be able to escape this whole thing, and safely?" she said timidly. Mark wasn't sure how to answer, because it was obvious it wasn't the truth needed, unless that truth was a yes. She was looking for much-needed reassurance and stability, a shoulder to cry on and someone she could rely on. "Yes, Chantelle, I promise you, I will do everything in my power to get you out of this situation, and out safely."

Chanelle realized Mark's response wasn't quite the glowing, definite response she was looking for, but she was more than willing to take it as it showed that they were a team, partners, and she had someone on her side, someone who cared about her well-being and whether she lived or died. Still exhausted from their night's adventure, they decided to retire for the evening, as they had an early-morning long drive back to Louisiana. They planned to start heading back at midnight for the long, almost seventeen hours' drive back. Chantelle not only needed to return the key to Dyna Corp on Monday, she needed to return before Gary's flight came in at 6:00 p.m., including responding to his calls before his flight from Atlantic City arrived so as not to further make him suspicious as to her whereabouts and her not returning home from her fabricated Sunday country drive to meditate. The ride from New Mexico back to Chantelle's Victorian house in Louisiana was done mostly in silence, with both of them in deep contemplation as Mark parked a block away from her house and let Chantelle out to walk with her stuff to her house. Mark felt bad, but they had to be as careful as possible not to be seen together and stoking any rumors and causing any suspicion in Gary and making Chantelle's escape that much harder and them finding out any more about the Dome nearly impossible.

CHAPTER 9

MUST GET AWAY

Chantelle arrived back to her house in Louisiana, after returning the key to Dyna Corp, around 4:30 p.m., she quickly unpacked, straightened up, threw out some old food in pretense of having been home and eaten some of it. Then she showered, and off she went to the airport to pick up Gary. Gary's flight was on time; he obviously missed her while being away, as he accosted her with a long and deep kiss. "Chantelle, honey, I missed you. You worried me so. I brought you a nice gift from Atlantic City," he immediately greeted her with these words upon seeing her. "Besides some lovely and expensive alcohol I picked up at one of the most expensive shops in Atlantic City, I also bought you something nice to remember my trip to Atlantic City fondly, but we will open it all when we get home. Did you miss me?" he said abruptly.

"Yes, Gary, I definitely missed you. The house was very quiet and lonely without you, but I kept myself busy, tried to use the time to connect to myself again."

"We'll, good," he immediately jumped back in. "Let's head home and have a romantic and quiet night together." And with that, they were off as Gary drove them home from the airport. As they pulled into the driveway, the neighbor was putting out her garbage bins and yelled hello to Gary and Chantelle as Chantelle started to get very nervous as she watched the neighbor approach them.

"Chantelle, where were you all weekend? Gary asked us to keep an eye on you to make sure you were safe and okay while he was away, yet I saw your car, but it didn't seem like you were home all weekend."

Both the neighbor and Gary now looked over to Chantelle for her response.

Slightly unhinged and wishing she was feeling the strength and security she was feeling while with Mark, she muttered barely audibly, "I was around, just keeping a quiet and low profile."

Then Gary jumped in to back his timid wife. "Yeah, you know Chantelle, Mrs. Fallow. She can be very introspective and mysterious. She was probably channeling and talking with her spirit friends or something," he said, and the two of them chuckled.

Chantelle found it very hard to barely break a laugh but forced a light giggle or two at her expense. While Gary showered, Chantelle prepared dinner which they enjoyed over wine and candlelight. They retired early and ended up making love, and afterward, Gary immediately fell fast asleep.

Next day, as predicted, Gary was up bright and early, ready to tackle more work and tasks for Dyna Corp. As soon as he left the door, Chantelle called Mark, who was staying at a hotel up the street so that he could come over and they could comb through Gary's home office Dyna Corp online files as discussed. Chantelle reminded Mark not to park anywhere close to her house and to possibly sneak in through the back door to come in, as she told him all about the neighbor's eyes on her activities and the information she already told Gary regarding her whereabouts on the weekend when he was gone, so they did not want to tempt fate or take anything to chance at being found out.

Mark arrived at Chantelle's house at approximately 9:30 a.m., giving them plenty of time to look at files and print out any and all information they needed to get all or as much as possible today because Mark needed to get back to Baton Rouge and tend to his PI business and some other clients that also needed his expertise; and even though he saw Chantelle as way more than a client, he needed to keep everything in perspective. He reminded himself that Chantelle was a married woman, and a married woman with lots of things going on, lots of dark and potentially dangerous stuff going on around her, so keeping levelheaded and not emotionally involved was imperative.

As they suspected, Gary's Dyna Corp account produced tons of detailed classified, secret information, much of which they couldn't spend time reading too exhaustively as they wanted enough time to print out everything, but just enough to read the jest of what was being downloaded and printed. They had hit the jackpot of information on Dyna Corp, it's other facilities throughout the United States and the world and, more importantly, the Dome and its detailed testing, experiments, and species being cultivated there, what they did with them, and in which communities the released ones had been residing.

Chantelle and Mark were happy with the day's work, which ended around 3:00 p.m., as Mark needed to head back to Baton Rouge and they were tired and had done as much as was humanly possible. Chantelle was becoming a bit emotional and sad, as her only stability and rock, the only other person to see the traumatic stuff she had seen at the Dome, would be heading off, one and a half hours away; and contacting him often without being traced or found out would be chancy, but she couldn't bear not talking to him for weeks on end like before. Mark understood her need for a safety net, kind words, words reminding her to be strong and that everything would be okay, so they decided to make a specific time and day of the week, every week, to talk on the phone, a time when she could talk without Gary around. They decided that Wednesdays at 10:00 a.m., Chantelle would call Mark from home or away from home, whatever she felt was best; and he would make sure he was always available to discuss the week's happenings and the progress in her situation, and more importantly, to concoct her exit plan, as she needed to get away—the sooner the better.

The final warning Mark had for Chantelle before leaving, knowing what they both knew now, was even more implicit and real: "At no cost must you allow Gary and Dr. Winston to do any more experiments and testing on you, awake or sedated. Tell him emphatically, no. If it becomes a fight or a contentious issue, it doesn't matter, as you are planning to get away, and being the loving wife, the yes wife will not help you get away. You need to be strong and stand up for yourself. Gary trying to force you to do something that you saw with your own eyes as inhuman should just fuel your anger, and strengthen your resolve to leave. Use it as your totem, your focal point to leave."

After Mark had gone, Chantelle lay in a puddle of tears for about an hour as a strong empty pit lodged within her and she couldn't shake the feeling off. She had to pull herself together, though, because it was now 5:00 p.m., and Gary would be home any moment and wonder what could have caused his wife this intense reaction. She would not know what to say as she was numb at the moment and really did not want to interact too much with Gary because her resentment toward him was building.

Chantelle pulled herself together, composed herself, got out of bed and straightened up her appearance and poured herself a glass of wine—the only solace she had when she was around Gary—and then started to prepare dinner, hoping the wine would quickly kick in and numb the intense anger that was building in her body at the moment. If ever she needed sedating, she thought, it was now. As Chantelle and Gary enjoyed a calm and nonconfrontational evening, they decided that now that Karen and Shawn were back from their honeymoon, they should have them over on the weekend for a nice dinner and hear all the details the newlyweds had to share from their honeymoon. Chantelle made the call to Shawn's apartment where they were living until they found a home. They were hoping to find one close to Gary and Chantelle's old Victorian house, and they gladly accepted their friends' invitation, so it was set for the upcoming Saturday evening.

It was fast approaching, the beginning of fall, which was a wonderful time in Louisiana, a great time to be in New Orleans and the surrounding towns; and the cooler weather was always welcome after the typical scorching hot summers. Karen and Chantelle worked at the gift shop together that Friday and had a fun and playful time just like when they were young and they decided to leave any conversation about their honeymoon and being newly married to the dinner party the following day.

Saturday Gary spent most of the day working in his office, as usual, and Chantelle spent the day decorating their home in fall décor and setting up dinner plates and chilling the wine and cocktail mixes for their dinner guests who would be arriving at 4:00 p.m. It was now 2:00 p.m., and Chantelle was going to shower before her guests arrived. When she approached Gary's office door to inform him of her plans, he asked her, "Chantelle, do you know who could have or would have been in my office and in my company account?" he asked in a rhetorical tone. Chantelle was immediately startled and frazzled by the unexpected line of questioning, and wondered how he knew. She just blurted out, "No, what would make you think someone was in your office and also in your company account? I'm the only one here."

He gave her a deep and dark stare without saying anything. Then he responded, "It just appears to have been tampered with—and in several ways, this is apparent."

Now shaking, Chantelle had nothing else to say but "No, I don't know how that would be possible unless someone was in the house when I was away. But it didn't seem to be broken into, and nothing is missing. Hmm," was all Gary had to say to her excuse as he stood up and approached her in an outwardly angry mood now. "When is your next scheduled testing with Dr. Winston?" he said.

Chantelle knew her next words would turn into an explosion but figured she had nothing to lose now. "I'm not doing testing any longer with Dr. Winston and Dyna Corp, Gary. I don't like it."

Gary was backing Chantelle at this time, looking at his desk until after she finished her sentence. He abruptly turned his head and his body, approached her with grave aggression, pinned her up against the wall, and spoke directly to her, face-to-face, eye-to-eye, with little to no space between them, and said, "You better believe you will be continuing with all and every bit of the testing and experimentation left even if I need to take you there myself, kicking and screaming."

Chantelle was in absolute shock and frightened out of her mind as she never saw this side to Gary, this aggressive, angry side. Chantelle was trying to rationalize that it must be the beer he was drinking while working in his office causing this anger, posturing, and abusive behavior. Chantelle tried really hard but couldn't help but have tears well up in her eyes and trickling down her face as she and Gary stood there eye to eye, without either one of them saying a word, just reading each other's expression.

Slowly, Gary started to unapologetically retreat and back up out of Chantelle's personal space, but Chantelle was still way too scared to move from against the wall until Gary left the room.

Chantelle did not know what to make of what had happened in Gary's den as she showered for her guests, who would be arriving in less than an hour. Gary was showering in the other bathroom and getting ready as Chantelle mulled in her mind how she needed to try to get the imagine of Gary and his anger out of her mind and focus on having a good night with her guests. A dazed Chantelle pictured a night with Karen and Shawn where it could very easily turn into a night of disaster as Gary seemed very angry about everything, including suspecting Chantelle, and possibly someone else, was snooping through his private, highly secret and classified Dyna Corp files. Chantelle was almost too frightened to leave the bathroom, especially while Karen and Shawn had not arrived yet to buffer Gary's intense and continued anger. Chantelle could sense, and feel Gary's intensity even while peering at him from across the living room as she scuttled to the kitchen to keep out of his way, looking busy preparing for their guests.

Chantelle poured herself a glass of wine and started sipping just in the nick of time, as Gary entered the kitchen dressed and ready for their guests but still very visibly angry. "Chantelle I'm going to ask you one more time, were you, and possibly someone else, snooping around my Dyna Corp files? And if so, what were you looking for?"

Chantelle replied with as much calm as she could muster, "No, Gary, I told you, I have no reason to go into your office or check Dyna Corp files. Why, what is so important or secret in there?" she asked coyly. 'You never mind what are in those files, just make sure you never go into my Den, more importantly make sure you never go on my computer, and into my Dyna Corp account, or, God forbid, you let anyone else go into my private personal files," he warned. And then he continued, "And as for your obligated Dyna Corp experiments and testing, don't ever tell me you are not going any longer, do you understand?"

"Yes," Chantelle replied, as she felt there was nothing more to say. She wasn't going to win this fight, and their guests would be arriving at any moment, and she desperately wanted the interrogation and the accusations to end, so she conceded.

Right at that moment, Karen and Shawn knocked on the front door. Chantelle was thankful, not only for their timely arrival but also that the front door was an old heavy door; otherwise they would have, for sure, heard Gary's barking, demanding, and threatening tone with her. How embarrassing Chantelle thought. Here they were, basically newlyweds themselves, having their best friends over to gush over their recent nuptials and honeymoon, yet the hosts for the night were miserable in their new marriage, or at least one of the hosts was.

Gary answered the door and warmly greeted his best friend and his new bride, as though nothing at all happened moments earlier. "Come in, you love birds," he gushed.

As Gary poured them drinks, Karen came into the kitchen to help with preparation. As she entered, she and Chantelle naturally gave each other a big hug.

"Hey, Karen, so how is married life treating you?" Chantelle tried to get the words out in the most nonstressed voice, careful not to signal any duress to her very observant best friend who knew her very well.

"Excellent," Karen exuberantly said with a smile that stretched from ear to ear.

"Wonderful," Chantelle said. "You will have to tell us all about your honeymoon as soon as I bring these hors d'oeuvres out to the living room. I'll be right there." Chantelle took in a deep breath, hoping this would calm her insides; but instead, her body then made an unplanned sigh. She was exhausted and defeated, and the only thing she could think of was needing to talk with Mark. The thought of Mark and his strong personality and what he would have said in this situation was what put a slight grin on Chantelle's face. Then she started thinking to herself, *She is a fighter. She is an Aries. She needs to stop feeling sorry for herself and figure out another way out of the testing.* Chantelle decided to play along with Gary, for now. *Play nice, as they say,* she thought. And that was exactly what she did for the remainder of the night. The night turned out well regardless of the shaky start between Chantelle and Gary. They managed to laugh, reminisce with their friends, catch up on all their honeymoon adventures and their post-honeymoon house hunting. It was a pleasant night. The rest of the weekend proceeded uneventfully, with Gary spending most of Sunday doing his usual Dyna Corp paperwork; but the elephant in the room, so to speak, was the obvious suspicion Gary still directed at Chantelle and him wondering what she could have been looking for on his computer. Chantelle figured he was probably wondering if she had figured out Dyna Corp's secret, which was probably verified by her refusing to do any further testing with Dyna Corp and Dr. Winston.

The week couldn't start quick enough as Chantelle was looking forward to speaking with Mark at their preplanned time, Wednesday at 10:00 a.m. Chantelle had so much she wanted to discuss with him and get off her chest. She needed to brainstorm with him on how she was going to get away in light of what new developments occurred with Gary—him knowing part of their secret, that someone was snooping around in his den and in his Dyna Corp account. It was only a matter of time before Gary started tracking Chantelle's movements, investigating more, and finding out about the weekend she and Mark spent in New Mexico, and why. If Gary found out that she had hired Mark, a Private Investigator, to not only investigate Dyna Corp and the Dome's activities but also himself, she thought to herself, "shit would hit the fan fast, and when it did, all hell would break loose! He would be livid.

Upon Gary's return home on that Tuesday, he informed Chantelle that she had a testing day with Dr. Winston at Dyna Corp scheduled for the following Friday in ten days, which was the earliest he could fit her in. He will be picking her up for her appointment around 10:15 a.m., as her appointment was at 11:00 a.m.; and, as usual, he would be staying there with her for her safety afterward, as Dr. Winston was sure to be using sedation this time, Gary's nice term for drugging her so he could do deeper testing, Gary spewed in a matter-of-fact way. Gary told Chantelle this news almost in a taunting way, as though he was trying to rub in Chantelle's face that there was nothing she could do to stop or change the testing being done on her. If Gary was trying to mentally punish Chantelle for suspecting she was snooping around in his office, he was doing a great job this week between barely saying two words to her since the dinner party with Karen and Shawn last Saturday and his boasting assertion of her imminent date with Dr. Winston for another round of human experimentation while being drugged, when he knew she suspected something was wrong and didn't want to participate. Gary was starting to really show his true colors—colors that frightened Chantelle to her core. Gary had become diabolical, conniving, dark, coldhearted, and threatening—the same characteristics his boss and Dyna Corp owner, David, showed. The stakes were obviously very high, and Chantelle was hoping that Mark had a chance to read through some of those files detailing how high the stakes were, for whom all this testing was done, or, at least, the reasoning and the full plan. There had to be a grand plan to all of this sick, illegal behavior, she thought.

Wednesday, right at 10:00 a.m., Mark called as promised. Chantelle could not answer the phone quick enough. She was breathless as she said "Hello."

Mark immediately sensed the panic and urgency in her voice. "What's wrong, Chantelle? Are you okay?" If Chantelle wasn't now petrified of being followed and found out by Gary, she would have gone down to Baton Rouge to see Mark and speak with him directly, as she really needed to see a friendly face. But she did not want to chance such a visit with Gary's suspicions at present. "No, not really," she told Mark, chancing even talking to him while in the house, seeing as Gary could now have added video and audio surveillance to track her activities at home, who she was speaking with, including catching her going into his den. Going into the backyard to speak to Mark wasn't an option either as her neighbors might hear, and she didn't feel any safer driving out to a parking lot as she could be spotted there as well. Chantelle was feeling more and more trapped in her own life, in her community.

"What's going on?" Mark said worriedly. "Should I come out there to get you?" The words came unexpectedly out of his mouth, even shocking Mark himself. Was he falling for Chantelle? he thought.

"You would do that? You would come down here and get me out of this place?" Chantelle asked, as this was something that never even crossed her mind, Mark sheltering her out of harm's way.

"If you were in grave and imminent danger, you bet I would, Chantelle. This whole situation is dark, evil, and way above even me knowing what to do about it, yet if that is what it would take while we figure out plan B, hell, yes."

They both paused a moment to think about all that was said. Then Mark asked again, "So tell me, what is going on?"

Chantelle proceeded to tell him about the heated exchange between her and Gary before the dinner party that Saturday and how he not just suspected but knew, that Chantelle, and possibly someone else, had been snooping around his home office and had gained access to his Dyna Corp company account.

Mark's eyes were wide open in shock. "No way," he said. "Oh my goodness, Chantelle, you must have been faint with fear at him accusing you of this and in such a matter-of-fact way. I'm so sorry I wasn't there for you. How did that all end?" Mark said in a genuine, consoling tone.

Chantelle went on to describe Gary's anger not only that day but every day since then—his mistrust and suspicion of her now, and him basically rubbing in her face that she would be doing more drugged experimental testing and going to like it. She told Mark about Gary going as far as booking the next session for the following Friday, reminding her that he would drive her because she was "sure to be sedated again." Chantelle half laughed at Gary's obvious choice of words, using *sedated* instead of the true word, *drugged*.

"Can you believe the gall, the bullying, and the controlling mind-set of Gary and Dyna Corp in general? I don't know what to do. I'm stuck at his mercy next Friday, and I wouldn't be surprised if the microchipping, and therefore tracking capability, will be implanted that Friday." She quivered in an exhausted, breathless tone.

"Okay, we will have to figure out something," Mark said. "Because if they microchip you that Friday, which I am almost 100 percent sure they will from what you told me—and they would be a fool not to, and we know they are not a fool, as they have way too much to protect for such a sloppy, foolish mistake. Gary knows that they need to monitor your activity, your daily whereabouts, daily interactions, and keep their *special human specimen* in check, so going to the appointment next Friday would be tantamount to doom for both of us," Mark finished as he was now trying to think of the solution.

"Well," Mark continued, "it looks like if you weren't ready to run and disappear before, you are now. You have no choice, Chantelle, especially seeing as they still don't know about me. You have a chance in hell at getting away fairly clean."

"Oh my God," Chantelle said in disbelief at her predicament. "I barely got a week and a half to get organized. I have nothing, barely any money. I will just be able to take some clothing in a suitcase,"

Mark said. "Don't worry too much about money as I will hide you at my place but make sure all traces of me and you ever knowing me are removed from the house before you leave. Right after Gary leaves next Friday for work, I will pick you up. You will first go to the instant teller and take out as much cash money as you can from your joint account and your personal account, so you have money for spending. Plus, you will not be able to use your debit card again after this, such traceable things like that. Things that can be traced right to your location are an absolute no-no." The private detective in Mark was really showing through now.

Mark knew all the tricks of this type of operation, "an operation on how to hide, and not be found." He continued, "Then when things settle down, we will get you new identification with a new name, a name which I will need to start calling you right away, at least in public. A new identity also includes you changing your look, your hair color, possibly even wearing color contacts, as there are always eyes and ears around watching, and it won't be long before people start searching for you. Tips will come in on sightings of you, and communities will be on the watch for you. Are you ready for all this, including not speaking with your family back in Massachusetts for a long while, or even longer, depending on who we find out is involved and was aware of the activities of Dyna Corp?"

"Like you said, Mark, I have no choice but to be ready if I want to survive, but yes, I think I can do this. Thanks for being there for me. That was a blessing, and one of only a few right moves I have made in a while, when I found you for my private detective, but I regret your whole life will be upside down now too." Chantelle started to cry in shame and in sorrow for putting him in this whole mess, even if he willingly wanted to help.

"Chantelle," Mark said, "now, now, no time for tears. You need to be brave, hear me?" he demanded as he waited for her sobbing to stop. Then in a very calm tone, Mark said, "I know you have it in you, Chantelle. We can do this, okay?" he said, finishing his pep talk. He reminded her that he would be calling her next Wednesday, same time, to finalize everything and coordinate a pickup. And that if she needed him for *anything* beforehand, or, if she needed to speak with him urgently beforehand, to feel free to call anytime. "Just do so from a concealed spot as much as possible. Trust no one," he reminded her. "Not even Karen," then he hung up the phone and went back to work.

Chantelle spent the rest of the day, before Gary arrived home from work, staring at the white walls in her kitchen, contemplating how drastically her life would be changing from next week. She was numb, no feelings left, and definitely no more tears left. As she sat there in the kitchen, she thought of all that she needed to do within the next week and a half. The most important things like, having final conversations with friends and family, without letting on that anything was going to be changing. Chantelle thought that it was like someone seriously knowing they would be moving ahead with their suicide plan and leaving a final note. Getting in all necessary information, talking points, knowing it was to be the last communication with their unsuspecting friends and family. She also thought of all the other things she needed to do to bring important itinerary documents, numbers, including packing any tiny reminders or important memorabilia and photos she wanted and felt a need to bring along in remembrance of her old lives, as she was really ditching two lives—life as a daughter and a sister in Massachusetts, and life as a wife and a friend in Louisiana.

Chantelle was so deep in thought she did not hear Gary arrive home and walk right into the kitchen, startling her from behind as he approached. "I'm home," he said sheepishly and smiled as Chantelle half jumped out of her skin. Chantelle slowly turned around and rose to her feet, eyes red from the hours of tears. She managed to calmly respond with a "Happy to have you home, Gary" and gave him a warm but not overly alarming smile.

"Why the tears?" he inquired as he approached her and raised his hand to wipe away a tear that was still lingering on her cheek.

"Just tired," she responded. "Emotionally and physically tired. Gary, I don't want to fight with you any longer,' she continued.

"Well, good, let's have a nice dinner, a quiet evening and night, and let bygones be bygones, as they say, agree-to-disagree sort of thing," he responded, as if talking to a social buddy at a sports bar. But Chantelle was okay with Gary's response; as long as he wasn't fighting with her, she could concentrate on her upcoming task at hand, preparing herself for her getaway, and she was fine with that.

Early Thursday morning, as soon as Gary left for work, Chantelle headed into the town for much-needed tying up of loose ends; but something seemed changed in Chantelle's environment, noticeably changed. It was like people knew she was going to be driving by before she approached them—people, young and old, would all peer back at her or at her car as it approached. She noticed that everyone seemed to be staring intently at their iPhones as she approached, even at the pharmacy, their iPhone text message tones going off constantly, and unfamiliar eyes watching her every time she looked up from the aisles. Was she becoming paranoid and just imagining people watching her every move, or was this really happening? She thought she would go into the bank and start withdrawing some money, holding on to it.

As she approached the counter, she heard, "Mrs. Moore, nice to see you again. What can I do for you today?" the young teller asked.

"I would like to withdraw one hundred dollars from my joint checking account," Chantelle said.

The teller started typing some information in, and then typing some more, and some more. And then she excused herself for a moment as she went to a desk in the back to speak with a senior advisor. When she returned, she said to Chantelle, "I'm sorry, Mrs. Moore, but it looks like that transaction cannot be completed at this time." Embarrassment turned to ire, and Chantelle responded, "How could this be? I checked the account this morning, and there was way more than one hundred dollars in the account, so what is the problem?"

"I'm sorry, Mrs. Moore. You will have to speak with your husband about the account. That is all the information I can give you at this time."

Mortified, and now shaken at the thought that Gary might be anticipating her trying to leave and furthering his efforts to control her, she left the bank in a hurry, but not before noting the nonchalant, unfazed, unfrazzled, unaffected, unchanging temperament and expressions of all the people there, including employees and customers. *Like programmed zombies*, her mind told her. The gentleman in the suit at the door entrance to the bank wished her a good day as she went rushing by, and she thought, did she just enter the twilight zone? *What is going on?*

Chantelle tried to compose herself in her car. *Oh my goodness*, she thought. *Should I call Mark? What should I do?* Chantelle knew that something was very wrong; it was as though today was the beginning of Operation S on Chantelle. *S* for stalking, surveillance, and the suspect, which was her. And everywhere she went, it was evident they were all doing the same thing. Chantelle even overheard a conversation of some people situated right behind her at the grocery store who started talking about New Mexico and should they drive or fly into New Mexico? Chantelle almost dropped all her items in the basket right there on the floor. Could it be possible they knew about her and Mark and their trip to New Mexico?

As soon as Chantelle left the grocery store, she knew she had to call Mark; but now, she did not know where to go and do that. She was already definitely being watched, stalked, harassed by the community on Gary's and Dyna Corp's behalf, but were her car or her phone bugged now too? Chantelle realized that it didn't matter now. They obviously knew things and were on to them already, and she needed to let Mark know. Funnily enough, she was sure there was still a payphone down the street from her home that she could have put quarters in to use, but mysteriously, when she went to find it, it was suddenly gone. Coincidence?

Chantelle felt the safest place to call Mark would be back at home in her backyard, so she tried to quickly head back home to make that call, as it was coming close to lunchtime. Occasionally, Gary came home for lunch, and somehow, she had a feeling that today might be one of those days. As she tried to weave between seemingly heavier-than-usual traffic, she wondered, *Where did all these people come from in this little town?* Chantelle never noticed such heavy and congested traffic in Pendle, as though they knew she needed to get home to make a call and was trying to delay her. Including making sure none of the lights this day were lining up, all going yellow to red as she approached, cars nearly hitting her several times, cars constantly coming out of parking lots to the side, many with lights beaming on her, cars lined up in unusual color-coordinated parades driving by her, most also with their bright lights on for no apparent reason—something she never noticed before today.

As she drove down another street, she would find several of the same-colored work trucks all lined up, against the same street roadway curb in a weird, unsettling formation. Chantelle started to remember her shopping experience this day, remembered the people coming up to her, right into her personal space, like mobbing her while at the stores, breathing down her neck, and other times surrounding her and blocking her in the aisles—all these she reviewed while sitting at another red light. Something, or someone, the whole community, was obviously trying to slow her down and stop her from making a call before Gary, who was possibly coming home for lunch, arrived. But how did they know? she thought. Was she already microchipped and being biometrically monitored like the others? Maybe she recently and unknowingly ingested it in something she ate as outlined in Gary's Dyna Corp playbook of activities, she snidely commented to herself.

Chantelle knew something was amiss. Everywhere she went, even approaching a high school with teenagers walking on the sidewalk, would be cause for all of them to pause and look back at her in her car. It was as though the whole town had snapped, gone into some type of attack mode, and now was showing its true colors. Chantelle didn't know what was happening and how a whole community could receive the obvious stalking and harassment orders to carry out without her getting such a message, but she knew that this type of coordinated activity could not be taught and orchestrated overnight. It must have been planned way in advance. It was like a cult, a conspiracy, a well-controlled, mentally and physically controlled, zombie people. Chantelle could feel their dark, evil intent shining through, loud and clear; and she wanted nothing to do with these people. But it was obvious they wanted her to be aware of them watching her and observing her every move.

As Chantelle pulled up in her driveway, she pondered, *If I didn't see for myself, the Dome, and the bizarre things being done throughout that facility, along with Gary's Dyna Corp documentation, I would never have believed such a thing could be real—a town of crazy, out-of-their-mind, mind-controlled cult people. Could all those years of rumors of conspiracy theory and a new world order be real?* Did she get pulled into a twilight zone of conspiracy that no normal human brain would be able to fully wrap their mind around? Nobody in their right mind would believe such people existed, that such a town existed, unless they experienced it themselves, had seen it firsthand, like she herself and Mark had. But it did, and now she had to escape with Mark, for her own well-being and sanity.

Sanity, she thought. What an interesting concept. Here are these townspeople, obviously mentally controlled, by cult, religion, power, and money, all in one. Yet if she didn't know what she knew, had Mark and the documentation to prove it, it would have been *her* they would have been calling crazy and trying to commit, she was sure of that fact. As she sat there in deep thought about what had gone on, Gary pulled into the driveway beside her, which was not surprising. He was home for lunch today.

"Hey, Chantelle, you just get home from shopping?" he said in a knowing tone—a tone of knowing exactly every detail of where she had been and with whom, she was thinking as Gary jumped out of his car to greet her. "Did you buy anything good for lunch, or were you just going to have leftovers today?" he said in an annoyingly happy, "checkmate, I got you" tone. She hated him at that moment. Chantelle was contemplating whether she should bring up the incident at the bank. It was obvious he knew about it, but if he asked what she needed one hundred dollars for, she wasn't quite sure what to tell him, as it was no one's birthday or anniversary. She couldn't even pretend she was buying Karen and Shawn a wedding gift as they had bought them one already.

Chantelle made Gary a sandwich for lunch as he only had forty-five minutes to eat and then needed to head back. Gary mentioned that he was going to be working late tonight, catching up on some paperwork, as usual. "What are you going to do with your free time tonight," he asked again in a coy tone.

"Not sure yet," Chantelle shot back in a monotone, unassuming way, trying not to play into his crazy cult mind-set. "Well, I shouldn't be too late. I will probably be home around 7:00 p.m." With a nod, Chantelle headed outside for some fresh air, as she had lost her appetite and couldn't stand being around Gary for too long anymore. Before Gary left back to work, he turned to Chantelle and said, "Oh, and by the way, Dr. Winston said he needed some preliminary blood work from you for whatever tests he will be running next Friday, so he wanted you to come down tomorrow and give a sample. I checked with Karen, and you aren't working, so tomorrow it is. Head down to give Dr. Winston that blood sample he needs." Not waiting for an acknowledgment response—because he wasn't asking her, he was telling her—Gary continued on his way to the car, blowing an air kiss to her as he walked down the driveway.

As soon as Chantelle thought it was safe to do so, she called Mark on his cell phone while sitting in the backyard. "Mark, can you talk?" she immediately started without even saying hi.

"Yeah, sure. Let me just shut my door… Okay, what's up?"

Chantelle was already breathless and was also trying to whisper, she knew, the eyes and ears were everywhere even outside. "Mark, they know. They probably know everything," she said. She not only detailed her last almost twenty-four hours, which included the community stalking, harassing, and the cars following her, she also mentioned the theater acting that was strategically placed right behind her in the grocery store, and the very specific conversation that was meant to be a reference to these people knowing about their trip to New Mexico. She told him about what happened when she tried to take a mere hundred dollars out of the joint bank account that had thousands, and all the other targeted attacks and monitoring she was experiencing. Including her once-quiet street now constantly having cars revving up and down the street, constant car horns beeping, constant car alarms, cars that were seemingly following her, and everyone but her had their headlights on.

"Very weird, cult, creepy behavior, Mark," she finished. "I need to leave, and leave now, before they drug test me again. I have already been told by Gary that I have to go tomorrow and get pre-experimentation blood work drawn, and Gary is acting more bizarre than ever himself. It's like the whole town has been programmed now to attack since we found them out."

Mark wanted to know if she was sure they knew who she was with, as he hadn't noticed anything unusual around there, as yet, but it might be a matter of time. Mark confirmed that the information he read through last night detailed her husband's own experimentation, the community she lived in, and also where else some of those Manufactured, those other beings were living. He continued, "It was quite eye opening—shocking, really. I didn't think I could be easily shocked after what we saw that weekend, but I was."

Even though Chantelle and Mark knew that it probably wasn't the safest plan, they decided to meet around Baton Rouge the next day, after her blood work, to talk about what he found out from the Dyna Corp files, even though much of it Mark didn't think Chantelle should hear about until she was well away from Pendle, Gary, and Dyna Corp. Chantelle insisted she needed to know what Gary had become, her friend Karen, and the others living around her. Before hanging up the phone, Chantelle and Mark agreed to meet early Friday morning, as she was going to get her blood drawn right at 7:00 a.m., when the Dyna Corp lab opened and then she would head to the park they agreed upon to meet, which was near Mark's office, to talk thereafter. Chantelle would call him on her way down.

Gary was home at 7:00 p.m., as he had predicted, and he was still in that giddy, condescending mood and frame of mind; but Chantelle figured it was better than the anger she had seen in him the week prior. Regardless of how uninterested or cold she presented to Gary, he still managed to be in the mood and wanted to show affection to his wife, which he did that night, in his quest for an offspring. Chantelle couldn't wait for it to be over; she immediately turned over and went to sleep, but Gary did not seem affected by her lack of affection at all. The next day, Gary offered to drive Chantelle to her early-morning blood work at Dyna Corp, and then said she could take a taxi home afterward. She flatly refused.

She arrived at Dyna Corp right at 7:00 a.m., ready to be first for the blood work, and get out of there fast, as she still had an hour and a half of a drive to Baton Rouge to see Mark that morning. Shockingly, she was placed in a waiting room with a few other people and had to wait for her blood to be drawn. Chantelle was starting to become suspicious. Did they know she needed to leave to go somewhere? And did they know *where* and with *whom*? Chantelle was becoming angry; she refused to be controlled by these people any longer. She stood up and went over to the nursing desk to ask what the holdup was: She had some things she needed to get done, she demanded, and didn't want to spend her morning there. Chantelle was assured that she was first to get her blood drawn and that someone would be with her in a few minutes to do her blood work. As Chantelle sat back down at her seat, the lady sitting a few seats over started talking to another lady in the waiting room about having family in Boston who owned an antiques shop, and how she was the middle girl with an older and younger brother.

Chantelle immediately thought, *Is this the theater acting harassment again, or just a coincidence?* She convinced herself to chalk it up to coincidence. Finally, within five minutes of talking to the nurse at the desk, she was called into a room for her blood work. While she was lying on the examination table, the door partly open, and waiting for the lab tech to arrive, Chantelle noticed two staff members, nurses, stop directly outside her exam room door. Within moments, one of the staff members started talking about making love to her husband the night before, how she was "disinterested and just turned over and went to sleep right after." With that, Chantelle snapped, which she knew was probably what they wanted her to do; but she thought, *Enough! I'm not going to be subjected to these crazy cult members, these human abductors and traffickers and their testing any longer.* She bolted out of Dyna Corp without the blood work done and went straight to Baton Rouge to see Mark.

She was flustered still, but happy to see him waiting on the bench for her. Chantelle immediately gave him the biggest, longest, tightest hug ever. She never imagined she would be so happy to see a *sane person*, and a friendly face, in her life. "Wow, Chantelle," Mark said after she told him about the events of her morning. "You know, there is a term for what you described they are doing. It is called organized stalking, community stalking, or gang stalking. It sounds like, along with the community's messed-up *cult mentality* and conditioning, they were also following the stalking, harassing, and blacklisting playbook to a tee.

"The real solution is to stop them and end the spreading cancer, the tumor, that they are in its tracks. But first, we must get you out of there," Mark concluded. He continued, "It would make my work easier if I knew you were safe, as criminal elements like them, with so many secrets they are trying to keep from the general public, can be very unpredictable, dangerous at best. And that is with us knowing probably only the tip of the iceberg on the real powerhouse backing this conspiracy, this cult operation, and the full depravity of its operation." Mark paused for a moment, and then he wanted to express the compassion he had for her because of her predicament. "You are going through so much right now trying to plan leaving Gary that I feel the majority of the information I found out from the files should be kept for when you are safely within my reach and we can talk about it fully. What I will tell you today is that the reason Gary is acting so unusual suddenly, like a Jekyll and Hyde light switch had been turned on in him, was because it probably was.

According to his own files, Gary had been implanted with the microchip that communicated information to him; could control his actions if needed, mentally and physically; and could monitor all his biometrics or vital signs. Gary had also voluntarily been injected with the Special Species genes and the Alien genes, making him official, what they called a Manufactured Human. Mark reminded Chantelle, "A Manufactured Human is a person who starts off 100 percent human and then voluntarily, or involuntarily allows the SS genes to be injected into their bloodstream. Over time, the genes would turn them to something close to superhuman: strong, better senses mirroring the pure Alien traits but to a lesser degree."

Chantelle wanted to hear more, but Mark was reluctant to keep going, knowing that the following part would be a lot harder for her to digest. Chantelle insisted, "It does go into them being instrumental in your union with Gary, wanted him to produce an offspring, due to your God-given *special abilities*, but not only with a Manufactured Human, Gary, but also with a Special Species. One last thing for today, Chantelle: the documents seem to elude to them, having taken out fertilized embryo specimens from you that are already being developed somewhere in the Dome. Do you remember any encounters with a Special Species? Chances are you were drugged, but I must ask."

Chantelle was speechless, flabbergasted really. Mark was right; she could not speak. She was shaking too hard, and her brain could not process what he had just said. "What" was all she could get out. She fainted, passed out cold; and when she awoke, she was in Mark's office, lying on his leather couch in the waiting room. Mark locked the door to his business. He had sent his secretary home with pay, for Chantelle's privacy and safety. As a precaution, he didn't want his secretary remembering seeing Chantelle there days before she would be reported missing. As Chantelle slowly started coming awake. Mark had a cool cloth over her forehead and a fan going. She still could not fully focus; she was disoriented.

"What happened?" she said. "What time is it?"

"It's only 10:00 a.m., Chantelle. You have been passed out for about thirty minutes. We were in the park, do you remember?"

"Yes, I do," Chantelle managed to whisper while sipping on the tea Mark had brought her.

"I knew it would be too much for you to comprehend, to process with all the other stresses you have been subjected to back at home."

Chantelle rose up a bit from where she lay. "No, Mark, I want to hear more. Tell me more. I must know," she said emphatically.

Mark couldn't believe what he was hearing, but he admired Chantelle for pushing herself and being strong, so he continued, "The New World Order—it might not be completely what people use to think it would be. It is a new and made-up world, put together, run, controlled by the wealthy, powerful, 1 percent, money elites—but from around the world. All cultures, all countries are involved, and they believe they are human gene cleansing, perfecting humanity, and producing utopia cultures that are free of crime at the same time. It is being controlled by these multicultural elites, who are all deeply into their own faiths, their own religions but agreed upon a joint religion, a coexisting religion, a *One World Religion*, for the purposes of the New World Order. A *One World Religion* built out of fear, chaos, and destruction of the masses, the blueprint for the main structure of the organization—a cult, I call it. This organization that is comprised of a combination of all the major religions, but as a subculture of people, who are permitted to still study, follow, and practice their subcommune religions on their own time. But when they come together, this New World Order, it is the *One World Religion* only, conformist for the greater-good type mentality; very dark, very controlling, very diabolical."

Chantelle listened quietly but couldn't believe what she was hearing. "The small town in which you, not so coincidentally, found yourself in, of just over 100,000 people and growing, all agreed many years ago, maybe ten to fifteen years ago, to be like a pilot project in guise, the promise of this utopia and a perfect, crime-free community. When it was agreed, as a community, to move forth with the project and transform their town to this New World, they were presented with the choices we saw at the Dome, but not before first being initially microchipped, preventing them from truly being able to think for themselves, and therefore tell anyone what they saw and were involved in. The controllers, or handlers, of these implanted people would know what they wanted to do beforehand and would have the ability to erase one's memory, or change their thoughts, reactions, etc. Other things that can be done once a human is microchipped is to control their bodily functions, implant thoughts, ideas, and actions in one's mind, produce a wanted outcome or reaction, and much more, all while they studied and documented these *pet projects*, like studying one big rat testing population. People were guaranteed money, land, cars, homes, insurance coverage, and medical care, in exchange for complying with the rules and living in this manufactured town. Many people, in your town, are these Manufactured people, as most decided to be injected with this Special Species genes in the name of learning, testing, experimentation. They were also promised that these injections, the mixing of their blood with these *special genes*, would make them stronger, smarter—a superhuman."

Mark was becoming exhausted with telling Chantelle all he had learned from Gary's Dyna Corp files, but he knew she needed to know, for both their safety. The saying "Knowledge is power" came to his mind as he went on, "Everyone's home has video monitoring going at all times, including streets and stores, so it was likely your home already has a video camera watching your every move. But it was weird that you were not microchipped as yet. It was just a matter of time. Maybe they thought you wouldn't resist so they weren't in a rush. Otherwise, you would have been. One last thing, Chantelle…"

Chantelle was nervous by Mark's tone, but she knew she had to hear it. "I really hate to tell you, but you were probably being drugged and subjected to frequent sexual encounters with various Manufactured People and Special Species alike, since the testing began on you. As Dyna Corp documented, a purple liquid substance that is made to ooze out of walls especially effective in the bathroom as the steam precipitates its coming out during showering and bathing. The substance builds up in the body over days, weeks, causing the exposed human specimens to go into deep sleep states. Once REM sleep is reached, basically, a hidden, covert type of date rape drug. This substance, once present, embedded in a special paint-looking coating, can be programmed to exude through the walls while you are sleeping, releasing this purple cold medicine–looking substance and accompanying invisible gas, puts its victim in an even deeper sleep, therefore removing inhibitions and, more importantly, memory of events to come, which is the sexual assaults. Nowadays, many of these events are videotaped using strategically placed, embedded video cameras, but often it is reported that they place various-sized drones above the victims', or specimens' home to not only monitor movement but also to video stream live the events in the home, the sexual encounters." Mark paused and just looked at Chantelle for her reaction when he was done speaking.

Again, Chantelle was short of breath and faint. She needed to lie back down while Mark got up and started to pace around the office foyer. "Why do they video stream it live, Mark?"

Mark cleared his throat while still pacing, in a slightly angry and thinking manner. "According to the documentation, it is so the various wealthy, powerful investors, and other, basically voyeuristic-type players, have proof of how and where their money is going and for what experiment and specimens, but the underlying connotations sound a little more nefarious, but that is neither here nor there, sick people any way you slice it."

Mark and Chantelle both agreed that it was enough information for her, for the time being. Plus, she did really need to get back. Chantelle came over because she needed to tell Mark about the amped-up harassing, stalking, and monitoring in person, but more likely because she needed to see a friendly face. Chantelle felt better by 11:30 a.m. and was ready to head back on her hour-plus drive back to Pendle. Chantelle wanted to avoid questioning from Gary on where she went after running out of the lab, which was going to be an intense conversation already. Mark promised to call again on Wednesday at 10:00 a.m. or earlier if either needed to talk; but the plans were already set for her escape on Friday morning after Gary left for work and before he returned to take her for her experimental day at Dyna Corp.

As Chantelle drove back to Pendle, approaching the New Orleans area, she started to notice more and more cars with bright lights racing behind her as though chasing her, like a group hunting down prey with their cars. Chantelle had to wonder what type of mental conditioning made a person, or groups of people, act so unusual; but she reminded herself that many are mind-controlled and this weird behavior was partly out of that control. These people didn't even see that they were mind-controlled and part of a cult, so all in a normal day's work to them. *How odd, and sad at the same time,* she thought.

Gary arrived home at 5:00 p.m., which was early for him, so Chantelle knew he was mad about the Dyna Corp lab incident, coupled with him calling twice during the day and her refusing to pick up or return his calls. Chantelle was in the backyard when Gary arrived home, stomping through the house, visibly mad and perturbed over her obstinacy. As he stood at the backyard sliding door, he yelled, "Chantelle, did you notice my calls to your phone?"

Chantelle nodded, pretending not to notice his anger. Yet she did not want to turn around, out of fear of his intense and angry disposition, which was more than palpable by this point. "Where were you today, Chantelle?" he continued, now slowly starting to approach her in the yard.

Chantelle quickly replied, "Gary, please, I do not want to fight with you. I just want to sit outside and think. I was home, but I ran out of the lab because I didn't want the testing, like I told you, and the people were acting weird, like they knew things about us, so I left. I didn't answer my phone because I knew you would be mad." Her explanation seemed to have appeased Gary for the moment, as he now said in a much calmer tone, "Chantelle, Dr. Winston agreed to come in tomorrow, Saturday morning, to draw that blood work, as he needs it for next week's experimentation, and it needs time in the petri dish to cultivate. I will drive you tomorrow for your 10:00 a.m. appointment, like I promised him. Traffic should be light, so it shouldn't take us more than thirty minutes to get there. Be ready by nine fifteen for us to leave, okay," he demanded in a rhetorical way. Chantelle wanted a quiet Friday night and knew it wasn't a yes-or-no question anyway, so she replied, "Yes, I will be ready."

Gary left the doorway and headed to their bedroom to remove his work attire and then to the kitchen for a beer, immediately retiring to his den shortly after and forgoing dinner at that moment. Chantelle knew Gary was mad, fed up, and pissed off, probably regretting marrying her to some degree, as he thought it wouldn't be such a fight to achieve what they wanted. Little did he realize that Chantelle wasn't a stupid, timid little girl he could use in this way. Use for a type of mental and physical abuse after marriage.

He doesn't own me, she thought angrily.

All Chantelle could focus on was her getaway the following week, and how scary and uncertain, even though necessary for any chance at a happy life, this would be. It would be like going into the abyss, the unknown. What would happen? Would Gary, Dyna Corp, and the community be looking for her for long? Chantelle started to think, *Maybe Mark and I should fake my death like in one of those movies so that no one will come looking for me and snooping around Mark. Otherwise, they might figure out, very early the nature of Mark's relationship with me, how we know each other, as it is bound to come out eventually. Maybe we should go to the police, the authorities, and tell them our plan, and why, so that they don't waste time looking for me, and maybe they will see the seriousness of the situation and investigate Dyna Corp and the Dome.*

Chantelle wasn't sure what the correct thing to do was, but she knew it was causing her a migraine, grief, and anxiety thinking about it. So she decided to go day by day for the next several days, just to hang on to her sanity, and worry about any new developments closer to Wednesday or Thursday, right before disappearance day. As she said those words in her mind, she started to feel sad and tearful again. She was not certain she could go through with this plan. It was a big step—disappearing, living on the lam, changing her name, her appearance, never speaking with family or friends again. She thought, *Maybe I should just lay in the bed I made. As they say, live and deal with my predicament, the experimentation. It might be an easier choice.* Chantelle was trying to convince herself, *Maybe running isn't the answer. Maybe I should stay, fight, and expose Dyna Corp and the Dome.* But she knew that was a crazy, unrealistic thought, because once they started the real experimental testing on her with the foreign gene induction, microchipping, and more, she would be more trapped, mentally and physically, than ever, barely able to think for herself, never mind able to try to get away. They would be able to track her anywhere, so this was definitely not an option. Chantelle consoled her mind with the thought that living around Mark and getting to know him better didn't seem so bad. He seemed like a great person, levelheaded, fun, yet serious when he needed to be, could help stop this organization, and had some legal and police contacts to help him do so.

The rest of Friday evening was uneventful. Both Chantelle and Gary were mentally exhausted and retired early. Saturday morning, Chantelle and Gary were up early, showered, and were ready to leave by 9:15 a.m., as arranged the night prior, so that they could arrive for Chantelle's blood work at Dyna Corp on time. Waiting for them was Dr. Winston, who didn't seem mad about Chantelle running out of the lab Friday or having to come in especially for her on Saturday; but he was curious about what had caused her reaction while assisting her to his examining table. Chantelle sat on the examination table facing Dr. Winston while Gary stood inside the room's door, like a bodyguard making sure she wouldn't run again.

"I'm not sure, Dr. Winston, what got into me. The staff was talking about things that bothered me, and I just wanted to leave."

Dr. Winston looked at her for a moment and then replied, "Well, I'm sorry. I will definitely remind my staff to watch their personal conversations when around patients, but are you sure something else isn't going on? It sounds hormonal—are you sure you are not pregnant, Chantelle?" he responded in an excited mood at the thought.

Chantelle was shocked that Dr. Winston would make such an assertion, or jump to such a conclusion, as it never even crossed her mind, what with everything going on. Chantelle panicked, thinking, *I hope to goodness that isn't the case.* But she knew it could be possible as Gary and she were still having marital relations, unprotected marital relations. Chantelle did not want to even think about a pregnancy with Gary, or any other way she might have become pregnant, so she blurted out, "No, doubt it," like it was impossible, end of story, so Dr. Winston let the subject go. But not without first inquiring to Chantelle and Gary both, if they were still trying to have another baby after the miscarriage several months ago.

Gary immediately piped up and said, "Oh, of course. We just haven't been blessed with that type of good news yet, but I'm sure it is just a matter of time before such blessed news again and the birth of our first baby." As Dr. Winston quickly looked back over at Chantelle for her reaction, Chantelle immediately gave him a confirmative smile, in agreement with Gary's sentiments and left that to be her answer. Gary and Chantelle did not have much to say to each other on the way home from Dyna Corp; but after dinner, Gary did tell Chantelle that he agreed with where Dr. Winston was going with his line of inquisition today. Gary agreed that she should already be weeks into a new pregnancy and wanted to try more aggressively at making that a reality. Gary felt it would be good for their relationship, a pregnancy again, and would give Chantelle something to focus her days on, something happy to look forward to. And with all that baby talk, he wanted them to start their attempt at pregnancy again that night.

Monday arrived fairly quickly, as the weekend was a quiet, pleasant, restful, one. Chantelle tried deliberately to stay out of Gary's line of view, line of questioning all weekend and all week, as she wanted to go internal and enjoy her last days at the beautiful home she had created, the home she had grown to adore.

While Gary was at work, she decided to call her family in Massachusetts which she knew would be at their antiques shop and spoke with her mother and her father, trying not to give away any clues that anything was wrong, or that it was their last conversation for a very long time, maybe forever—she wasn't sure of the future. After ending a calm, unassuming, and light, conversation with her parents, even having a chance to speak with her brothers for the final time, Chantelle felt good that she was able to relay many, deep personal feelings and thoughts to her family. In a light reminiscent, matter-of-fact, conversational way, Chantelle felt able to get a few pressing issues and feelings discussed, even if they didn't know why she was suddenly bringing up those issues for discussion.

Tuesday morning, both Gary and Chantelle had work. Gary drove Chantelle to work and then off to Dyna Corp he went for a full day of meetings with international investors, which always made him a little nervous and uneasy, Chantelle noted. At work, Chantelle enjoyed light conversations in between some deeper conversations with not only Karen but also with a few of her closer coworkers such as Eunice and Lenore, who were working at Mardi Gras on this day. Chantelle always found it amusing how these two young girls had such old Victorian age names. She always meant to ask them but figured they were probably named after passed-on or very old family members, like a grandma. The workday was coming close to an end, a busy tiring day, yet it was a pleasant shift. Chantelle wanted to spend a night out with these girls, knowing in her mind that it would be her last for a very long time, possibly forever.

"Karen, Eunice, Lenore, why don't we all head down the street to the sports bar for a little girl fun—drinks, food, and chatting," Chantelle shouted over to them as they headed to the staff area to get ready to leave. With a nod of their collective heads and agreeing that it would be fun, the girls called their boyfriends, or husbands in the case of Karen and Chantelle to let them know their plans; and then off they went, down the road, staying in the French Quarter, to a quaint little sports bar. It was Tuesday afternoon, almost evening, and not too busy at the sports bar, as it was a weekday. Even though they looked barely eighteen, they were never carded for age, as many of the local businesses knew them and befriended them, so it was never an issue.

They sat down at a large booth with the perfect view to the outside to see all the eclectic, eccentric, and just plain interesting people going by, hanging out on the streets. The ambience was set. They started to order appetizers and drinks. The girls' night out had begun. The girls spent several hours laughing about old times even if many of these times did not include Chantelle, the newcomer to the group. Chantelle still enjoyed hearing about their adventures as it gave her a bit of comfort knowing that Karen would have some good girlfriends to spend her time with when she was gone, so she encouraged the stories and the reminiscing of these ladies. As she sat carefully and intently watching her best friend and coworkers, knowing that they were part of this whole scheme, this whole dark plot of this new world. She wondered how they could act as though nothing was wrong in the world, in their world. Was it because of the mind control, the mind conditioning, that they could not remember any other type of existence or a combination of all these things? It baffled and perplexed Chantelle, but she reminded herself that now was not the time for such deep and upsetting thoughts. She commanded herself to stay positive and have fun, and so she did. It was now 8:30 p.m., and the girls all agreed it was time to wrap up the party for the night. A couple of them had to work again in the morning. Chantelle called Gary to pick her up, as she didn't want Karen, or any of the other girls, to make a special trip out of their way to drive her home, seeing as some had to work in the morning.

Gary would be arriving shortly, "approximately twenty-five to thirty minutes," he said, so the girls took their time hugging each other and waving good-bye to each other. Chantelle's girlfriends had barely driven out of the parking lot of the sports bar when Chantelle spotted Gary pulling in. She ran out to his car and jumped in. Gary was unexpectedly happy to see her and greeted her with a big, deep, lingering kiss before driving off with Chantelle. "How was your night?" he inquired. Chantelle couldn't help but wonder what could have caused Gary's about-face, his change in attitude toward her. Chantelle could only think that David from Dyna Corp possibly spoke with Gary and reminded him of how they needed, and wanted, her for their projects, and that keeping the peace at home was the only way. For some reason, this explanation came through loud and clear in Chantelle's mind, like a discarnate voice speaking to her, similar to when she was young and she *just knew* something to be true. Chantelle knew it was best to play nice, even if she was not truly feeling it, as that would be the only way for her to get through the next less than seventy-two hours she had left with Gary.

As soon as Gary left for work on Wednesday morning, Chantelle showered and got ready for Mark's 10:00 a.m. call. She was both excited and anxious to hear if he found out anything more, that she didn't already know, from the files they downloaded and printed out from Gary's Dyna Corp company account. As to be expected from reliable, predictable, a man-of-his-word Mark, he called promptly at 10:00 a.m., which couldn't be that easy in between trying to manage his other clients and other calls at his office, Chantelle thought. She felt a little bad when she thought of how his life must have changed, had taken a 180-degree turn since meeting her, yet he hadn't complained, or even voiced out wanting to jump ship once. He was a solid guy, a hard-to-find, rare specimen of a guy, she told herself.

"Morning, Chantelle," he immediately greeted her on the phone. "How was your week?" Mark asked with some concern that it might have been a tough and emotional week. Chantelle reassured Mark that she actually had a fairly pleasant and productive week, making last calls, and amends, as much as necessary with those closest family and friends. Chantelle confessed to Mark that being able to express and get off her chest what she needed and wanted her family and friends to know did make the whole upsetting situation a little easier, but not much. Chantelle had to constantly remind herself not to feel guilt, or take on their pain, it was them who created this whole terrible, dark situation, not her, she was just trying to deal with it, to survive, and, hopefully, end their evil plot of world domination, world change, and world control.

Mark did have more, a lot more, information to tell Chantelle as he nightly combed through Dyna Corp's secret, classified, information, but nothing that terribly new and pressing that he wanted to waste time on the phone explaining and chancing being picked up on surveillance, videotaped, or listened to by phone tap. Mark told Chantelle he would leave all new information to the time where they were together, seeing as Friday, the pickup day, was only thirty-six hours away.

"It looks like we will be spending a very long time together, at least initially, until we figure out what to do about Dyna Corp and its facilities, and then see who we can trust to help us infiltrate and stop them," Mark reassured Chantelle. He gave her the game plan again. We will go day by day. There's no rush. Rushing could cost us our lives, or at the very least, our safety and our freedom, like they are already stealing from all those mind-controlled minions, including some willing wayward victims." Apologetically, Mark said he had to go, as another client was coming shortly. But he would be in their agreed-upon location on Friday at 10:30 a.m. Mark also reminded Chantelle that he would be in her town by Thursday night, if she needed him, as he planned to be parked within surveillance view on Friday morning to monitor Gary's departure and make sure that all was clear before they began.

Chantelle felt better, as usual, after talking with Mark; he seemed to always know what to say, what to do, or at least have a plan B. But she couldn't think about that right now. She needed to start packing covertly, including figuring out what she really needed to take with her and what she could leave behind.

Thursday evening, Gary picked Chantelle up from work, and knowing it was her last evening with Gary, she encouraged him to pick up a nice dinner from their favorite Italian restaurant. On their way home to enjoy their meal, Gary inquired, "What is the occasion? Why did you insist on a meal at our favorite, and pricey, I might add, Italian restaurant on a Thursday night? What's the occasion?"

Chantelle noted his slightly hostile tone but was hoping it was just him being hungry and tired talking, and not him suspecting or, worse yet, knowing that something was going on. "No reason, Gary," she tried to convey in her best matter-of-fact, unassuming way. "Just felt like a nice dinner, something better than leftovers, tonight."

Gary perked up. "Maybe you are pregnant." He laughed in a partly hopeful way, knowing that she wasn't pregnant, or at least she wasn't physically presenting as being with child.

When they arrived home, Gary went immediately to shower while Chantelle started getting the table ready for dinner. Then she showered quickly before they ate. Gary and Chantelle enjoyed a long and leisurely dinner, with very little conversation; but Chantelle was just content spending quiet and effortless time with Gary, ending in Gary trying to produce that much-wanted child. A child that Gary was convinced Chantelle didn't want as much as he did. But he would work on producing it anyway.

*****

October in Louisiana and a cool-feeling Friday morning. The day had finally arrived. It had seemed as though the last few weeks moved in slow motion in some ways, as every little moment was studied, significant, and seared in Chantelle's memory bank for later remembrance. Gary woke up very early, as usual. He showered and kissed Chantelle good-bye, but not without first reminding her where he left money on the table for her to take a cab to her doctor's appointment today, because "some very important last-minute meetings had been scheduled at Dyna Corp, and I won't be able to get away this morning as planned, but I will be meeting you at Dr. Winston's office by early afternoon, probably before you have even completed the experimentation, so I can drive you home."

Chantelle managed to slightly nod her head while still pretending to be in a semi-deep sleep. She lay very still in bed awaiting the front door, to open and close, marking Gary's departure for work. It was an unusually late, unorganized morning for Gary, who always liked to leave for work much earlier than 8:00 a.m., when he had important meetings with international investors, like he did today. When Chantelle felt he was well gone, and most likely close to arriving at work, she got out of bed, showered, grabbed her hidden partly packed bag and finished her packing in full and uncontrolled tearful, crying mode. She was still partly in shock and couldn't believe that such a day would ever need to arrive. Just over a year earlier, she had gotten married to who she thought was the love of her life, who swept her off her feet in a whirlwind romantic nine months of dating. It was now almost 10:00 a.m., and Mark placed a call to Chantelle's phone to make sure she was all right and ready, and to see if there was anything she needed him to do. He was even willing to sneak into her house to assist her with bringing out what he hoped wasn't much luggage, which would cause a stir in her neighbor's eyes, and minds. He reminded Chantelle on the phone that he could always buy her things she couldn't pack, so not to worry. He really did not want her walking down the street with anything more than an un-noteworthy duffel-type bag, and maybe a tote bag and her purse.

As Chantelle approached Mark's car with these items, obviously very emotional and with her eyes bloodshot, he came around her side of the car, gave her a quick but solid hug, and whispered, "Everything will be all right." Then he put her bags into the car and assisted her into the passenger seat. Then they whisked down the road before anyone could study what was happening and start noting details. Mark was driving down the street only a few blocks from Chantelle's house when she told him she wanted to attempt taking money out from her usual ATM machine in Pendle before leaving, as she really would feel better having a little money of her own. She gave Mark detailed directions on where to go, seeing as his fight-or-flight, pacing energy had started presenting itself. He was becoming nervous hanging around Pendle for this additional time. He parked the car and waiting for Chantelle, who was now at the ATM, and thinking how he would feel better just getting Chantelle out of Pendle. He didn't care about her having money. He had enough money for them both, but of course, she insisted, even though he understood why.

Chantelle was happy at that moment. Maybe it was her lucky day, she thought. Everything would be all right. She was doing the right thing because she was able to get the money from the ATM without trouble this time. But she knew it was more likely due to the fact that Gary had no inkling of her leaving, which made her a little sad to think of it again. Still, Chantelle was delighted to be able to withdraw five hundred dollars from their joint account—money she had worked for too, so it wasn't like she was taking money that wasn't partly hers.

Mark and Chantelle drove the hour-and-a-half drive from New Orleans to Baton Rouge in close to silence. They were both deep in thought over what was happening, what to do next, and the fact that they would be living together now—big life changes for both of them who were strangers just months earlier. They pulled up in front of a fair-sized, newer home in the suburbs of Baton Rouge. Marks's house was painted a warm and inviting light blue on the outside. He quickly grabbed Chantelle's bags and whisked her inside the house before anyone could see her or the events unfolding. He did have a back alley with a detached garage; he could have pulled his car into it due to its location in the backyard, the back-alley way, which would have been more private to use for this occasion. He decided that for this one time, he just wanted to get her inside, and he felt it would be safe as she was not reported missing as yet, and most of his neighbors were at work during the day.

After Chantelle had settled into her room and unpacked her bags a little, she asked Mark about work. She was hoping he didn't close his office and miss a day of work for her again. Mark reassured her that his secretary was there at the office working and holding down the fort, so to speak. But he did have to head back as soon as she was settled in and comfortable as he had pressing matters to take care of at the office. Chantelle was actually very happy to hear that he was going to be leaving her; even if this was an unfamiliar surroundings for her, it was a safe place, so she reassured Mark that she would be fine and that she had everything she needed. In fact, she promised Mark she would start on her hair dying while he was gone, because in a few hours, when Gary returned from work, after not finding her at the testing, it would be obvious that she was gone. Chantelle did leave a note explaining, in general terms, her reason for leaving, basically blaming it on the testing and the experimentation by Dyna Corp that she didn't want to endure and participate in any longer, but she was mindful not to give away where she was going, and whether she ever planned on returning. So she needed to change her look, and fast.

Chantelle looked through Mark's house, trying to become familiar with where everything was. She did note that his room was directly beside her bedroom, and even though it was a comforting feeling, it was a confusing feeling. Chantelle knew in her gut that she was way past starting to develop strong feelings for Mark. She was there, but she had to remind herself that she was still married, and that she and Mark had a lot of problems ahead of them to face, so becoming emotionally involved with him was probably not a good idea. But Chantelle wasn't sure if she could control her growing feelings for him—feelings she was pretty sure he had for her also.

CHAPTER 10

NEW LIFE

D r. Winston called over to Gary in his office by 11:30 a.m., worried because Chantelle never showed up for her appointment, and he was wondering if Gary knew where she might be. Gary said to Dr. Winston, in disbelief, "How can that be? We agreed this morning that she would take a taxi down to Dyna Corp for her appointment with you, seeing as I had meetings this morning and into the afternoon. Chantelle was to wait for me, knowing I would be picking her up after to make sure she got home safely," Gary explained to the doctor. He then thanked Dr. Winston for calling, apologized, and told him he would update him on what happened with Chantelle the next day. Gary did not want to be too alarmed and didn't want to alarm David, seeing as they were both unable to leave Dyna Corp any earlier because they had meetings with VIPs, extremely wealthy, investors and contributors, and needed to keep these meetings due to many being there from out of town; some even came in from completely across the world—China and Japan—and had to fly back in a day or two.

Gary called Chantelle on and off all day, now more frantically, and at every free moment he had since talking with Dr. Winston this morning, wondering why Chantelle was not answering her phone. The first thing Gary thought was that Chantelle was playing a childish game, and how mad he was going to be that she put him through this again, twice within the last two weeks. Gary decided to head home early, arriving at 4:15 p.m., the earliest he could get home that Friday afternoon from the barrage of high-pro-file meetings.

He noted Chantelle's car in the driveway, but as he walked into the house, he noted that all the lights inside the house were off, and there was no sign of Chantelle anywhere. As he approached the kitchen, he noticed a two-page letter on their maplewood counter, and immediately, a heavy, worrying, painful feeling embedded itself in the pit of his stomach, like a pile of bricks. He knew the note would not be good; something was wrong. He read through the note, going from sadness and tears to outrage and anger. He was thinking, *The gall of this girl. She would do such a thing as pack up and leave.*

Gary frantically started calling, first Karen's place, as he figured she must have gone there for solace. Karen answered the phone but said she had just gotten home from a half day at work but never heard from Chantelle at all. The last time she spoke with her was Tuesday night, their girls' night out. Gary barely said good-bye or finished telling Karen to contact him if she heard from Chantelle. He hung up the phone and was now trying to pull up the number of her parents in Massachusetts. He thought, could she have possibly flown back home to get away?

Chantelle's mom answered the phone, and Gary told her what was wrong and read her the letter she left for him. Chantelle's mom was now also very scared and worried over where her daughter could have run off to. Gary could not believe this was happening. How could none of her close contacts know where she was? Where could Chantelle possibly be? He was even starting to think that maybe she had been abducted, kidnapped, and that this was a forced or made-up note; he just couldn't wrap his brain around Chantelle vol-untarily leaving. He then decided to call David at Dyna Corp, the only other person he could think of, mostly for advice, as this situation involved Dyna Corp and the testing, the experimentation, all the reasons Chantelle cited as her reasons for leaving.

"David," he started frantically as soon as his boss answered the phone. "You haven't by chance heard from Chantelle, have you? She was supposed to have experimentation with Dr. Winston today, and when she didn't show up for her appointment, he called me. I have been trying to get a hold of her all day on the home phone and her cell phone, with no answer. I came home as early as possible after our meetings at Dyna Corp, and she had left a note, saying she basically left me and staying in an undisclosed location due to the experimentation and testing she did not want to be subjected to any longer," Gary finished, more frantic than when he began, and even more breathless.

The seriousness and the gravity of what was going on was sinking in for Gary, more and more as he called everyone and anyone he could think of, looking for Chantelle. David and Joyce decided to head down to Gary's house to console him and to try to make sense of all of this, not only as his friend and employer but also because Dyna Corp was directly involved. When they arrived at Gary's house, Gary answered the door, still wearing his work attire and clinging on to the two-page note Chantelle had left. It was apparent he had been reading it over and over again for clues to her whereabouts and with whom.

David and Joyce were being like detectives now, asking Gary a bunch of questions about her behavior the last few days to weeks, whether she was hanging out with anyone unusual or new, if she made any large purchases lately or bank withdrawals, and if she had said anything to him, in hindsight, that was a clue, as these are all the questions the police would be asking. Gary knew he had to call the police soon and file a missing person's report. Gary thought calling the police was not only embarrassing, but also suspicious. The police would think he had something to do with her disappearance, or ask why she would leave voluntarily. What was going on in the marriage,? The digging into their private life would be unbearable. Chantelle mentioned Dyna Corp in her letter, so a full investigation into the company, the other facilities, and the experiments she mentioned in the note would be questioned, opening Dyna Corp to unwanted, worldwide negative attention.

Gary was wondering if they should destroy the note before calling the police because the note was extremely incriminating and detrimental to Dyna Corp and all involved with the companies. Gary would need to tell the few people who had been made aware of it, such as Chantelle's mother and Karen, not to mention it to any-one, especially the police. They would understand why. Gary, David, and Joyce agreed, and quickly after they read the note one last time, burned the letter in a receptacle, and let it outside to blow away for good, knowing that the fireplace, being part of the home, was where investigators would also be looking when they searched the house. It pained Gary to burn the letter written by Chantelle, the last and only current connection to her, but he had to for his and Dyna Corp's protection—the greater-good mentality like they were taught. Gary knew he had just committed another crime along with his accom-plices, David and Joyce; but the activities at the Dome would most definitely land them all in a federal prison anyway, so what was burn-ing a note that no one would ever mention knowing that it existed. It was time, hours had gone by, and Chantelle was still not answer-ing her phone, and no one knew where she could possibly be. Gary contacted the local police, but not before calling back Chantelle's mom, Karen, and Chantelle's close friends, reminding all that the note never existed and that no one was to mention it ever again.

The police arrived at Gary and Chantelle's home within min-utes. These events rarely, if ever, happened in this small town, so it was newsworthy and notable. Gary, David, and Joyce gave all the information they knew about Chantelle, including her hometown in Massachusetts and her coming to Louisiana. No one mentioned test-ing and experimentations, and no mention of any letter; that evidence was forever gone. The Pendle police, who now called in assistance from the New Orleans main police department, combed through Gary's house for evidence, clues on the disappearance of Chantelle. Gary agreed with law enforcement that if he still was unable to make any contact with her in a few more hours, and they could find no clue to what could have happened to her, he was to have a TV news brief, pleading for her safe return, and for anyone knowing of her whereabouts to contact the police.

When the police left, David and Joyce offered to stay with Gary or have him over at their place so he wasn't alone, but he refused. Gary did not want to leave the house in case Chantelle returned or called, somehow made contact, as he was hoping she would change her mind, maybe even miss him, and decide to come back home on her own.

*****

Back in Baton Rouge, Chantelle had just finished dying her hair a very light yet warm brown when she heard the front door. Mark was home. Home, she thought. An interesting concept, seeing as she didn't know where that was anymore. Would it be back with Gary one day in Pendle, here in Baton Rouge with Mark, or somewhere else altogether? Her future felt very uncertain to her. As she came running down the stairs to greet Mark and to show him her new hair, he immediately commented on how nice the color was on her. He had picked up fast food for dinner, and they sat down to eat. Mark scrambled to find proper plates and tableware, confessing that as a bachelor, and since breaking up with the fiancée, he was rarely home to eat, and when he was, paper plates and plastic cutlery would suffice as he hated doing dishes or any such cleanup.

Chantelle laughed. "Well, don't worry around me about being formal and proper. I can eat with silver cutlery or plastic—it really doesn't affect my judgment of the person serving and providing the meal. You will still be a great host in my eyes." She gave him a big and grateful smile. During dinner, Mark wanted to discuss important points to this situation that needed to be enforced for both of their protection.

Chantelle listened with her full attention as Mark carried on, "Okay, so first you dyed your hair, which is perfect. When we go upstairs, I will give you the color contacts I purchased online that you must wear when we are out, even in the yard, as a hair color change will not be enough for your new identity. Also, if you could cut it in a little bit different style, length specifically, these are all things that law enforcement and all people looking for you will note. Next, your name. I can still call you Chantelle in the house, but when we are out, again, even in the yard, I must call you your made-up name. How does *Cindy* sound?"

Chantelle nodded in agreement with everything Mark was telling her so far.

"Next," he continued, "we will also have to figure out a story about who you are, the woman now living with me, and is with me all the time. Do you want to be a college friend visiting indefinitely from out of state, or do you want to be the live-in girlfriend?"

Chantelle broke out in a hysterical, uncontrollable laugh, and Mark joined in. It was very comical and partly mysterious and alluring, all rolled in one.

"Well, let me see," Chantelle pondered, pretending to really need to think about it when she knew what she wanted to say almost immediately. But she still paused. "Okay, I think I would rather be the live-in girlfriend. Sounds sexier and more exciting." She gave Mark the biggest smile and then laughed.'

"It's set, then. You are my live-in girlfriend. Let's hope we don't have houseguests, or then we would have to sleep in the same bed," Mark threw in as a final thought to see her reaction and to mess with her a bit further. Then they abruptly stopped laughing, almost at the same time, as the danger and seriousness of the situation came flooding back into their minds, simultaneously. "Back to reality," Mark said with a poker face. "Changing your name on legal documents, a driver's license, or any permanent legal proof of your new name will be next to impossible without going before a judge who will allow this name change after you have told him why. Such drastic changes are allowed only with convincing proof of needing to get away from an abusive situation, and such proof we are not yet ready to provide as the investigation of Dyna Corp and the Dome has barely begun. Plus, going before a judge before ready with the evidence would be chancing being found and many other legal problems involving police, missing persons, possible abduction charges—the list goes on, especially if Gary turns everything around and wants to press charges for me keeping you hidden. So for now, you can't show anyone your real identification documents, such as driver's license. If asked, say it was stolen, and you haven't replaced it as yet, therefore, everything we do must only involve me showing identification, or you are bound to be found, which we don't want until at least we know what to do about this situation."

Mark stopped and looking into the blankness, the dimness of the room, trying to think and then continued, "I can't think of anything else right now. Any questions? Because these things are extremely important and must be followed to the letter, Chantelle, a.k.a. Cindy." He laughed.

Chantelle nodded in agreement and then replied, "Just one question, Mark. Do you have any wine? After that deep and serious talk, I need something to relax me." They both started laughing again as Mark jumped up to oblige. "I have always got wine, spirits, and beer stocked in the house, Chantelle. This is Louisiana. What is a home without some social drinking with the festivities? Feel free to indulge anytime. Just do so responsibly," he reminded her, especially seeing as she was very young. But he trusted her level-headedness and maturity.

As they sipped on their drinks and watched TV, the news flash came on, a live video of Gary, David, and Joyce doing a news conference with the police, pleading for "anyone with information on the whereabouts of this missing woman, wife, and friend, Chantelle Moore, five foot five inches, dark-brown hair, hazel eyes, approximately 120 pounds, last seen early this morning. Please contact the 1800 number on your screen or your local police station if you have seen her. A reward for tips leading to her safe return will also be given." Chantelle's picture splashed larger than life across the TV screen. She could not hold her emotions anymore. She went running into the bathroom sobbing.

Mark chased after her, but she slammed the bathroom door in behind her. Mark started lightly banging on the door. "Chantelle, are you okay? Come on, talk to me, Open the door. You knew that was coming, and we knew it would be hard to watch, but it was necessary. Now we know it is official—you are classified as a missing person, with pictures being circulated, and even with a reward for tips leading to you being found is being offered."

While Mark continued talking, Chantelle felt sick to her stomach. She was hanging over the toilet, ready to vomit her meal and drinks. The night was over; she just wanted to go to bed now. Mark settled her into her room and bed for the night, and then went to his room and right to bed himself. He had a long day at his PI office the next day. He had a Saturday meeting with a client about an ongoing case he was already staking out, doing undercover work for. He had to meet with the client to give the updates, and this was the only day that fit both his and his client's schedule. When Mark was ready to leave for the office at 9:00 a.m. the next day, he knocked on Chantelle's room door to see if there was anything she needed before he left, and when she assured him she was fine, he left for work.

Chantelle got out of bed around nine thirty that morning, feeling better than she did the night before, but still shell-shocked. She made a pot of strong coffee but refused to put any TV or radio on, in fear of what she might hear and see. Seeing herself as a fugitive on TV again, she knew it would make her feel sick to her stomach again, and she just couldn't take it emotionally. She guessed in some ways she was already missing Gary and her old life, including her beautiful Victorian house that had the perfect ambience for her; but she worked hard at not remembering these things, at least not at the moment; the wound was too fresh.

Chantelle sat in the kitchen looking straight ahead with a glazed look on her face, sipping her coffee. She remembered the weird, premonition-type dream she had that night. A dream about the letter she wrote to Gary and seeing it burning, leading to a huge house fire that destroyed parts of their Victorian house. Chantelle started to think, *I wonder why I dreamt about my letter to Gary, and with such odd surrounding circumstances.* Then she started to wonder why during the TV news cast on her being missing there was no mention of the letter, and Gary had said during his interview, he had no idea why his wife would leave, that maybe someone took her and wanted ransom, he wasn't sure. Chantelle pondered this for a while but couldn't figure it out. Would the police have told Gary not to mention the note, the reason for her leaving, or was there another explanation on why it wasn't mentioned? Chantelle gave herself a mental reminder to ask Mark about this when he returned from the office. She was thinking maybe she should contact Gary so he knew she was okay, she was safe; that way, he wouldn't worry about her as much and would stop the manhunt looking for her. Chantelle wasn't sure if this was the right thing to do and knew she should check with Mark before making such a potentially detrimental move. Mark arrived home from the office later than he expected. He thought he would only need to go in for a few hours and ended up not returning until just after 3:00 p.m. Chantelle decided to make dinner, seeing that Mark had all the ingredients for lasagna and this was something she knew how to make fairly well.

Mark appreciated the gesture as they sat down to a nice, quiet late-afternoon dinner. He asked Chantelle, "How was your day? Feeling better? Any new developments?"

Chantelle looked up from her plate and slowly looked directly into Mark's beautiful, kind baby-blue eyes. "Didn't watch TV or listen to the radio all day. I couldn't take hearing about me missing, seeing my picture on TV again, or the fake pleading by Gary, David, and Joyce for my safe return." She continued, "Mark, did you wonder why Gary said in the interview he wasn't sure why I was missing and that maybe someone wanted ransom—wasn't that kind of strange seeing as he knows exactly why I left? I stated my reason in my two-page letter. And should I try, block, calling him, in case, somehow, he didn't get or see the letter, and tell him 'I'm fine, just not returning, and don't look for me' so he could call off the police and the country from looking for me?"

Mark agreed that he did note that Gary didn't mention the letter she left, and that he found it to be a bit odd, mentioning someone wanting ransom, like this situation was a possible abduction. But Mark wasn't 100 percent sure of the reasoning behind it. What Mark did know was that Dyna Corp and all its players tell a lot of lies and would use any means to hide the truth. Just then, Mark got up and went to his computer room and pulled the Dyna Corp files they had printed from Gary's computer. He opened to a section he was looking at from last night when he read it before he fell asleep. He told Chantelle, "It cited a woman they called X Human and talked about how they finally had her in their facility for experimentation and testing after years of working on isolating this single woman from friends and family by lying about her to them, demonizing her to them, trying to frame her for crimes, and sabotaging every and all efforts she attempted at dating or finding someone, as this would affect them getting her if she married or had someone who loved and cared about her. They then mentioned how they worked on sabotaging her financially, over the years, and other dark, devious endeavors, all in their sick plot to eventually, basically, abduct her, take over her life, with no one caring or asking where she had gone. This is Dyna Corp, it's facilities and all the people involved. This is how they operate. So I have a hard time feeling sympathy for Gary and his cohorts knowing what they had planned for you, and what they have already done to so many others."

Mark took a few deep breaths to try to calm down and then continued, "You are away from there, you need to stop feeling sympathy for Gary, and remember what he was making you do. You need to stop thinking about your whole life back there right now because I'm not convinced anyone in your previous life had your best interest in mind. And lastly, *no*, about calling Gary. Not only does he not deserve the courtesy, or peace of mind, from a call from you, it will not change anything. He will still lie about you, along with Karen, David, Joyce, Dr. Winston, and all of Dyna Corp, and act like it is poor, crazy, and mixed-up Chantelle who left, and that they had no idea why she would every want to do such a thing. Your best bet at sanity is to forget them forever and treat all of them like strangers, so we can move on and get the task at hand done, which is stopping these people and having them face justice for their terrible deeds, period." Mark was obviously angry, but Chantelle knew it wasn't directed at her. She actually found it endearing that he had taken on this problem as though it was directly affecting him, made her feel safe and like all, would be okay one way or another.

They finished dinner, and Chantelle cleaned up—the least she thought she could do around there was keep the home clean, seeing as Mark wanted nothing in the way of payments from her. Mark was now working for free on her case, seeing as access to her bank would be cut off and would give away information about her location, if she did attempt taking money out. Mark decided to retire to his den to finish office work for the night, but not before saying one more thing to Chantelle: "It's best for right now if Gary and the rest of them are not sure if you are alive or dead. Trust me, it will make things easier. He will eventually stop looking for you if he isn't sure you are even alive. If he knows you are alive and living somewhere, it will drive him crazy, especially as a man, and he's still married to you, he obviously felt that he owned you, and therefore, he would hunt you down. So no calls. Just stay calm and focused, okay?"

Chantelle nodded as she knew Mark was right.

As the cool fall days, nights, and weeks leading up to Halloween fast approached filled with much work for Mark, including evenings and nights combing through files, and more files, from Dyna Corp, looking online for all information, and everything they could, on Dyna Corp and its facilities, especially the Dome, on which virtually no extra information was available. Not surprising due to its extremely secretive, deliberately covert nature of the operation. Mark wondered if they needed to take another trip to New Mexico to try to find out more about what was going on in there, maybe talking to people living around there also, to see if they knew anything. Mark wasn't sure if another trip inside would produce any further information unless they were actually able to remove petri samples, people, something from there that was tangible. As Mark spent days and nights figuring out their next move, Chantelle spent the time decorating for fall and for tonight, Halloween, her favorite night, a night she wished they could have had people over and had fun or a party, but she knew that was out of the question—knowing people that closely and allowing them to come to the house.

Mark had a better idea: "Why don't we go out for Halloween? Must be a party or somewhere fun we could hang out with other strangers for the night, as long as he didn't have to dress up," he said.

Chantelle laughed while stating, "But you would make such a great vampire." She checked the local papers, and there were events going on in Baton Rouge. It was Louisiana, home of voodoo, Magick, and the rest of it, so it wasn't too hard finding just the perfect spot to settle down for the night.

While Chantelle and Mark laughed and enjoyed their night at the local pub bar, a friend of Mark's from high school and college, whom he hadn't seen in several months came over. "Hey, Robert." Mark immediately got out of his chair to greet his friend.

"Sit down"—Mark gestured to Robert—"Long time no see. Where you been?"

"Oh, here and there," Robert said nonchalantly while looking over at Chantelle. "And who is this?"

"I was just going to introduce you," Mark said. "Robert, this is my girlfriend—my live-in girlfriend, Cindy."

"Hi, Cindy," Robert said. "Why do you look so familiar?"

Mark immediately interjected, "Cindy, this is my good friend from high school and college, Robert, who I obviously lost touch with in the last several months."

"Yes, last I saw you, Mark, you had a fiancée," Robert retorted.

"Yes, that ended," Mark said matter-of-factly. As Robert excused himself to go to the bathroom and to get a drink, Mark quickly whispered to Chantelle, "First, don't forget you are now Cindy. Secondly, just don't talk too much, because like me, he is in the investigative field, more into cyber intelligence but will ask you a million detailed questions. You noticed how he already thought you look familiar? I will need to keep his drinks coming and get him a little drunk until I can talk to him privately tomorrow or the next day. Because now I think of it—he is a good guy, a guy I can trust, known him for years, and his cyber infiltration knowledge and techniques could be helpful to us. Maybe he can gain access to the Dyna Corp's system, so we could do some private snooping without them knowing. Helping us keep up to date on the latest information inside Dyna Corp, and more importantly find out more about the activities at the Dome."

Robert hung out with them for the night, and Chantelle found him to be a very entertaining and an easygoing personality. They all had a great night.

Early November, a few days after seeing Robert at the pub, Mark invited him over on a Saturday to discuss business, cloaked in a casual evening, at his home. Mark's intention was to assess Robert's willingness to try to stop a company like Dyna Corp and the Dome. Once he told him all about it, showed him the files he had on Dyna Corp, and then saw if he would be willing to come on board with him to help then possibly ease into Chantelle's true identity and why she might have looked familiar to him, a tall order for the night. Robert arrived by himself as specified by Mark, as he did tell him the conversation of the night would be private and not appropriate for a casual date to be privy to. The guys started with drinks and appetizers while Chantelle finished up some last-minute preparation in the kitchen for the guest, and to give Mark and Robert a chance to start talking before she joined in.

Mark started with having Robert catching up on what he had been doing over the last several months, which companies hired him for his expertise but partly because Mark wanted to make sure that Robert could be 100 percent trusted and had no conflicting interest, in what he needed to tell him. Once satisfied that Robert could be trusted, like Mark suspected, he pulled out all the files and went over parts of it with Robert, the most pressing and important parts. Mark told Robert about the trip to see the Dome, and about all that they witnessed there. Mark could see Robert's face visibly change. He had been privy to some gruesome and covert dark web operations before, but nothing ever like what Mark was describing to him, and that Mark was an eyewitness to, as being true, not just rumor, made it all the worse. As the men continued talking, Chantelle was ready to sit down with them for a bit before dinner, seeing that no one felt ready to eat yet, and they were enjoying Robert's company. When Chantelle sat down, Mark decided it was time to go into the rest of the story and Chantelle, a.k.a. Cindy's real identity and the manhunt for her throughout Louisiana and the United States.

Seeing as Mark knew he could trust Robert, now it was time for the full story. Again looking shocked, Robert replied, "Well, you guys are just full of surprises tonight, aren't you." Robert wasn't mad; he knew that was the nature of the business he and Mark were in. What good would they be if they couldn't keep secrets? Then Mark had one last part to the story: he needed to know if he would be willing to come on board and help them with this very fluid and dangerous operation, but he understood if Robert didn't want to get involved.

Robert agreed to help without hesitation. He couldn't believe such a company, with such an operation, was allowed to flourish and no one reported it; and in fact, so many people were covering up for them. Mark was elated that Robert wanted to join in and help with his cyber hacking intel expertise, he knew he would be a valuable part of the takedown of Dyna Corp and the Dome. Mark, Chantelle, and Robert had a great Saturday night; it was like old friends, the three of them, reuniting. Similar to what Chantelle felt for Mark while they were driving down to New Mexico, Robert had that same knowingness about him—an ease, a calm, a very familiar aura about him, Chantelle reviewed in her mind, as though she knew him before this week. After Robert left, Chantelle and Mark sat on the couch side by side laughing about their night with Robert and Mark telling her old stories from high school and college of the two men; and without knowing where the emotions or the thought came from, they found themselves kissing for the first time.

Mark pulled back and apologized for what had happened, but Chantelle refused to accept the apology. "No, Mark, I didn't mind." They started to kiss more passionately, and they eventually found themselves in Mark's bedroom, for a long night of uninhibited, unadulterated, enjoyable, sex.

Sunday morning, when they woke up side by side, naked in Mark's bed. Chantelle felt embarrassed; she felt she was betraying Gary and their marriage vows. Mark insisted on her telling him what was suddenly wrong. Chantelle said she was still a married woman, and this was wrong, barely a month away from Gary and now sleeping with him.

Mark couldn't believe she was still worried about Gary and what was right and fair treatment for him. "Chantelle, if you said you felt uncomfortable about what happened between us because we haven't known each other long enough, I would better understand that than you saying it has anything to do with a guy that would rather see you dead and miserable than happy and living control free. Please stop wasting guilt and energy on feelings and thoughts of Gary and his evil crew." Slightly perturbed, Mark got out of bed, and went to the bathroom.

Chantelle knew she had offended Mark somewhat and decided it was best if she got up as well. She headed to her room, showered, and went downstairs to put on coffee and some breakfast. When Mark joined her downstairs for breakfast after his shower, he poured some black coffee, took a sip, and said, "Look, Chantelle, you know I like us to be honest with each other, so I will start. I like you. I like you a lot. I think I liked you more than I should have from the time I picked you up for our trip to New Mexico. I know you are still technically a married woman, and that probably won't be changing on paper for a long time, but I like you, and if you want to be more than just pretend girlfriend and boyfriend, I would gladly oblige. But I would never want to pressure you into anything, so if you need more time or are just not interested, it will not change how I feel, and it wouldn't change me wanting to help you, I promise."

Chantelle walked over to Mark and gave him a light kiss on the lips. "Thanks, Mark. Thanks for being honest. I do like you also. I'm not sure how I feel about the boyfriend-girlfriend thing as yet, seeing as I was just living with my husband about a month ago, even if he is a terrible person who never had my best interest in mind, only Dyna Corp's interest. I didn't know that, so I was in love with him, and I need a minute to fully detach, from those feelings. If you could be patient and understand, I know I will get there. I just have too much on my mind right now." They both agreed her answer was not upsetting and very understandable to Mark, especially the way she expressed what she was feeling.

Mark and Chantelle were enjoying a quiet and leisurely Sunday when the phone rang late afternoon. It was Robert, and he wanted to see Mark first thing in the morning at his PI office, as he thought he knew how to break Gary's Dyna Corp code and gain access into his corporate account. Mark was happy to receive that late breaking news and agreed to see him first thing Monday morning. Even though Mark and Chantelle agreed to not be officially a couple, they both were having a hard time not showing the affection, the passion, the attraction they felt for each other as they spent another night together in Mark's room, this time unapologetically.

CHAPTER 11

CAN I TRUST AGAIN?

Monday morning, Mark could not get to his office and get ready for his friend Robert's arrival early enough. He wanted coffee, doughnuts, and bagels with cream ready and waiting for his friend, as he knew Robert would be proving why Mark trusted bringing him on board; he was a solid, smart guy who could be counted on in a crunch. Robert arrived promptly at 9:00 a.m., a few minutes after Mark's secretary. Mark and Robert locked themselves in Mark's office and reminded his secretary to hold all calls and take messages, unless absolutely necessary. "A call that was absolutely necessary like from Cindy," Robert followed up. "Sounds like you and Cindy are becoming close," he said as he put his hand in a quote-unquote gesture when he said "Cindy."

Mark didn't deny that he was falling, and falling hard, for Chantelle, and that they were not only pretending to be involved, they were becoming involved, but he quickly reminded Robert that, that was not the reason he was there and would prefer conversation about his real purpose in him coming by rather than his complicated relationship with Chantelle. "Besides, she knows to call my cell phone."

Robert agreed. "All right, then," he said, while Mark proceeded to log on to his computer. Robert helped himself to a bagel with cream cheese and some coffee while waiting for Mark's computer, which seemed very slow this day, not the unusual for high-tech PI Mark's computer. Once in they had gone on to the Dyna Corp website employee login, Mark typed in Gary's full name and the account username he remembered. Then while the cursor was hovering over the password area, Robert pulled out a little black device that he attached to the back of Mark's computer tower, as immediately, letters and numbers started flashing on the computer screen in a search for Gary's login information. Once found, it flashed on the screen. Mark quickly wrote it down and then immediately opened Gary's Dyna Corp account.

The two men spent the first several hours of the morning going through vast details regarding the investors and the countries of these wealthy investors, the activities in the other facilities, including Dyna Corp and, most importantly, the Dome. Robert could not believe the extent of such activities, experimentations, and the transformation of towns, as they found out that many other communities throughout the US were part of the pilot plan and to think they could go unnoticed and undetected by government and federal authorities for so long—how could this be possible? Robert was appalled, outraged, and determined to help Mark in stopping these extremely wealthy, powerful people before it was too late for the world. Robert mentioned to Mark that he did have a friend he had known for years who was in the FBI, and once they had done more of their own investigation, he would contact him for assistance from official authorities. Robert mentioned that he also had a special tiny device that if they could place it anywhere in the Dome, it would give them access to live viewing anywhere in the Dome facility due to its special wide-frequency capability.

Mark had to admit to Robert that he knew bringing him on would prove invaluable. He was already worth his weight in gold. Thank you, Robert."

Robert bashfully accepted the compliment. "Okay, enough gushing. Down to work. I have the password we pulled from Gary's Dyna Corp account. I will comb through all the files and catch up with you on all that you already know. Also, look for any new, important leads and information. I will call you later, buddy," Robert said as he grabbed his device from the back of Mark's computer, grabbed another bagel, and off he went.

The rest of Mark's day was uneventful. He arrived back at home around 5:30 p.m. to find Chantelle visibly upset and staring blankly at the TV. "Hey, what's up, Chantelle," Mark greeted her in a cheerful tone, hoping everything was better than she looked. When Chantelle did not reply or even look over to him, he said, "What's the matter?"

Chantelle finally started to move her body, so that she was now facing Mark with tears in her eyes. "Not sure, Mark. I just feel so out of place, so homesick, so bored, and by accident, I caught an updated live TV pleading for my safe return by Gary, and that was all I needed. I had a breakdown."

Mark walked over to Chantelle, knelt beside her and gave her a big hug and a kiss on the forehead. And then he whispered, "Trust me, Chantelle. Everything will be all right. I actually have some good news, good progress in this situation from my meeting with Robert this morning. We will discuss things over dinner. Let me just go and change." He gave Chantelle one more hug before getting up and heading upstairs.

Chantelle got up to set the table and get the roast and potatoes out of the oven. Then she placed a nice bottle of red wine along with two lit candles on the table. She couldn't help but muse at how much of a Molly Homemaker she had become, even though she wasn't sure that was a title she wanted, but it was all she had at the moment to call her own.

Mark came back down within ten minutes. He went to the fridge, grabbed a cold beer to drink, and sat down at the table for dinner. "Chantelle, you really need to keep yourself busy during the day with something other than deep thinking, watching TV, or watching any other, depressing news outlet. As soon as Robert and I get everything in order, we will make one more break-in into the Dome, so you can join in with that, if you want. It will make you feel that you are doing something productive about resolving issues from your old life, your old situation. You need to stay calm and focused. I know I keep saying it, and it's easier said than done for me, as I didn't go through and experience all the pain and trauma you have been subjected to, but you must stay mentally strong until we bury these people and this organization, and we will stop them," he said defiantly before ending his nightly pep talk.

"Yes, you're right in everything you tell me," Chantelle said. "I do play back during the day when you aren't here, but at times I get flashbacks of what must be, what happened while I was drugged. Other times I wake up with vivid dreams that are a playback of what happened. It never ends. And at other times, I'm reviewing in my mind what my family in Massachusetts did know, what my best friend knew, what my coworkers and the community knew, and all the stalking and harassment activities. When will these crazy people's reign end, and how many people and communities are like that out there across the U.S. and the world? Are we too late to stop this new world organization? Have they infiltrated too many big-money companies in all levels to control them? These are all the thoughts that go through my mind almost daily, Mark," she concluded in an exhausted tone.

"I know, I think of those things too. But one step at a time is all we few can do. The first step is identifying the full scope of their dark activities. Next would be getting the proof to present to people we can trust, the federal authorities, who can do something about it and stop them. Robert said today that he personally knows a guy that works for the FBI, and he will talk to him when the time is right. So please stop worrying, Chantelle. Let me do the worrying for you. You take this time to relax. Relax your body and mind during the day, take a hot bath, read a book, light thoughts, nothing too deep for now. Let yourself heal. You have had a lifetime of trauma, it sounds like; but you are safe now, and I will take care of everything, I promise."

I promise, Chantelle thought. Last time she heard "I promise," it was her wedding vows. *And we know how that turned out*, she thought with anger and cynicism, but she wouldn't dare say such a hurtful thing to Mark, as he was only trying to be kind and helpful. Thankfully, they enjoyed a leisurely dinner with light conversation and a few jokes thrown in here and there, mostly by Mark, to lighten the melancholy atmosphere.

*****

The weeks flew by, and it was already the first week of December. Chantelle had been living with Mark for about two months now, and things were quieting down with the search for Chantelle, and things were heating up with what was now mainly Mark and Robert's investigation into the Dome. Before they knew it, it was almost Christmas. Chantelle could predict that her slightly better mood over the last several weeks might take a severe hit over the Christmas holidays as she hadn't spoken with family and friends for many weeks, and by Christmas, it would be close to three months of absolutely no contact and them having no idea where she was, and if she was alive or dead. Chantelle thought, *Isn't this separation thing supposed to get easier with the passing of the days, not harder?*

Mark mentioned to Chantelle a cabin he had in the woods, a retreat he liked to go to now and then when taking time away from work and from being a private investigator. He was thinking that over Christmas might be a good time for them to spend there instead of going to his family's house, which might cause even more upset and melancholy in Chantelle, and suspicion in his family regarding her identity.

A getaway to a quiet cabin, just her and Mark—no family, no phones, no TV, no Internet, no other social contacts, no Dyna Corp, no nothing—might be exactly what she needed over the holiday season, Chantelle thought. She and Mark would have each other's undivided attention, which could reveal a lot, good and bad. But Chantelle welcomed the chance to get to know Mark at a core level, a level she was, usually, good at reading and homing into, a chance to assess his feelings toward her, his intentions, his heart.

Chantelle wanted to go Christmas shopping for Mark and also buy something for Robert to show her gratitude for his help, and maybe even Mark's parents, who she spoke with a few times on the phone and met once briefly but didn't really know well. Mark's parents and sister knew Chantelle as the girl living with him, but it was apparent they never took their relationship that seriously, figuring it could end like Mark's ex fiancée and him did after five years together. Their attitude toward Chantelle came across clear as until otherwise advised by Mark of the true seriousness of the relationship, they would play it very casual, slightly aloof with her, which didn't offend Chantelle, as she didn't know what the outcome of her relationship with Mark would be either. Besides, Chantelle and Mark had some big obstacles to get over, such as her real name wasn't Cindy as his family knew her to be; she was still married and so couldn't get married to Mark yet, even if she wanted to; and, surprise, she was the missing woman from the Pendle area. Running away to the cabin for Christmas and New Year's was sounding better and better to Chantelle as she thought through everything around the whole Christmas season, including Mark's family, something Mark warned her not to do. No deep thoughts—they always got her into a dark and upsetting state of mind, called the truth, called reality.

So it was settled in Chantelle's mind: the cabin it was for the Christmas holidays. She would confirm with Mark tonight, so he could tie up all loose ends, including informing his family, early, so as not to upset anyone with preconceived expectations of them being there for Christmas. Chantelle still had the five hundred dollars she took from the ATM on the day of her disappearance, and she wanted to use it to buy her Christmas gifts for everyone. The only thing she needed was for Mark to drive her to shop and pick her up after. When Mark arrived home from work that evening, Chantelle had a lot of conversation for him, but it was all presented in a happy, positive, upbeat tone. She deliberately made sure of this delivery—no negativity surrounding the Christmas holidays, she reminded herself. Chantelle was finding it extremely easy to talk to Mark about anything, even things he didn't want to hear, he listened to, and he thought on it before making a judgment or giving his opinion either way. Mark had traits that were really making Chantelle fall deeply in love with him; even more than his rugged, strong body and good looks, his heart was genuine and real. He was a straight shooter; he told it as it was to people, but not in a hurtful way. He had the art of tact, something Chantelle confessed she didn't always have but admired in Mark.

Mark was happy to see her feeling better, happy she agreed the cabin for two weeks over the Christmas holidays was a great idea, and he gladly agreed to drop her off for her shopping expedition on

Saturday. The only caveat Mark had was that Robert would need to come up once or twice to the cabin during their time there with his laptop, so they could go over some much-needed important business. Mark promised to keep the details of the Dome operation out of Chantelle's earshot as he wanted her to not even think of Gary, Dyna Corp, or the Dome—not even once over the holiday period. Chantelle had to promise to Mark that she would not think of Pendle or Massachusetts, which she reluctantly did, reluctant only because she wasn't sure if she could keep the promise, but she would try.

Saturday shopping went well. Chantelle managed to get all she wanted for those she was Christmas shopping for, and she even sat down and had a hot chocolate at a café after, while waiting for Mark to pick her up. It was now December 20, and Mark and Chantelle thought it would be the perfect day to buy a real Christmas tree after Mark got off work, as the new batch had just come in. They picked out the perfect blue fir even if they were only going to enjoy it for a few days before heading to the cabin for Christmas. They spent the night decorating it while drinking eggnog. That Thursday, two days before Christmas, they went to Mark's parents' home where his sister also resided, and they all enjoyed a pre-Christmas get-together, handing out gifts and enjoying each other's company. Mark and Chantelle would be driving up to the cabin the following day, Friday, Christmas Eve, to begin their two-week holiday retreat.

On Christmas Eve, both Mark and Chantelle were excited to be heading to his cabin to begin their two weeks of holiday festivities and relaxation. A retreat of getting to know each other, eating, drinking, gift giving, and merriment, and no talk of Chantelle's past life at all by her, and very little by Mark, only due to business purposes, with Robert, as agreed. Other than their personal effects, like clothing and toiletries, they also drove up with their gifts for each other, some wine, and spirits, as alcohol was very pricey at the town's store near these cabins. Mark drove toward northern Louisiana, a woodsy area near Lake Clairborne, which was where his cabin was. They were looking at a good four-hour drive ahead of them, lots of time to talk—something Mark did not mind doing, even though Chantelle was complaining of feeling very sleepy and tired. Even though Chantelle slept well the night before, she chalked up her tiredness to an iron or vitamin deficiency, something she would need to buy when they arrived. They planned that when they arrived and were settled in, Mark was going to head into town, which was only twenty minutes from the cabin, according to Mark, to pick up some groceries and baking goods for the night, seeing as Chantelle wanted to bake. And now she would have him pick up vitamins for her as well. They started out nice and early, before 8:00 a.m., for their four-hour trip to Mark's cabin, but figured it would probably take longer with the holiday traffic. About one hour into the road trip, when they were safely away from the city traffic, Mark came up with a game. "Are you ready to play *our* game? The game of what do you want to know about me that you already don't know, or want to know more about game?" And they both started laughing, causing Chantelle to almost spit out the soda she had just taken a sip of all over Mark's new truck's interior.

"You go first, Chantelle. What do you want to know or know more about?" Mark said.

Chantelle thought about it a moment. "Okay, tell me, do you have a Christmas tree for us to put up when we get to your cabin?"

As they both started laughing again, Mark replied, "How lame, and yes, I do. Okay, Chantelle, my turn. Are you in love with me yet?"

Chantelle was shocked by the blunt question, and immediately replied, "Wow, Mark, you take no prisoners, right to the point."

He nodded in agreement, and it gave her a little time to study him and think on her feelings, even though she never really wanted to frame her feelings for Mark in those terms, with the multitude of problems around them; but she knew she did—she had fallen in love with him. "Yes, Mark, I do love you."

"Good. Finally!" he quickly retorted in a joking tone to lighten the seriousness that came over them with the question. "Is it my turn again?" he asked, as Chantelle stopped talking. Chantelle was starting to feel really worn out, really tired, and didn't know why; but she wanted to be fresh and awake for their night's festivities, so she asked Mark if he would mind if she just napped for a bit, and to wake her up right before they arrived to the cabin, and he agreed. Traffic for the holidays was heavy even going north toward the cabins and camp areas. They were finally almost pulling into the area where Mark's cabin was located when he woke her up. Chantelle had been sleeping for a solid three hours but confessed to feeling a little better.

Mark did most of the unpacking when they arrived, allowing Chantelle to keep her energy. Then he took her inside and gave her the grand tour of the cabin, leaving the bedrooms last, where he started to give her a deep kiss, and they made love right there and then. After the christening of the cabin by Mark and Chantelle, Mark helped Chantelle put away some items, and then got the list from her of what she needed from the local grocery store for her Christmas Eve baking. Mark was starving and needed a deli sandwich to eat before heading to the grocery store, but as he turned to ask Chantelle if she wanted one as well, she went dashing to the bathroom, barely making it, and vomited all over the toilet seat.

Mark came running behind her, worried as he came into the stomach-turning scene. He rubbed her back while she was still hugging the toilet bowl, vomiting, retching. Mark asked if she was all right. Chantelle knew for sure that there was something very wrong with her, but she was in denial, as the last time her body behaved like this was when she was pregnant with Gary's baby. A baby she supposedly lost fourteen weeks into the gestation, but now, with the information she and Mark found about Dyna Corp's the Dome and its activities, she was wondering if she truly lost her baby that day, or was it alive somewhere at the Dome?

As Chantelle knelt there bringing up the little she had left in her stomach, her mind started racing. *Tell me this isn't so*, she thought. *I can't be pregnant again after all this time, and who is the father? Mark, Gary, something else?* All that thinking started a barrage of vomiting again. She had to stay calm. Chantelle was so deep in her own thoughts, so deep in her worry, that she almost forgot Mark was standing beside her rubbing her back as she continued to vomit. When Chantelle felt that the vomiting was over for the moment and she could safely stand up, she immediately headed to the bathroom sink to splash water on her face. Her complexion was now what they called looking green in the gills. She looked and felt dizzy and shaky. Chantelle took the opportunity to clean her teeth and freshen her breath, hoping this might help to stop the sick feeling that was developing again.

Mark was waiting for her in the kitchen. "Feeling better?" he immediately inquired. Chantelle barely got out a nod when Mark continued with his line of thought, "Maybe you're pregnant, Chantelle." His statement was more telling her than asking, because even though she did not want to admit it to herself, the signs were pretty obvious, even to Mark. Chantelle did not answer, as she was still hoping she was not; it was too soon after leaving Gary to have a baby with Mark, if it was his.

"I will purchase a pregnancy test at the grocery store while there, okay," Mark said softly, and Chantelle nodded, as he headed toward his truck and drove off toward town. As Chantelle waited for Mark's return, she had no thoughts or words. She refused to think. She just wanted to be, be still in her space, and be happy to be alive—that was how she coped for the moment.

Mark returned just over an hour later, fairly quick for all the items on the list she had given him, and also for driving twenty minutes each way. Chantelle met Mark at his truck to help bring the groceries in, and there, sitting on top of one of the bags was the pregnancy test. He did not let himself forget the test, and he also remembered the multivitamins, which Chantelle was pleased about. Mark brought in Chinese food with him from the only Chinese restaurant in that little town, and they didn't deliver, so he figured he should get it while he was there. Chantelle started to prepare the table for dinner, including starting her baking, which always took all of Christmas Eve night to complete. Mark got the Christmas tree down from the attic and started to put the artificial tree up. He had finished assembling the tree and decorating it while Chantelle placed the second batch of cookies already in the oven.

Mark and Chantelle were ready for dinner. They both decided to forgo festive cocktails, before and during dinner, until Chantelle took the pregnancy test to see if she could partake in adult beverages. During dinner, Mark wanted to know if Chantelle was scared, happy, or sad to take the pregnancy test. What was she feeling? Chantelle admitted to being scared to take the test, because if she was pregnant, the question became, who was the father? Mark understood her worry, but he reminded her not to worry, let the doctor, when they returned to Baton Rouge, first tell her how far along she was. Then they could figure things out from there. "For now, let's take the test and be happy with whatever results we get."

Chantelle wondered how Mark could always be so levelheaded and calm. *He must be from another planet*, she joked in her mind. After dinner, they were ready to take the pregnancy test, and it came back positive in less than a minute. But neither one of them was surprised. She was obviously pregnant, and for some reason, Mark felt confident it was his.

CHAPTER 12

BABY MAKES THREE

Mark was excited about the thought of having a baby even if it ended up to be Gary's or something else's. He loved Chantelle, knew he wanted to marry her and spend his life with her, so they would figure it out. He was ready for whatever challenges the new year would bring. *Might as well add this to the mounting pile of problems we have currently on our plate*, he thought while he finished cutting wood in the front yard for the fireplace. When Mark returned inside, Chantelle was ready for him to get the fire going while she put out the first batches of her Christmas baking goodies, along with some eggnog, punch, and beer for Mark. She wanted Mark to not feel that now that she was pregnant, he couldn't, or shouldn't, drink; but even though he appreciated the gesture, he decided that during this pregnancy, he wasn't going to drink either. They would wait to celebrate after its birth. Chantelle gave Mark a big smile, his perfect words reminding her exactly of why she fell in love with him so quickly.

Christmas morning, even though Chantelle wanted to get up early, excitedly running to the tree to open gifts like every year before, her newly pregnant body was not providing her with any extra energy. She was still exhausted from the baking fest in the late night and into the wee hours,. She rolled over to Mark, seeing as they now had decided to be a couple since coming to Mark's cabin. They agreed it was pointless for them to sleep apart when obviously they were more than just roommates.

Chantelle wanted to wish Mark Merry Christmas first, but before she could fully get it out, he planted a big and loving kiss on her and said, "Merry Christmas, beautiful." Then immediately, he jumped out of bed, grabbed his robe, and headed downstairs to put some coffee on while yelling to Chantelle, "Do you want breakfast in bed this morning, or were you feeling up to coming down to eat?"

Chantelle needed to think about that question for a moment as she was feeling way too tired to get out of bed, and the thought of breakfast food was making her feel queasy again. "I think I'm going to stay in bed for maybe a half an hour more, Mark. If you could just bring me some coffee with a light amount of cream and a dash of sugar, that would be great. But no breakfast, please!" she yelled back.

Twenty minutes later, Mark returned with her coffee and one gift. He didn't mind if she was too tired for gift giving right now, but he wanted her to have this one gift while she lay in bed. As she opened the palm-sized rectangle box, she thought, surely it couldn't be an engagement ring already. And she was right, but it was a gorgeous, brilliant pure sapphire, gemstone pendant, one of Chantelle's favorite stones. She loved it and gave Mark a huge hug and a loving kiss, leading to another intense lovemaking session. Chantelle started to think pregnancy was making her feel friskier than when she wasn't pregnant, yet she didn't remember feeling this increase of passion when pregnant with Gary's baby, so it couldn't be that, she pondered.

"What are you thinking?" Mark asked just then. "I'm thinking we should get up, shower, open gifts, and start this day while my energy is good right now." Immediately, Mark and Chantelle headed to the shower together and then downstairs for Christmas gift giving. The day flew by; it was now 9:00 p.m. They finished dinner and cleaning dishes for the night. It was a great day, "a perfect Christmas," Chantelle told Mark. They both retired early, shortly after Christmas dinner that night. Robert was expected the following morning, as planned, to discuss the newest developments on their investigation into Dyna Corp and the Dome with Mark.

Even with the over-four-hour drive to Mark's cabin, Robert still managed to arrive by 1:00 p.m. They had planned for him to stay overnight at the cabin, so they had plenty of time for everything they needed to take care of.

"Merry Christmas, my friend," Mark greeted Robert at the door, as his SUV pulled up to the cabin driveway.

"Merry Christmas, Mark." They shook hands and proceeded inside the cabin where the fireplace was already going in full glory. It was a nice, cozy atmosphere that brought back many memories to the men of the other occasions they shared at Mark's cabin fishing, hiking, and having guy time.

"Where's Chantelle?" Robert inquired.

"She's doing yoga and meditation in another room, as we agreed no thinking about Gary, Dyna Corp, and the Dome for her this whole holiday season. She needs a mental reprieve from their dark grip."

"Well, good call this time, Mark, because some of the information I found in Gary's Dyna Corp account would be way too much for Chantelle to take in right now." With that cryptic statement, Robert had Mark worried, yet intrigued. Robert started opening the printed-out files with the information, and then he started to say, "It turns out that due to Chantelle's many gifts and abilities, they have been interested in her since birth. Basically, these people signed some contract with her parents, unbeknownst to Chantelle while young, the men in black she saw as a child. Probably a contract that had to be continued even when she left Massachusetts. That's where the so-called chance meeting, whirlwind love affair between her and Gary came in, securing them further having full access to her, even after marriage."

"No way."

The look on Mark's face was now one of awe as he tried to find his seat."

There's more," Robert continued. "Chantelle has been the victim of experimental cloning since young, and carrying over through these years, into marriage. The newest gene, embryo cultivation and, growth of a new species is a fairly new part of these people's biometric and genetic labs activities. But the cloning, they have successfully developed a couple cloned Chantelle's over the years, according to the files, all in an attempt to study her genetics and have full access and knowledge into her special gifts, but they still need the original host, Chantelle. Now we need to know where they are, these poor cloned humans, and find out more about that part of the program, also the Special Species gene-mixing experiments."

Mark was speechless. He could not figure out what to make of these illegal and unethical practices Robert just told him about being done to the person he cared about, the person he now loved, and the person to be the mother of his child.

"Robert, we mustn't tell Chantelle anything about this for a while. We just found out she is pregnant, yesterday, and with her other stresses around this whole situation, this would be way too upsetting for her and the baby. Me and you will get all the information and facts needed to prove what has been and is going on at the Dome without giving Chantelle details of these newest findings until after the baby's birth," Mark concluded.

"Wow, we are both full of surprises today, aren't we. Congratulations, Mark," Robert replied, a little shocked himself, with Mark's news. "It is yours, right?"

Mark couldn't help but start to laugh at Robert's frankness and said, "Well, that is the million-dollar question. is it mine, is it Gary's, is it"—Mark paused—"something else's."

Robert knew exactly what Mark meant, so the men left the conversation at the congratulations part for now. With all that unnerving and dark information, the guys decided to have a beer to settle their nerves, as Chantelle was still meditating and doing other metaphysical practices in another room and wouldn't care either way if Mark's promise to not drink until after the birth was already broken.

Mark and Robert took Robert's laptop that he brought with him from home to the room Robert would be sleeping in for the night, for some privacy and to further talk about Dyna Corp and the Dome. Robert said he had an idea on how to plant that device inside the Dome, the special surveillance device he had, that once inside a room, or building, could live-stream a wide range live video activity of up to a street block; in other words, if he could somehow get this device into the Dome, they would have 24/7 live access to the whole facility—every room, every hallway, every office. But they needed access to the Dome to hide the device somewhere, anywhere. Robert had come up with a possible plan for getting this device in the building, either taking it there himself dressed as a delivery guy, say, delivering flowers to one of the women, from an anonymous admirer. Robert did have a friend he could borrow a florist truck from, or just send a delivery there, flowers, a gift, or something else that would be opened and handled by employees and something they would keep in the facility and not throw away—a little chancier way, but possible.

"Brilliant. Let's do it!" Mark said. "Once the device is placed in the facility, I have specialized monitoring equipment that can view from nearly every angle, split screen, multiple rooms, you name it, very entertaining when I had to use it." Robert laughed. He had to leave early Monday morning back to Baton Rouge for business he needed to take care of, including getting the device planted in the Dome facility, so he promised to have Mark updated in a week or so.

Chantelle was already awake, meditating and doing yoga in the other room, when Mark came in. "Do you meditate and do yoga most mornings Chantelle? I never noticed you doing it before." Mark was curious and intrigued.

"Some mornings, not all. Come sit beside me, Mark. I want to show you something."

Mark came over and sat beside Chantelle with slight hesitation as to what was going to happen next. Chantelle held the palms of her hands up in the air and toward Mark and told him, "Place the palms of your hands against mine. Now take some deep breaths, long breaths, and concentrate with your eyes closed. I want you to feel through your hands, starting with the palm of your hands. I want you to feel me, feel the transfer of myself, my essence to you. What do you feel, Mark?"

Mark didn't say anything at first while they both continued to do what Chantelle instructed. Finally, Mark started to speak, now in a very relaxed and slow tone. "Wow, Chantelle, I feel tingling, I feel emotion, not my emotion but you, your emotion. I feel love, I feel relaxed"

"Perfect," Chantelle interjected and then slowly broke the hold with Mark. She said, "This is some of the things I'm good at doing, building portals from this world and the outer world, person to person, spirit to spirit, also bringing forth such entities if they so choose to help over here. Tell me, do you have a wish, Mark?"

Mark agreed he did have a wish right now. He wished for the baby to be his and for it to be a girl." As she walked over to a table where she had an old-looking brass, almost teapot-looking container, Chantelle said, "Good, then. I will have you rub my special brass container and call my special friend King Yasir three times and then tell him what you wish for."

Mark thought it was unusual but also thought, what could it hurt? So he did as Chantelle instructed, and when he was finished, Chantelle thanked King Yasir and then placed the old brass container back. Chantelle then said, "I guess we will see in the new year if your wish was fulfilled. That is another thing I am known for, Mark. I can summon what I call my friends, what others call, what is collectively known as the djinn, genies, and other such entities. Some people believe, and some people don't, but either way, *it is what it is, I say.*"

In awe, Mark laughed and said, "Well, I hope it is what it is, because I would love to have my wish granted."

The week flew by, and before they knew it, it was New Year's Eve. They were both very excited and ready to ring in the new year— in fact, Chantelle felt ready to head back to reality after enjoying a week of peace and respite, but Mark had planned for them to be there for another week, which he really felt they both needed, quiet time away from others, away from TVs, and electronics.

New Year's Eve, Mark and Chantelle had a nice late dinner. All seemed, unplanned, easy, natural, until unexpectedly, and shockingly, due to Mark never giving away any clues, and he wasn't nervous at all during the day, right before the stroke of midnight, Mark said, "Happy New Year!" to Chantelle, followed by, "Will you marry me?" as he pulled out a black satin box, got down on one knee, and revealed the most breathtaking diamond ring.

"Yes!" Chantelle shouted as she bent down to him to give him a hug and a kiss. "Yes, I most definitely will." It was the perfect ending to an already perfect holiday season, and the wishes and dreams they had wanted for this time away had been fulfilled.

*****

It was now the second week in January, and Mark had found a local, Baton Rouge female maternity doctor, and Chantelle agreed to see her for her first prenatal appointment that week. Chantelle and Mark were both very nervous as they would need to reveal Chantelle's real name and explain what was going on, why the hiding. Mark hoped Chantelle wouldn't be recognized as the person from the missing person's reports months earlier, before they had a chance to explain things to the doctor. Mark had spoken with the doctor, Dr. Clemence, on the phone beforehand to prepare her and the office nurses for the seriousness of the matter and the need to be absolutely confidential, therefore he didn't want to explain their personal matters in front of a room of other clients and patients, but he promised to fill the doctor in while in consultation with Chantelle. As Mark drove Chantelle to her appointment, they both confessed to be a bit nervous, because if her identity got leaked out, it would mean not only the authorities coming down on them both, but, more troubling, Gary, Dyna Corp, the whole dark organization, and community knowing Chantelle's location.

The prenatal appointment was going well with Dr. Clemence sympathetic to Chantelle's situation even though they couldn't tell the doctor all the specific details, just that the whole situation with her ex-husband was abusive. Dr. Clemence and her auxiliary staff seemed to be on board. Everything was progressing well, with their secret being kept, including notes being left in Chantelle's chart, noting the need for this extra confidentiality measures. Dr. Clemence figured Chantelle was approximately at ten to twelve weeks' gestation but wouldn't be able to give a more exact time until they did an ultrasound at her next appointment, but all looked healthy with the fetus. Mark reminded the doctor and her staff to send the bill directly to his office. He would call in a payment at that time. Chantelle and Mark were relieved to hear all was good with the baby and still very hopeful that it was Mark's, as the timeline was correct; still, they knew it was open to any possibility but did not want to worry about such matters for the moment.

*****

The weeks were going by quickly. It was a week after Valentine's Day already, and Mark and Robert had begun inside surveillance of the Dome. Due to Robert's geniusly planned trip to New Mexico the week earlier, he managed to get the surveillance device implanted within the Dome facility. Robert explained that after finding out the name of one of the single women working at the facility, he went there as a flower delivery guy, delivering flowers and a present to her from her anonymous admirer. He further lucked out when the guy manning the back door of the facility took him directly to this woman and had not taken the flowers and the gift himself, giving Robert access inside the facility to leave his monitoring device directly. In fact, Robert decided to leave an extra one there in another spot near a bathroom, the bathroom he excused himself to before leaving the facility, just in case the first device was found. Robert took a few additional days at his house, getting all the monitor camera angles synchronized and set with the devices implanted at the Dome. Robert and Mark spent much time watching live video stream of the facility and the people coming in and out, and when they weren't there, live-stream watching. The device was always on record mode, recording all activity for future evidence, future viewing.

*****

Mark knew that the wonderful peace, serenity, and happiness he and Chantelle were experiencing was too good to be true, and then true to form, he found out by early March, the bill from Chantelle's doctor's appointment had been inadvertently charged to her husband's medical insurance account, and therefore the bill was also sent to the home in Pendle. When Mark found out the mistake he was livid and let Dr. Clemence and her staff know it, but now he had to break this news to Chantelle, as it was a matter of her safety. Any moment, her location and pregnancy would be known to Gary and all those around him. Chantelle had another prenatal appointment a few days away to find out, through an ultrasound, the specific week of her pregnancy. And now Mark was also going to let the doctor explain this terrible mistake regarding her privacy to Chantelle, as he didn't have the heart to give her such bad news when things had been going so well. During Mark and Chantelle's drive down to her prenatal appointment, Chantelle was wondering why he seemed so quiet, and introspective, but thought that possibly Mark had a tough day at work and a lot of things on his mind.

Inside the doctor's office, the doctor first asked Chantelle how she was feeling regarding nausea and the baby's movement. Chantelle confirmed that all was well. Still, Chantelle noted that the doctor was acting as though something was wrong. She was becoming worried about her pregnancy again. Dr. Clemence proceeded with the ultrasound, which still confirmed the same timeline as she had given originally, which was now seventeen to eighteen weeks pregnant but probably not more than twenty weeks along. Still not enough difference in time to know for sure if it was Mark's baby conceived after Halloween, or Gary's baby conceived a few weeks earlier, the night before Chantelle's disappearance, an answer they would have to wait for, definitively, after the birth, when they could get an official DNA blood test. After the doctor gave Chantelle and Mark all the positive updates with the baby's development, it was time for the negative information. Mark started the conversation but let the doctor finish explaining what happened and why. As the doctor left the room to let them talk and allow Chantelle to get dressed, Chantelle was in shock. She started to break down in tears. "Now what, Mark? What will we do?" she asked in a panicked tone. Mark was visibly mad and told Chantelle to finish getting dressed, and they would discuss what they needed to do at home.

At home, Mark was visibly shaken. He called Robert to update him, and so they could coordinate any new video information, with incoming information coming from Gary's Dyna Corp account about the Dome, and specifically regarding Chantelle. Mark knew that regardless of what he was feeling, he needed to keep calm and strong, for Chantelle and the baby, he didn't want her miscarrying like she did during her last pregnancy, at fourteen weeks, with Gary's baby. As Chantelle entered the room, Mark gestured her over to talk. "Okay, sit down, Chantelle. And I want you to stay calm and relaxed, for yourself and the baby, while we talk."

Chantelle agreed, and Mark continued, "Maybe this happened for a reason. We needed to confront the situation, so we could move on with our lives. What you are going to do tonight, when Gary gets home, is call him. I'll be right here with you. He will see your number come up, but when he gets on the phone, tell him you just wanted to let him know you are safe, but like your letter states, you are not coming back due to Dyna Corp and the experimentation being done to you and to the others, but don't go into too much detail about what you know, and say nothing about the Dome," Mark reminded Chantelle.

Chantelle was not sure if she could do this. She was too intimidated by Gary knowing what evil things he was capable of, and to his own wife. Chantelle wanted to know what to say if he already received the prenatal insurance papers and wanted to know about the baby? Mark wasn't sure what she should say to Gary, either. So he told Chantelle, "Just let him know you are all right. It's not his baby. Tell him, under no circumstances is he to come looking for you, and then just tell him good-bye, have a good life. Be firm, and unwavering, Chantelle," Mark told her.

Easier said than done, she thought, but she knew she had no choice. This was the only option now that the doctor's office had exposed their secret.

*****

It was 7:30 p.m., and Chantelle was pretty sure Gary would be home from work by now, so she made the call to his cell phone. The phone rang a few times before Gary picked up. "Hello," he said, winded and obviously not noticing the number that had called his phone.

"Gary, it's Chantelle." She paused for his reaction.

"Chantelle!" he said, surprised but not overly, as though he was expecting her call or to hear from her. Maybe he had already received the papers from the doctor's office, Chantelle thought. "So, you are not dead, and you aren't very far away, I see, Chantelle. Why would you do such a thing, Chantelle, as hiding out for five months now and not let anyone know if you are alive or dead?"

Chantelle knew that was a rhetorical and sarcastic statement by Gary geared to intimidate her and make her feel bad, a blame-the-victim mentality, but she remembered what Mark said—"Be firm, be strong"—as she looked over to him for support.

"Gary, I'm not calling to talk about all of that. I'm calling for no reason other than to say I'm fine, I'm safe, I'm not coming back ever, and you know why. I told you in the letter I left on the counter that day, that I didn't want you looking for me," Chantelle said in the strongest tone she could bring forth.

Gary was obviously becoming very angry. His tone was now very loud on the phone. "You don't want me looking for you. Chantelle, we are still married, and according to the paperwork, you are carrying my child, so I demand you return immediately, or I will be coming to get you."

Chantelle did not know what more to say, but she could not leave the conversation like that so she ended calmly, telling Gary, "I wouldn't come looking for me, Gary. I am not going back, and if you do come, I will call the police and tell them about the experimentation being done on me against my will. You will not receive any more bills. It was a mistake, sorry. Good-bye, have a good life." Chantelle abruptly hung up the phone. Mark and Chantelle knew that conversation did not go as well as they would have liked, and Chantelle had to really watch out for her safety even though she rarely went out, and never without Mark; but they knew Gary and Dyna Corp would not let it end there.

*****

It was now the beginning of April, nearly three weeks since Chantelle's ill-fated conversation with Gary and happily more than halfway through her pregnancy as her official due date was August 8, just four months away. Chantelle and Mark decided to see a divorce attorney and serve Gary with divorce papers as they had been separated and not living as man and wife for more than six months now. Even though they didn't want to stir the pot with Gary as things seemed quiet since the uncomfortable conversation weeks earlier, other than a few weekly prank calls to the house, but they thought it was time for the next steps if Chantelle was to be truly free of Gary and Dyna Corp.

Soon after the divorce papers had been served to Gary was when the nightmare that showed itself a few weeks before her disappearance started to rear its ugly head again—the stalking, harassment, break-ins, and the petty theft behavior began again, and this time even Mark wasn't immune. He started to receive death threats and hang-up calls constantly at his office, extending to the house and at all hours of the day and night. Mark was followed, mobbed, harassed, and even some blacklisting had begun at the various local food chains, banks, hotel/motel chains he used for surveillance work and other large and small store franchises and chains—all the signs were there of the organized stalking activity starting up again, now that their location was known. And Mark noted that it was apparent that larger private corporations, including city facilities and utilities alike, *were being paid* to participate in this stalking, harassing, blacklisting activity, as their private accounts and information related to their TV, cable, Internet, water, gas, and electricity were all affected and interfered with on the directives of this criminal organization and corporation. Mark knew they paid their cell phone provider for their account information as their cell and home phone accounts were also accessed by this criminal organization in order to tap into Mark and Chantelle's phone calls and home computer to embed their spyware into their systems, allowing them to divert their calls and online website searches to fictitious ones.

Mark and Robert had to organize more investigations into Dyna Corp and the Dome, as they were becoming more threatening, angry, and violent, knowing Mark and Robert had secret information and files about Dyna Corp and its facilities. If they were ever going to successfully and permanently stop this evil, dark, cult organization, they had to act fast, as this organization was hell-bent on destroying Chantelle, Mark, and now Robert, before ever chancing being found out by the masses with all their covert activities. But even with all that Mark and Robert already knew about Chantelle being cloned and other criminal activities, at Dyna Corp and the Dome, it still wasn't easy, mainly because so many people were being paid to be involved and keep their dark secrets. In addition, Mark and Robert needed more live video evidence of the clones, information on where these clones were living, and more information in general on the Dome's vast genetic-mixing activities. They needed more tangible evidence, to present to authorities, before they could expose the company. But Mark decided that he and Robert needed to wait until after Chantelle gave birth to tell her what they knew and have her help with going into the Dome again. They also needed information from her regarding what more she remembered from her childhood, like the day the men in black came to visit, the drugged experimentations, and more. Mark was fairly certain that none of the new information on Chantelle's cloning, was something she was aware of, and that was how Mark wanted it for now.

It was now August 7, and Chantelle couldn't wait to give birth as she was feeling very big, bloated, and with the added stress of the constant stalking and harassment from Gary, Dyna Corp, and all those paid trolls, as they liked to refer to them. It was all proving too much for Chantelle; she wanted the pregnancy to be over so that she felt less vulnerable. Chantelle took a long hot bath on the night of August 7 and immediately fell asleep beside Mark when done. Three o'clock in the morning, Chantelle woke up feeling wet, like there was a puddle underneath her. Her water had broken in the bed, and she was having strong contractions. She was in labor, and even though petrified and scared out of her mind, she was happy the baby was coming on time.

Mark grabbed the hospital overnight bag they had prepacked and headed to the hospital while calling the doctor to meet them there as Chantelle was going into labor. The labor was long and painful, as expected. Chantelle needed an epidural for the pain halfway through her labor when she couldn't take the pain any longer, but it all paid off, because by 6:09 p.m., August 8, she gave birth to a healthy baby girl, eight pounds and three ounces. Mark and Chantelle were elated. As the new parents continued their adoring of having this beautiful baby girl, which Mark right away commented on, saying he thought she looked just like him, they realized they never thought of any names, what with all the problematic days leading up to the baby's birth.

Immediately, a name came to Chantelle's mind, like a soft whisper. She blurted it out, "Reign. Why don't we call her Reign?" Mark loved the name. They unanimously agreed that her name would be Reign, and with *his* last name on the birth certificate, Ryerson. Reign Ryerson. He liked the sound of that.

Mark was smiling from ear to ear, happy to be holding his new daughter, Reign. Chantelle couldn't help but remind him, "See, your wish to King Yasir has already half come true. You got your girl." They smiled at each other, content for the moment at what love could do, and forgot all about the evils that awaited them when they left the hospital.

NOTE FROM THE AUTHOR

I t was hard, with many obstacles encountered, to stop this book from being published; but with awareness of this global growing problem, these criminal and civil rights atrocities can be stopped, if we all band together against them and say no to joining and conforming to such organizations, groups, and people.

If you are the victim of human trafficking; organized stalking (corporate, community gang stalking); harassment, surveillance, blacklisting, and discrimination, know that those activities are illegal and must be stopped through awareness. Please contact organizations such as the ones listed below for assistance on how to fight back and reclaim your life. These are *human rights organizations*, available to help and combat these *global issues*:

ICAAACT.org
freedomFCHS.com
mindjustice.org

Also, Cyber Crimes can be reported at these FBI sites:
https://www.ic3.gov/default.aspx

or the general FBI website at:
https://www.fbi.gov/

and your local FBI department- see online listing for your city

CPSIA information can be obtained
at www.ICGtesting.com
Printed in the USA
LVHW040156230719
624964LV00002B/534/P